NO ONE But You

The Orlinda Valley Series

DONNA R. MADDEN

MARCUS HENRY
PUBLISHING

This is a work of fiction. All the characters, organizations, and events portrayed in this novel are either products of the author's imagination or are used fictitiously.

No part of this book may be reproduced, or stored in a retrieval system, or transmitted in any form or by any means, electronic, mechanical, photocopying, recording, or otherwise, without the express written permission of the publisher. 1st edition.

Copyright © 2024 by Donna. R. Madden, all rights reserved.

Printed in the United States of America

Paperback edition ISBN: 979-8-9877343-7-7

Cover Art by: Champagne Book Designs

Also By Donna R. Madden

More Than Enough series
More Than Enough
Your Love is Enough
You Are Enough

Orlinda Valley series.
No One But You

This book is dedicated to
everyone who believes in the importance of family
and the power of love.

NO ONE
But You

Chapter 1

KORA

"What the fuck?" The familiar ride down the back country road turned into bumpy, out-of-control chaos as my car, which was perfectly fine a second ago, suddenly swerved and veered all over the road.

I slid to the shoulder, jammed my foot on the brake, and slammed the gearshift into park. "Damn county roads filled with potholes the size of craters. When are they finally going to pave these terrible pieces of shit?" I slammed my hand on the steering wheel, opened the door, flung the rhetorical question into the open field, and jumped out of the car. Someone had to inspect the tires.

As I suspected. Front passenger tire. Flat. As a pancake.

I stood with my hands on my hips and kicked the now worthless tire. "Dammit. I'm gonna be late for my hair appointment." With a strong exhale, I reached into the back seat of my SUV and grabbed my phone. I needed to let Summer know I'd be late.

My phone rang and rang, but no answer. "Dammit, Summer." I clicked the call end button and sent a text to my best friend for life, Darlene. She would be at the salon. Her son James had spent the night with his grandma, who was also my aunt, Tonya. Tonya—I don't use the aunt—spent her Saturdays bothering her best friends who own the salon, so Darlene was meeting her at Shear Perfection.

She could give Summer a message.

I was staring off over the pasture and watching cows munch the grass when the phone notified me of an incoming text.

I glanced at my phone. "What the hell?" It wasn't Darlene. It was a text informing me my last message wasn't sent. I gritted my teeth as my face heated, and it wasn't because of the humid morning we were already dealing with this late in May. It was my skyrocketing blood pressure. Who wanted to be stuck on the side of the road in Bumfuck, Egypt, and in this heat?

I stalked around the car, held my phone high, and gave it an evil eye. Still no bars. *Of course not.*

"Dammit!" I yelled at the top of my lungs. There was nothing around. Nothing. Except birds, cows, and a rabbit hopping across the field.

The cows stopped munching the grass, and the rabbit even stopped hopping to stare. "What? Am I bothering your busy day?"

"Moo," the cow responded as he chewed his cud without a care in the world, and the rabbit hopped off.

"See? I figured as much." I trudged to the rear of my black Nissan Rogue and opened the hatch to get to the spare as a memory hit me.

Shit.

I wouldn't see a tire unless I got lucky and my father had helped me out. I lifted the floor panel slowly and squeezed my eyes tight. As soon as the panel was all the way up, I wedged my eyes open slowly, hoping I would see a tire where the spare tire should be. I stared into the abyss of the undercarriage and no such luck. It was empty.

Last December, I went out Christmas shopping and needed more storage for all the gifts I was going to purchase. I had a feeling they wouldn't all fit in the back seat and trunk. Yeah, I know it was a little overkill, but my cousin, Bryson, is married to Darlene, and they have the cutest little boy, James. I can never say no to him, so to make sure I had the space, I took the spare tire out of the car—who uses it anyway—and had more space to stash presents.

I glanced up at the cloudless blue sky and at the sun already shining hot and bright at nine in the morning and shook my head. I could hear my father discussing—as he never yelled—all the reasons why taking the spare tire out of the car was a bad idea. I could also hear him reminding me to put the tire back in the car "in case of an emergency, and you hit one of the many potholes on the county roads."

"Damn, I always knew he was able to see the future." I slammed the hatch closed and peeked at my phone again. Still no bars. This was the one dead zone between my place and downtown, and I was about ten miles away from the nearest house.

I could walk. It wouldn't be the first time I'd walked the roads to town.

The air was getting thick with humidity, and sweat had already formed at the nape of my neck. I pulled my hair up in a high ponytail, leaned in the car, and plucked the emergency scrunchy from around the gear shift.

This was an emergency.

My stringy, straight, auburn hair would get nasty quick. I twisted the ponytail into a loose bun on top of my head, leaned against the hood of the car, and sighed.

It was so damn hot—desert hot.

If this was any indication of what kind of summer we were going to have in Tennessee this year, I'd better be prepared for anything, and in this moment, I was so *not* prepared. I left in a rush this morning, running late as usual, and didn't grab a water bottle or even a second cup of coffee. Death by dehydration suddenly became a possibility, and walking the ten miles to the nearest house was out of the question. "Where am I gonna get water?" The brown cow who had his head in the grass munching next to the electrified fence stopped pulling up grass, gave me a glance, and went back to munching.

How rude. "Fine. Don't share your water source, cow. See if I sacrifice my hunger next time I'm at a barbecue and have a choice between a burger or chicken. I promise you. I'm eating that burger."

The cow eyed me with disdain.

God, I must have really been losing my mind to be arguing with a cow. Maybe dehydration didn't take as long as I'd thought.

A loud, rumbly growl, along with the sound of gravel crunching, caught my attention. "Wonderful. Help from the calvary. No thanks to you, cow!" Yeah, I hollered at the cow. It was hot, he was rude, and I was thirsty.

I turned away from my nemesis and watched as a beat-up silver Ford pickup pulled up to the side of the road. To say the man who climbed out of the truck and strutted toward me was striking would be an understatement.

He wore a beige Carhartt button-up and a baseball cap on backward. His eyes, which were a unique silver-gray, held mine and caused my heart to do a strange fluttering thing, and they popped in contrast to his sun-tanned skin and, from what I could see sticking out from under his hat, jet-black hair.

My eyes traveled down his tall, muscular body. He wore work boots which had seen better days, and faded, paint-splattered jeans that were well-worn and perfectly tight, hugging his thighs. I stalled at the bulge right under his hips, and my mouth went dry.

Good Lord. Keep moving, eyes.

A loud moo pulled my attention away from the gift strutting toward me and back to my adversary in the field.

"Just go drink that water. You water hoarder," I spat in its direction. I don't know why, but that cow really pissed me off.

"I can't figure out why that cow would be walking away from you. He was keeping you company, and you sure don't seem grateful." His voice was deep, smooth as whiskey, and sexy as hell.

I started to pull my gaze from his, and a distinctive scar, which started by his brow and dipped below his eye, caught my attention. It was the shape of a crescent moon, roughly two inches long, and stood out clearly, suggesting it had been a part of his skin for quite a while. The scar's edges were jagged in places and added a bit of intrigue to his boy-next-door good looks. The couple days' worth of scruff on his face, which I yearned to rub my hands over, gave a rugged allure to his chiseled jawline, and he carried himself with confidence, which increased his overall irresistibility and caused a tingling throughout my body.

What the hell, Kora?

I was taken so off guard, I needed to clear my throat to make my voice work. "Yeah, well, the cow was keeping me company, but when he wouldn't share his water source to keep me from dying of dehydration, I threatened to skip the chicken and eat his cousin instead next time I was at a barbecue."

"Well, I'm sure that's what irritated him." The corner of this stranger's mouth ticked up, and a sexy-as-hell dimple appeared in his left cheek.

Just when I thought this man couldn't get any hotter, I was mistaken. I smirked to hide the blush I was sure colored my cheeks and nodded. "Yeah, well, water would have been nice, but a tire would be even better."

"I guess you hit one of those craters back there?"

"Yeah, I did. I wish this county would spend a little bit of money to fix these back roads, since most of their citizens live back here. But they're so cheap. It's much more important that city hall has a newly paved parking lot and cute rocking chairs on the front porch."

"Those rocking chairs are a perfect place for the locals to hang out and play checkers. I think it's a great addition."

Really? I glared at him through lowered lashes. "You can't be serious."

There was that dimple again.

Did the heat just tick up a notch? I puffed out a breath. "Look, this has been great, but you wouldn't by any chance have a tire in the back of that beat-up truck, would you?"

"Wow." He took a step back. A flicker of annoyance crossed his features, and his brow furrowed. "You don't even know me, and you're bashing Matilda. No one bashes Matilda."

Okay, now that was funny. It looked like poor Matilda had been bashed on multiple times. I laughed out loud. "You're right. I shouldn't be bashing your truck. I'm sorry."

"Matilda."

"Your truck is really named Matilda?"

"Got a problem with Matilda?" he asked as he stepped forward, his hand out. "I'm Kai."

My brows rose. *Nice name.* I smiled and shook his hand. "Kora." His hands were rough like he wasn't scared of hard work, which matched his clothing choice perfectly. "I haven't seen you around before. Are you new, visiting family?"

Kai shook his head and pursed his lips. "Nope. No family. Just got into town yesterday, so I guess that qualifies as new."

"So, what brings you by this way?"

"Well, a woman on the side of the road looking like she's in need of assistance." Again, I noticed his voice: deep yet soft, and totally sexy.

This guy was amazingly hot, had a unique sense of humor, and a sexy as hell dimple. *He can assist me anytime.* Again, I needed to clear my throat—probably a lack of water. "Yeah, well. The woman stuck on the side of the road appreciates your help, but I meant Orlinda Valley. What brings you here? Business, pleasure?" I turned my face up to see him better. He was tall, at least six feet four. And built. God, was he built.

He wiped his hands together like he was preparing for battle. "Let's deal with this tire. Where's your jack and spare?"

"Yeah, about that."

His brow ticked up.

"Yeah, well, at Christmas, I needed the space under there for presents and never put the tire or jack back in my car. It's sitting in my aunt's garage."

"You don't have a tire or jack in your car? Isn't that Driving 101?"

It sounded so much more ridiculous when I divulged the situation to him. *I hope he doesn't think I'm the stereotypical female. All about shopping and have no common sense. That is so not me. Well, I do like to shop.* My shoulders met my ears.

"Figures," Kai muttered and shook his head before walking to the back of his truck.

Hell no. He is not going to go there. My hands flew to my hips. "Excuse me? Did you just say *figures*?"

"What, you heard that?" Kai pulled a small tire from the back of his truck and carried it to the car. Then he went back to his truck and returned with a jack and a tire iron.

My gaze followed him back and forth as a heavy weight lodged in my gut. "I'm not deaf, you know. Explain yourself. What figures? Is it that I'm a female?" I eyed the tire. It didn't look big enough for a go cart. "Are you sure that tire will fit on my car?"

He didn't answer as he jacked up the car, loosened the bolts, took off the flat tire, and quickly replaced it with the donut he had taken from his truck. "To answer all your billions of questions—it figures that you don't have a tire. It *is* such a female thing, and yes, this will fit. It came from my sister's car. I gave her a full-size spare before she drove across the country. Oh, and you said it, sweetheart, not me."

Did he just call me sweetheart? I sucked in a big breath and took a beat to keep from saying the first thing that came to my mind. I scrunched my face. "I said what?"

"That you're a female, and that's the reason you were stuck on the side of the road." Kai stood up and brushed his hands against his pants.

Is this guy for real? "Are you always this rude to people you just meet?"

"Rude? I didn't say anything rude. Just pointed out the obvious and answered your million-and-one questions."

I could stand a lot of things, but I couldn't stand being treated like a weak female. Okay, maybe I did something stupid when I didn't listen to my father. I should have put the spare back in the car, but being needy and weak was not something I wanted people to see me as, especially not this irritating, yet hot, stranger. "You know what?" I walked over to him and stepped on the dead tire. "Keep this here. I don't need any more of your assistance. I'll deal with it myself."

Kai peered at me, then down at the flat tire, then back. "I can just toss it in the back of my truck and take it to the garage I saw in town. It's not a big deal."

My hands flew into the air and brushed him off. "Nope. Please don't. I'll *toss* this into my car. I wouldn't want to be seen as needy."

"You sure?"

What a jackass. I rolled my eyes toward the sky. "Yeah. Thanks for your help." My gaze rested on his, and I squinted in disgust. "Next time, though, keep driving."

Kai stepped back and lifted his hands in defeat.

Good. He might be a jackass, but he listens well.

I bent down and attempted to lift the tire off the ground. *Shit.* Even flat, it was heavier than it appeared. I slowly drag-carried it to the back and opened the hatch. I took a big breath, bent at my knees, heaved it into the back, and then had to take a second to catch my breath.

God, that sucked.

I slammed the hatch closed and froze as I caught a glimpse of my hands. They were black. I brushed them together. Still black. Then I brushed them on my pants, and the dirt smeared. "Shit."

"What's wrong, princess? Little grease on your hands?"

I shot Kai a glare, one that could kill.

I waited and watched.

No luck. He still stood there, breathing. "No big deal. Nothing soap won't get rid of," I answered with fake confidence. I'd be damned if I'd show weakness over grease.

"Yeah, maybe, but your shirt will need a little TLC."

I glanced down. There was a streak of black on the front. Must have been when I lifted the tire. "Shit. My favorite shirt."

"Dish detergent will get it out. Scrub it with an old toothbrush and rinse with cold water. Should be fine."

Dish soap. "I knew that." I pushed past him to the driver's side of my car, then stopped, and my shoulders drooped. *Be an adult, Kora, and don't be so bitchy.* I pulled myself up as tall as my five-foot-six frame would allow and shot my hand toward him. "Thanks, Kai. I appreciate your help."

He wrapped my hand with his, and warmth seeped into my skin. My chilly attitude melted instantly and caused me to forget where I was for a beat. I blinked repeatedly to regain my composure before I said, "I know we've started off rough and had a bumpy patch, but I hope everything's been fixed." I chuckled at my joke. It was funny.

He glared at me.

Okay then, maybe the heat that melted my attitude was all one-sided. *Let's try to break the tension between us one more time.* "There's a great place to eat in town—Jerry's Pub, if you want to catch a bite or anything."

"Thanks, but I've already been told about it and was planning on doing just that." He turned and strolled away.

My eyes were glued to his ass in those jeans. *Nice.*

He reached his truck. "It was nice meeting you. Stay clear of the potholes and get the spare back in your car. Maybe I'll see you around town."

"I sure hope so," I muttered to myself as I got into my car. I waved as I pulled away. The last thing I saw was his dimpled smile—maybe it was a smirk—and his fine-as-hell body as he climbed into his truck. "Orlinda Valley just added another hot-as-hell asshole to its population."

Chapter 2

KAI

I leaned my elbow on my open window as I sat in my driver's seat and watched the Nissan until it disappeared around a curve. "This small town keeps looking up," I said aloud to the cow standing by the fence.

The cow lifted its head before it let out a soft moo and headed on its way. I chuckled, feeling unexpectedly good. I patted the steering wheel as I cranked the key. "Sorry, Matilda, old girl. You don't need to listen to those words. You've always been reliable and had my back."

She revved high, then loud, then purred like a kitten. Okay, maybe it was closer to roaring like a lion, but the point was, she was still reliable even after all these years—the most reliable thing in my life—even more so than any person had ever been, including my parents.

I drove back toward town and enjoyed the scenery as the open country, with scattered houses, gave way to sidewalks and houses closer together with cute fenced-in yards. Driving out to the country had been useful. The land I had looked at, five acres surrounded by woods and farms on one side and bordered on the other by the Red River, was perfect, peaceful, and exactly what I wanted. As soon as I could get the papers signed, I'd pull my fifth-wheel camper onto the property, get the septic in place, and start building my dream home. It was time to lay down roots and stop roaming the country. Orlinda Valley was the perfect out-of-the way town to call home and live a quiet life, and since I'd met some of the occupants, it became even better.

Finally, the bumpy road came to an end—the county really did need to make fixing the roads a top priority—and I pulled into the parking lot and into a spot at the front of Jerry's Pub. Gary, my realtor, better not have been wrong about Jerry's having the best sandwiches in town. I was ravenous.

Jerry's Pub was a brick building that had been painted beige. There was a covered deck off the side with tables and an outside bar with a garage door that could probably open up on nice nights to expand the space and let the fresh air in.

I walked through the door and was greeted by country music playing through the speakers. There were televisions on the walls. One was on a local news station, and a ball game was playing on most of the rest. High-top tables and booths were scattered around, and the space was decorated with local high school sports team pictures and jerseys, and artifacts from an old fire station. It was a cool atmosphere, and I made myself comfortable at the bar and opened a menu.

The bartender placed a coaster in front of me. "Hey there. I'm Trevor. Welcome to Jerry's Pub. How can I help you?"

I glanced at the menu for a second longer, then closed it and pushed it away. "My realtor told me you have the best sandwiches in town, but looking at the town, I'm not sure if that's a compliment." I tried to make the statement sound light and funny, but I might not have succeeded, and it could have seemed slightly condescending.

Luckily, Trevor seemed to have a good sense of humor. "I thought you were new in town, and yes, that doesn't say much as there's not a lot to choose from, but it also says a lot. Because it's so true, no other restaurants have ever tried to compete with us."

Tension left my body, and I relaxed. "Good to hear. What do you suggest?"

"Nico, our chef, makes a mean Reuben. The fries are seasoned and amazing, and we have some great local craft beers."

"Well then, a Reuben and fries would be perfect, but I'll just take a Coke." Though the beer sounded good, I could do without it.

Trevor smacked the bar. "Coming right up." He tapped on the computer screen, then pulled out a hose and filled a cup with Coke. "Here ya go." He placed the Coke on the bar.

I took a sip and leaned back on the stool to have a better look around. The pub had a typical American small-town vibe. There was an entire wall dedicated to Orlinda Valley High School sports, and another with the University of Tennessee orange decorating the area. It was relatively empty, but seeing as it was just one o'clock on a Saturday, it wasn't surprising.

There was a group of older men in a corner booth laughing and cutting it up. There were four teenagers, two boys and two girls, at another table. I sipped my Coke as I watched them. I tried to decide if they were on a date or just hanging out, but I gave up.

"Here ya go. One Reuben and fries." Trevor placed the basket of food on the bar. "Can I get you anything else? Ketchup, Tabasco?"

"Here's a weird question, but could I have a side of mayo and some Tabasco?"

"Not weird at all. Be right back." Trevor pounded on the bar again, disappeared behind the double doors, and quickly reappeared with a small bowl of mayonnaise and the hot sauce.

"Thanks." I shook the Tabasco sauce into the mayonnaise, stirred it with a fry, and ate it. My mouth was accosted with flavor. "Damn. Those are some amazing fries."

"Right," Trevor agreed. "And I've gotta say, you're the first one I've seen do that." He pointed to the mayo and Tabasco concoction. "I've mixed that combo together for years and have gotten some strange glares. Until they try it, of course."

"Nothing's better." I dipped another fry into the mayo and popped it in my mouth. Delicious.

"Let me know if you need anything else," Trevor said as he refilled my glass.

"There is something else. Can you tell me if there's anyone in town needing a handyman? I've got full-time work, but really want to keep myself busy and can do all types of home repair and small remodeling jobs."

"You know what? Shear Perfection, the hair salon just across the street, needs an addition. Let me make a call and talk to Diane and Kaye."

"That'd be great. Thanks."

By the time I was finished eating, I had a meeting with Diane and Kaye, the owners of Shear Perfection. It sounded like a simple addition. They just needed a storage area turned into additional shampooing stations. I didn't think it would be difficult or take too much time.

"Thanks, Trevor. You were right. The food was delicious." I handed him my card to pay for the meal. "And thanks for the reference to the salon."

"Glad you enjoyed it, and not a problem at all," he said. "Don't want to pry, but do you have a wife or kids who'll be joining you in town?"

"Nope." I shook my head. "Just me. I'm hoping to settle down, build a house, and see what happens." I placed my card back in my wallet. "What do you do for fun around here?"

"You're looking at it. Friday and Saturday nights, this place gets full. You should stop back by tonight. The cornhole competition starts, and it can get competitive."

My brows shot up. Cornhole was the weekend fun. "Sounds interesting."

Trevor laughed. "Yeah, the expression on your face says otherwise. If you don't come for cornhole, come for the females. We have quite a nice group of single women in this town."

I had to agree. If Kora was any indication of the type of women occupying the town, I was looking forward to getting to know them. Maybe Kora would show up. I wouldn't mind seeing her again.

Chapter 3

KORA

I blew through the door of Shear Perfection like a tornado on a path of destruction. God, I hated being late and hated the attitude Summer always got when she was held up. "Hey, Summer. So sorry." I plopped my ass into her chair and pulled the scrunchy from my hair, letting my wavy mass of auburn hair fall past my shoulders. I had to suck in deep to get my breathing under control.

"You're fine. I need to finish up in back really quick. Get comfortable, and for God's sake, try to stop sweating."

I chuckled at Summer. She was as sarcastic as a wasp was mean, but she made a perfect friend. She was always honest and wouldn't let you walk around looking ridiculous.

"Hello there, Kora honey." My Aunt Tonya was at the salon as usual on a Saturday morning, more to feed her best friends the local gossip she'd heard during the week than get her hair or nails done. She wrapped me in a one-arm hug, then backed up with a grimace.

"You're as sticky as a strip club floor at closing time. What the hell have you been doing?"

My mouth dropped, and Tonya laughed, which always sounded more like a cackle than a laugh. Everything about her was loud, and she was always the life of any party and the perfect aunt. "Tonya," I said, shaking my head. Yes, Tonya was my aunt, but she always said aunt made her feel old, so she banned me from using the term early on.

"You do know we have customers in here, right? You need to find a filter." Summer appeared from the back room, her hands filled with towels.

I took some of the towels from her and helped her put them in the cabinets above the sinks. "You know we should be used to her by now."

"Yeah, you should," Tonya agreed. "Sometimes, Summer, you act older than me. No wonder you're still single. You need to relax a little," Tonya said as she sat in Kaye's chair, a stylist and co-owner of the salon.

"T, be nice," Kaye replied. "Not everyone needs to be as eccentric as you."

"Eccentric?" Summer's face scrunched up with disgust. "Tonya is far from eccentric. She's just loud and obnoxious. Adding a filter once in a while would make her more bearable."

"Oh, pooh, Summer." Tonya tilted her head mockingly. "Better?"

Summer rolled her eyes and turned to me.

"Sorry." My shoulders met my ears. "That color's new and looks amazing on you." Maybe I could get Summer's attention on something else. Change the subject. "You really pull it off." It was true. Summer's hair was an out-there color—as usual. Her naturally brown hair was dyed midnight black with blue tips, but in true to Summer form, her petite five-foot-three frame easily looked natural with the short choppy cut and colorful locks.

Summer always was the unorthodox one and stood out like a sore thumb in our conservative, small-town high school, and that was how she liked it. She was loud, boisterous, and unpredictable, and had been since we were kids.

Darlene and I had been friends with Summer since kindergarten, but neither of us would put her in the class of bestie. Summer didn't do besties. She just did friends. If she had to pick a best friend, though, she'd probably choose Rowan, my cousin and Tonya's youngest son of her three boys.

"Thanks. I did it last week." She pulled a brush through my hair. "I liked it then, but now I don't know. Rowan wasn't a fan. That's for sure."

"Seriously? That's a surprise. He loved the blonde with blue tips you did last year."

"I know, but he said this color is too dark and makes me look like I'm going back to my Goth stage. He hated my Goth stage."

"No offense, Summer, but we all hated your Goth stage. You were a little depressing and scary."

Summer bopped her head back and forth. "True. That was my way of getting back at my parents for their divorce."

Summer was a freshman in high school when her dad came home, told her mom he had stopped loving her, and packed and moved out to California with his young secretary. Summer took her parents' divorce hard and went immediately into a rebellious stage and became a little much to deal with. Rowan, though, could always keep her from doing something totally stupid and regretful. She'd had nothing to do with her father since then.

"So, how is Rowan? Military still treating him well?"

"So far, but I'm not sure how much longer he's going to be in. It's already been eleven years, and he was only planning on two enlistments and he's on his third." Rowan graduated from high school with Summer, Darlene, Trevor—his best friend—and me. We all hung out daily, and even though Rowan was my cousin, he was always closer to Summer than we ever were.

"I can't wait till he gets home. It's been a while."

"Yeah, well, you know how things were when he left. So, whatever." Summer pulled at a knot in my hair.

My hand went immediately to my hair in defense. "Ouch. What the hell, Summer?"

She slapped it away. "What happened to you this morning? You're never late, and your hair is all matted. Were you hanging outside in this heat?" She grabbed her bottle of detangler and carefully brushed out my matted mess.

"You know me too well. Yes, I was." I cringed as she worked. "It was a fucking nightmare."

"Language, niece. We all need filters so we don't upset any customers." Tonya's voice dripped with sarcasm from across the salon.

Summer squatted by my ear. "Can I shoot her a bird?"

I muffled a laugh. "She'd enjoy it too much. I'll handle this. Sorry *Auntie*," I sang in the sweetest and most condescending voice I could muster. I scrunched up my mouth and made a face at Summer. Like Tonya wasn't the one I learned that kind of language from.

Summer chuckled. "So, what happened to cause the effing nightmare?"

"My tire was eaten by one of those pothole craters back on Old Fort Road, and when I tried to call you and Darlene . . . nothing. Not even one bar."

"Not surprising. That's the county dead zone." Summer placed a towel over my head.

"You should tell Mayor John. He needs to know," Tonya said.

"You should mind your own business, old lady. We aren't talking with you," retorted Summer.

"Enough, you two." Kaye turned Tonya's chair to face the other direction.

Summer wiggled her brows at me in the mirror.

Those two were always on each other's case and were very entertaining. "The county wouldn't do anything about it. It doesn't bother them any," I said as I followed Summer to the shampoo chairs and laid my head back on the sink. I closed my eyes. This was the best part of getting my hair cut and colored. I loved the hair wash and scalp massage.

"I bet he'd listen to you, T, if you pull John to the side and give him a little gift," Kaye answered as she wiggled her shoulders.

"You're so right. You know he's always asking for a little something, something," Tonya whispered loudly.

Summer and I flinched.

"Oh, my God. I really need to find a new place to work. Hearing their sex talk all the time is so cringey," Summer whispered.

"You need to learn how to whisper, girlie. We aren't so old that our hearing's going," Tonya said.

"Sorry, Ms. Tonya." Summer's voice oozed with sarcasm.

"The girl's not wrong though, T. You were quite explicit last weekend with your dating experiences."

"Well, I'm no longer interested in John, anyway. He and I are yesterday's news." Tonya caught Kaye's gaze in the mirror. "Go easy on the blonde. I don't want the young bucks in town to think I'm too hot."

"I gotcha, T. Light on the blonde but heavy on the sexy." Kaye chuckled as she started to prepare Tonya's hair.

"Do you think we're going to be that . . ." I sat up as Summer wrapped a towel around my head.

"Crazy?" Summer said.

"No, I was going to say young at heart."

Kaye spoke to Tonya in the mirror. "I've always liked your niece, T."

"Yeah, I think she's a keeper." Tonya blew me a kiss.

I air-kissed her back and sighed. "You could have given me a longer scalp massage, Summer. With the morning I had, I deserve it."

"Yeah, well, with the morning you had, I'm now running behind and have an eleven o'clock coming in like thirty minutes, so let's get your hair cut and styled ASAP. I'm gonna be playing catch-up all day and starving by the time I'm done with my last cut. I want to join y'all at Jerry's tonight as soon as possible."

Jerry's was short for Jerry's Pub, the best place for sandwiches and beer in the county. Jerry no longer owned it, as he passed away years ago, but a group of local firemen purchased the pub, added on, and what used to be a small hole in the wall had become a place to hang out all weekend and take part in one of the many tournaments going on. On this particular evening, it would be cornhole.

"That's right, Bryson and Patrick are playing tonight, aren't they?"

"Yep," Summer replied as she passed a comb through my hair, much easier this time. "So, what are we going to do with this stringy mess?"

I made eye contact with Summer in the mirror and put up my middle finger.

"Not smart. I have scissors in my hand."

"Ha ha," I said as I ran my fingers through my wet locks. "Honestly I was thinking of adding layers, framing it around my face, and cutting it just below the shoulders."

Summer leaned back. "Are you sure? That'll be a big change. You're not one for big change."

"True, but I'm also tired of dealing with it just hanging and having to put it up all the time."

"Okay then. Let's do this." Summer combed some hair up, measured a length to take off, and made eye contact.

It was a little longer than what I suggested but shorter than usual. She knew me too well. I nodded.

"Good. I'd rather go a little longer at first, and if you still want to go shorter, we can take more. We just can't put it back on if you don't like it, and I don't want to hear you bitch till it grows back out."

"You sounded so genuine at first. I wondered if you were abducted by aliens. But no."

Summer made a duck face in the mirror, and I returned it. "So, you never finished your story. Your tire was eaten by one of those craters." Summer encouraged me to continue as she combed and snipped.

"Well, I pulled over because I ended up getting a flat, had no service, and was wondering if I would die from dehydration if I walked into town when this truck pulled over to help."

"Who was it?"

"Someone new. Anyway, he helped me out, but was such a jerk and a sexist pig. You know—it was like he expected me not to know how to change a tire."

"Well, you don't."

"Not the point. And then he was rude when I told him I didn't have a spare because I took it out to make room for Christmas shopping."

"You still hadn't put it back?"

I shook my head.

"Didn't your dad tell you to take care of that before he moved?"

"Again, not the point."

"Interesting. So, where's the old tire?"

"In the back of my car. I'll take it to Bubba's. He'll dispose of it for me when he puts on some new tires." Bubba owned Tyson's Brakes and More.

"It was nice of this stranger to put the tire in the back of your car."

"He didn't. I did."

"I'm guessing that would explain the smudge I noticed on your shirt."

"Yep. It'll come out with dish soap."

"Okay, so a guy stopped by and was a gentleman, and helped you out, which you ladies nowadays don't like. But was he a looker?" Tonya asked.

Nothing was ever sacred in this hair salon. Not with the town gossips, slash book club, slash my aunt and her best friends, always within ear shot. "Yeah, he looked good, but looks aren't everything, you know. Personality and respect are number one, *Auntie*," I replied.

The bell over the door jingled, announcing the presence of another in the salon.

"Yeah, and helping a woman in distress isn't very gentlemanly," Tonya mocked.

"T, leave the ladies alone," Kaye answered. "They'll figure out how to find a gentleman when they're ready."

"Hey, everyone." It was Darlene, my best friend since birth. "Don't put me in the same category as my friends here. Remember, I've already figured things out. I have my husband." She was married to Bryson, Tonya's middle son. "And he's pretty amazing."

"Thank you, honey." Tonya blew her a kiss. "His wife's pretty amazing as well."

Darlene placed a coffee on the counter in front of me.

"God, you're a lifesaver. Thanks, Dar." I leaned over to pick up the coffee, but Summer yanked my head back by the handful of hair she held. "Ouch. Crappy customer service," I said as I reached up to rub my head.

Summer smacked my hand away.

"Jesus, Summer. That's the second time this morning you smacked me. Your customer service truly sucks."

"If you want me to take out a big chunk of your hair, fine. But I don't want to hear you complain about it forever, so sit still."

Darlene chuckled and sat in the neighboring chair and crossed her legs. "You better take her seriously, Kor. We don't want a repeat of senior year."

Yeah, that sucked. I had always been Summer's guinea pig when it came to needing a model for cosmetology school. Senior year, Summer was pissed at me for something that happened on the volleyball court and "accidentally" cut off all my hair. We didn't talk for months after.

I met Summer's gaze in the mirror and raised a brow.

Summer winked. "Don't worry. I've matured since then."

Darlene let out a loud, hearty laugh, and Summer got a snort from me. One thing we knew as a fact—Summer would never grow up.

"So, get back to this mysterious stranger who helped you this morning," Summer replied.

"Mysterious stranger?" Darlene leaned forward in the chair; her brows raised intently.

"Yeah, I got a flat tire, and a hot guy helped me."

"Oh, so now he's hot." Summer pursed her lips. "Earlier he was just good looking."

"Hot, good looking. Whatever. He helped out and was especially annoying."

"Interesting." Darlene stared at me intently. I knew her too well. Her mind was grinding. "Did you get his name?"

"Yeah, Kai."

"Nice name." Darlene leaned back and sipped her coffee.

"Hot name," Summer answered.

Darlene nodded slowly. I closed my eyes and tried to ignore the silent discussion going on between the two of them. They were always looking to set me up with someone even though I had just broken up with Patrick four months ago. It was annoying how Summer got away with never being bothered about dating someone. It was always me.

Well, one thing was for sure, Kai was not going to be the next guy in my bed. Nope. Wasn't gonna happen. Not even with his sexy body, or those crystal eyes, or that seductive voice. I forced my eyes open to get his picture out of my mind.

Darlene's gaze met mine. She had a shit-eating grin on her face, and her head continued the annoying bobbing up and down.

Friends were so much trouble sometimes. I rolled my eyes and tried my best to ignore her.

Thirty minutes later, my hair was cut and styled. It felt much lighter and already looked so much healthier. "It looks amazing. I love it, Summer." I shook my head from side to side. My hair flowed gently and lightly touched my shoulders.

"If you would get your hair cut more often, it wouldn't be such a mangled mess."

"Gee, thanks."

"Any time. Now, in two weeks come to get that color we've been talking about."

"Yep. I will." I grabbed my coffee and took a big drink. "Shit. It's lukewarm."

"Like your heart." Summer blew me a kiss.

"Maybe a mysterious stranger could warm that heart a bit." Darlene wiggled her brows.

"I'm sure a night of amazing orgasms would do the trick," Summer agreed.

"Oh, my God. Y'all." I stood and held up my hands to stop them. "Why do I even talk to y'all?"

"Because you love us," Darlene said.

"And we're your only friends," Summer answered.

"Whatever." I grabbed my purse. "Dar, if we're still going shopping, then to the pub, I suggest you stop this crazy talk now, or I'll just go home and spend a quiet night with my goats."

"The only guys she spends time with are those damn goats," Summer said as she swept her station.

"You're right," I spit back. "Percy, Jackson, and Baby Goat are sweet and expect nothing but food, petting, and unconditional love. They are the perfect men."

"As far as I can tell, all men want is food, petting, and unconditional love. Goats seem to be no different." Summer swept the hair into the wall vacuum.

"I don't know, Summer. My man enjoys my company and is one of my best friends," Darlene interjected.

"Exactly like Kora's goats."

An older woman, Mrs. Ledbetter, entered the salon.

"Hello, Mrs. Ledbetter," Summer greeted her next customer sweetly, then turned to us, her sweet demeanor evaporated. "Now you two get out of my salon so I can make some real money, and I'll meet you at the pub when I'm finished."

"We should be there around five. Maybe if Bryson and Patrick win the first round, they'll celebrate with some free drinks," Darlene said.

"Perfect. I have my final cut at four. I'll show up after." She turned to Mrs. Ledbetter. "Hi. Take a seat, Mrs. Ledbetter."

"Hello, girls. It's so good to see you."

Mrs. Ledbetter had been our first-grade teacher. She had to be about seventy by now, but she still looked good. "It's good to see you too, Mrs. Ledbetter," I answered.

"Yes, ma'am. it is," Darlene agreed.

I turned to Summer. It had been a while since we had all been out together. Summer always bailed at the last minute, giving some lame excuse. I knew it was because she wasn't a fan of Bryson and tried her best to avoid him. "We'll save you a seat, Summer. You can't back out this time." I pointed at her.

"I won't," Summer answered as she placed a cape around Mrs. Ledbetter.

"Friendship swear?" I asked.

"You're serious?" Summer stood with her hands on her hips and looked more than irritated, as I knew she would be. She was downright pissed.

"I'm always serious." I held out my arm.

Summer rolled her eyes but linked elbows. We crossed our arms, kissed our palms, then tapped each other's cheek.

Summer hated this friendship swear the three of us made up in elementary school. Well, Darlene and I made it up, and Summer just had to follow. "Perfect. See you tonight."

Summer turned to Mrs. Ledbetter, our cue to leave.

We said goodbye and gave Tonya and Kaye quick hugs.

Shopping, then margaritas at the pub. No better way to spend a Saturday night.

Chapter 4

KAI

I pulled Matilda into the parking lot of Shear Perfection just before one and sat inspecting the building. It was an older, updated house and was next to a small strip of stores on one side and an old drugstore, Orlinda Valley Drugs, on the other.

I walked through the door and was greeted by the heavy ammonia smell of hair products mixed with fresh-brewed coffee. It's a smell only women would see as relaxing and comforting as it burned my nose. The sounds, though, were relaxing. A low murmur of conversation along with the buzz of hair dryers.

"Hi there, hon. Can I help you?" I was greeted by a woman, maybe late twenties or early thirties, with black hair which had dark blue tips.

I caught her eyes as they floated down, then back up. I had to hide a smirk. I was always amused when I caught a woman staring. "I talked with Trevor, from Jerry's Pub. I'm supposed to be meeting

Diane and Kaye." I put on my best poker face and acted like I was clueless and didn't catch her gazing at me, but standing there in the salon, I felt like a fish out of water. This was nothing like anywhere I'd ever been. Give me the chaos and dirt of a garage, or the loud cacophony of a construction site any day. But a hair salon?

"Diane, this is . . ." The woman with the black and blue hair shot her brows up in a questioning look.

"Kai," I finished for her.

Her eyes bulged, pushing her brows up a bit higher.

I ticked up my brow up to match hers and held her gaze. The look she was giving me was intense, like she expected me to break out in dance or something. *What was that was about*?

I didn't get a chance to ask because three ladies, one with pieces of her hair wrapped in foil, walked toward us.

A middle-aged woman with dark hair put out her hand. "Hi there, Kai." I shook her hand. "Thank you for coming so quickly. I'm Diane, and this is Kaye." She gestured to the woman to her right with shoulder-length blonde hair. "We own the salon."

"And I'm Tonya," the one with foil in her hair stated. "Their nosy friend." She held out her hand, and I shook it as Tonya's gaze flicked down quickly, then back up, just like the first woman. Then she nodded.

Talk about feeling scrutinized and judged. For a small town that had been so welcoming, the women in this salon had a way of making me feel like a piece of meat.

"Ignore her," Kaye said, pushing Tonya out of the way. I chuckled at the look Tonya threw at Kaye. "Follow me. I'll show you what's going on."

We walked into a back room that turned out to be a small kitchen, likely the break room. Kaye, Tonya, Diane, and the one with colorful hair followed. *Do they all really need to be a part of this?*

"Would you like a cup of coffee? It's fresh," Diane asked.

"Thank you. I think I will." I filled a mug with coffee. It smelled amazing, and one mouthful told me it was much better than what I drank at the crappy hotel I was staying in just outside of town. I couldn't decide what was worse, the coffee or the lobby it was brewed in. My taste buds and insides thanked me for the amazing, rich coffee flavor seeping through my blood. I could almost feel the caffeine taking effect. "This is great. Thank you, Ms. Diane."

Diane brushed away the gratitude. "Don't thank me yet. You haven't started anything."

The lady with the silver foil in her hair, Tonya if I remembered correctly, leaned on the counter.

I squirmed a little as she looked me up and down again. It wasn't the first time I had the older ladies intrigued. "So, ladies. Maybe I should introduce myself correctly. I'm Kai Lawson, and just got into town. I'm working with a construction company, currently on a site in Nashville, so I'm looking for extra work at night and on weekends." I sipped my coffee and started to relax. "I've had years of experience and love doing little fix-up jobs around houses and small businesses."

"Well, Kai Lawson, I'm Tonya McKendry. It sounds like you have the experience needed to fix up this shithole."

"Watch it, T. The owners of this shithole could leave your color in too long and fry those lovely locks of yours. Then where would you be?" Kaye replied.

"Looking my age, I guess."

"Exactly."

Tonya rolled her eyes. "If you weren't one of my oldest friends, I wouldn't keep putting up with your abuse. Anyway." She turned her full attention toward me again. "So, you think you'll be able to fix up this sh—I mean amazing hair salon?"

"Better." Kaye winked at her.

I chuckled. Tonya might have been a little off, but there was something about her that made her fun. "Well, if this is how it'll be, at least it won't be boring around here. But first I need to see what you need done."

"Follow us." I did as instructed and trailed after Diane and Kaye through a side door, and we spent some time looking at the room and discussing what they wanted done. I took measurements and asked questions. It really was a simple job. Pulling out some old shelving, adding additional plumbing, and electricity possibly, then putting up walls and stations.

"I think what you're asking will be relatively straightforward. Not a problem at all."

"Do you often do whatever women ask of you?" Tonya asked in a sultry voice.

I was in the middle of swallowing coffee and choked, spitting some out of my mouth.

"Tonya! Don't scare the man off already. We need him to stick around," Diane yelled as she slapped Tonya across the arm.

"It's good. Trust me." I held up my hand and tried to get control of my coughing fit. "Keep the coffee coming, and I'll be here forever. The coffee where I'm staying is a close cousin to mud, which shouldn't surprise me since the motel could use a total overhaul."

"Where are you staying?" Diane asked as she mopped up the bit of coffee I spewed on the floor. I tried to take the mop from her, but she brushed me off and made quick work of cleaning up.

"I'm staying at the motel at the edge of town."

Tonya stepped away from the counter, a horrified look on her face. "Motel 256?"

"Yeah, that's it."

Her eyes went wide as saucers, and she shared a glance with Diane and Kaye and a head gesture.

I had no clue what was going on between them. It seemed as if they were communicating without words. When you were friends as long as they seemed to have been, I guess you could. I wouldn't know anything about that as I never had good friends growing up, and lately I hadn't been in one place long enough to set down roots and make friends. Someday I really hoped that would finally come to an end.

Diane spoke up. "You know, we have a small office space with a single bed we turned into a couch. We don't use the room anymore. You're more than welcome to use it. It's clean, and you'd have full use of the kitchen."

Did she just invite me to stay here? They don't know anything about me. I'm all for small towns being friendly and everything, but that's a little bit crazy. "I don't know. I don't want to put you out."

"You won't. Just think about it."

"Thanks. I will. If you don't mind, I'll take some time, write up a plan of action, and make a list of everything I'll need and get a quote for you before I leave today. It looks pretty simple. If you agree with what I write up, I could start as early as tomorrow. As soon as you close, I can start demoing."

"That sounds great. Take your time, and if you have any questions, just let us know," said Diane.

"We would be happy to help you with anything you might need," Tonya said. "And welcome to Orlinda Valley."

"Thanks. I appreciate it." I went back to the room and started to take notes and make lists. It didn't take long for me to get into the groove of what I was doing and lose track of time. Before long, I knew where the electric would need to be moved to and planned out the new plumbing. The most difficult part would be tapping into the existing plumbing. That wasn't my strength, so I'd have to find a reliable and local plumber to help.

It was a while later, and the salon was surprisingly quiet, when I finally finished. I walked out of the back room. The only ones there were Diane and Kaye.

"Hey. So, how'd everything go?" Diane asked.

"Everything went just fine, ma'am. I don't think it will be hard at all to do what you need done."

"Handy and mannerly. No wonder Tonya was at her best today." Kaye faced me. "Excuse our friend. She's never had a filter, and her mouth tends to run as quickly as a river after a hard rain."

These ladies were a lot of fun. I'd enjoy working near them. Their banter between each other was sure to keep me entertained. "Not a problem." I laid my notes on the counter. "I have here a list of materials I'll need, and a quote I put together. I will send you my references, and as soon as you okay things, I can get started."

Diane swiped away his words. "We don't need any of that. Just give us the quote and let us know how you want us to pay. We don't need your references."

They sure were trustworthy. I really needed the job and the extra money it would bring in to get things at the new property going quicker. "Great. Then once I get the wall down and everything pulled out, I'll be able to start the build. If I can get in here tomorrow, it really shouldn't take too long."

The bell over the door announced a customer. I turned automatically. A man entered with a young child. Kaye walked around the counter and scooped up the little boy just as he propelled himself at her. She planted many kisses all over his face and made him squeal like a pig. "Kai, this adorable little one is James, Tonya's grandson. James, say hi to our new friend Kai."

James narrowed his eyes. I was more uncomfortable because of this little boy and his gaze than from all the adults who gave me the same scrutinizing stare all day long.

"Please excuse him. He's not great with strangers. I'm Bryson, James's father." Bryson poked James in the stomach, making him wiggle free from Kaye's hold.

He walked over to the bucket with suckers and opened and closed his hand. "Pweese?" His brown eyes were large and wide as he pushed out his lips and placed his hands in a praying gesture at Kaye. I may not have been into kids, but he sure was a cute one and already knew how to play the women.

"Of course, handsome," Kaye answered as she plucked a sucker from the bucket and handed it to James.

Bryson chuckled and glanced at the plans on the counter. "I guess you're the one they hired to do the upgrades?"

I leaned on the counter and started to explain to Bryson the plans, then led him into the back room. "It really shouldn't be difficult or take long. The hardest part will be adding the plumbing. I'll be looking for someone local and dependable to help me out. I'll have to do that after hours, or on a Sunday, so the women don't lose business."

"It looks good. You seem to know what you're doing, and I'll get you Blake's number. He's the best plumber in Orlinda Valley." Bryson's eyes bored into me.

"Yeah, I've done my share of remodels over the years." Why did it seem like Bryson was giving me the third degree before I took his little sister to prom instead of doing work which was like second nature? "Is there a problem?" I held Bryson's gaze.

I watched as he sucked in his cheek and shook his head. "Nope. I think everything's good. Sorry if I seemed a little rude, but you know, you just came into town and are doing work for my mother's friends who are like family. Just making sure everything's on the up and up."

"Is Ms. Kaye your mother?" I asked.

Bryson chuckled. "No. My mom's Tonya. Their loud-mouthed friend. She was here today. She's always here, so you probably met her."

I couldn't forget Tonya. "Yeah, I met your mom. She's a hoot."

"That's one way to describe her." Bryson's gaze was frozen on mine.

I knew he was just looking out for the women. I totally understood. If I had a mother I was close to, and some strange man showed up from out of town to do work for her or her friends, I'd be suspicious of him as well. "I promise I'm on the up and up. I'm a certified electrician for the state and currently work for Warren Construction. If you want to check on my background, feel free to call them." I turned to gather my supplies. "I'll be back tomorrow to start demoing the room." I reached my hand toward Bryson. "It was nice meeting you."

"You too, man." Bryson returned the handshake, then turned to leave but stopped. "You know, there's a group of us going over to Jerry's, the pub just down a bit. It has great food and beer, and the first round of a cornhole competition is tonight. If you don't have any plans, you should join us."

Yeah, I didn't have any plans, and I needed to eat. Hanging with people I didn't know, though, was not quite my thing. Just at that time, my stomach let out a deep rumble. Well, again, I needed to eat, and eating at Jerry's two times in a day didn't seem like a bad thing. "Sure, why not. I'll run back to the motel to clean up a bit and meet you there in about what, forty-five minutes?"

"Sounds good. What motel are you staying at?"

"According to Diane and Tonya, the nasty one on the edge of town. Shouldn't surprise me any. It's a shithole."

"Ugh. I can't believe that place still rents out rooms." The face Bryson made gave me another reason to possibly accept Diane's offer to stay here for a little while.

"Yeah, well . . ." I shrugged. "It's cheap. Diane did offer me the small backroom here."

"You should take it. It might be small, but it's clean. Just lock the door. My mother can be a little creepy at times, and you never know what she'll do."

I laughed. I could see that. I turned to Diane. "Ms. Diane. If you don't mind, I think I'll take you up on your offer of the room. As long as it doesn't put a burden on you or anything."

"Oh, please. No burden at all. And just call me Diane."

I drove back to the motel, showered with my slides on because who knew when the shower had seen a sponge or soap last, threw my things into my bag, and checked out early. Thank you, Diane and Kaye.

I drove back to town to the pub. Meeting new people would be a good thing. It was time to step out of my comfort zone, and making friends would be a good first start.

Chapter 5

Kora

Darlene, Summer, and I sat at a high-top table on the patio of Jerry's Pub. The night was calm and a perfect sixty-five degrees. Mild for a late May night. We shared our typical pitcher of margaritas and a platter of nachos.

"So, finish telling us about this hunk who helped you with your tire." Summer said as she took a large sip of her margarita and held my attention.

"I don't think I said anything about him being a hunk." I replied and raised a brow. Ever since Summer joined us, she kept finding ways to bring Kai into the conversation.

"Well, I used my amazing inferring skills."

"Wow. Inferring. Fancy word," Darlene answered.

Summer turned toward her. "I know. My teacher friends should be very impressed."

"They are, and if you use a little alliteration, they might buy the next round of margs." I shook the now empty pitcher in front of Summer's face.

"Well since hunk didn't do it for you, how about handsome, hot hunk?"

"Good alliteration." Darlene held up her margarita glass.

Summer clinked hers against it. "See. I have been listening all the time you both get your teacher nerd on."

"Whatever. I'll be back." I pushed my chair away from the table and went to the bar. Quicker service this way, and I really needed to have some space. Summer was being weird. Well, weirder than normal. I leaned on the bar and showed the empty margarita pitcher to Trevor.

He gave me a thumbs up, so I watched the baseball game on the flat screen television on the wall while I waited. It was getting crowded in the pub, and the bar was busy. Since it was before seven, everyone was taking advantage of the tail end of happy hour. Good business for the pub.

Finally, Trevor placed a fresh pitcher of margaritas in front of me. "Thanks, Trev." He nodded and slapped the bar as he went to fill the order of one of the servers. I picked up the pitcher and made my way carefully through the maze of bodies.

The cornhole tournament must have started because the crowd got tighter as I got closer to the patio, making it more difficult to get through.

I stood tall and twisted and turned through the crowd, concentrating hard on keeping my pitcher of margaritas away from the onslaught of arms and people.

Suddenly a man backed up, and as he turned, he ran into me. "Dammit." I seethed as half the beer from one of the glasses he was holding sloshed all down my front, and a good amount of the margarita as well.

"Shit. I'm so sorry," he apologized.

I stood with my arms in the air, one open and the other with a now half-empty pitcher. The rest of the liquid seeped down my arms and through my shirt.

Damn, it was cold. Really cold. At least the drinks they served were the best—nothing but quality at Jerry's.

No decent words came to my mind, so I bit my tongue to keep a string of curse words from flying.

A chuckle that sounded vaguely familiar entered my ears as my gaze slammed into the beer spiller's. His disheveled black hair and amazing crystal gray eyes caused a rock to lodge in my stomach. "You again." Fucking seriously? Why, of all the men I could have had spill their beer down the front of me, it was—what was his name—Kai from this morning?

Kai was still blocking my path. I passed my gaze over his body, his dark jeans, and his beige flannel. He really needed to get out of my way so I could grab Summer and borrow her sweater—she always had a cute cami under everything she wore. Just in case she got hot.

"Kora, right?"

"Kai." I gave him a nod and squeezed by.

I really needed to get to the table and as far away from him as possible.

Bryson stood when I got closer to the table. That's a bit much, even for Bryson. He wasn't usually so kind as to give up his chair, especially when he was next to Darlene.

"Hey, you made it," Bryson greeted Kai.

My mouth dropped open. How in the world could they know each other?

"Kai, this is Summer, Kora, and my wife, Darlene. Kai's doing the addition to the hair salon."

"Nice to meet all of you."

He was right behind me. I could feel my insides churn with frustration. I couldn't stay there any longer. "Sorry to interrupt," I said, not even trying to keep the frustration from my voice. "Summer, I need to borrow you in the bathroom. I'm wearing quite a bit of margarita and beer and would really like to no longer smell like tequila and a brewery. I might have to borrow what you're wearing."

"Yeah, you look awful, but if I give you my sweater, what am I going to wear?"

"You always have on a T-shirt or cami. You can share."

Summer glanced at Kai, then back to me. A look flashed in her eyes, but I couldn't figure out why. "Fine. Let's go."

Thank God. I need to get away and get dry. "Darlene, finish what's left in that pitcher, and maybe you could get us another since I'm wearing most of this one." I needed a drink before; now I could really use one. I threw a hard gaze at Kai.

He touched my arm, and a shock ran from that spot up to my heart, causing it to skip a beat.

First, he tries to drown me, now kill me by stopping my heart. What a guy.

"Sorry. I didn't mean to bathe you in beer."

The look he gave me was apologetic, almost like a sorry golden retriever—well, a golden retriever if they had striking gray eyes. Really striking gray eyes. A sigh escaped my lungs. "It's not a big deal. I was on my way to the restroom, anyway. I'll just clean up while I'm there." *Idiot!* Frustration finally coursed through my veins. "Come on, Summer."

I grabbed her and stepped around Kai. I really had to get to the bathroom, and soon. I smelled more like an old frat party by the second. It was disgusting.

I entered the restroom with Summer close behind and turned on the faucet. I caught a glimpse of my reflection in the mirror and shook my head. My T-shirt, which was white, was now see through and my bra was visible for all. No wonder Kai's eyes were large and struggled to focus on my face. I thought it was because he was embarrassed, but it seemed as though it was other interests that kept him from looking up. "Men."

"What's wrong with men?" Summer asked. "He couldn't keep his eyes off your boobs."

I huffed and shook my head.

"It could be worse. Dude is hot." Summer unbuttoned her sweater and handed it to me, and as I predicted, she had on a silky black tank top underneath.

"I would feel bad taking this sweater from you if I thought you'd be embarrassed to walk around in that all night."

"Why would I be? With these jeans, maybe I'll get the new dude to take notice of me." She tucked her top into the waist. "Did you see those eyes?"

"Kai, not dude." I peeled off my shirt, dried my bra the best I could, and slipped on Summer's sweater. The knitting was large, which made it easy to see the bra underneath. I modeled in the mirror and shrugged. "Looks good. Just glad I'm wearing a cute bra."

"It does." Summer stepped from the stall and washed her hands. "So, Kai's the one you had a thing with this morning."

I entered a stall and said nothing until I finished peeing and was drying my hands. "He *changed my tire* this morning."

"Amazing eyes is the hot, handsome hunk you were talking about earlier," Summer stated.

"Correction—you were talking about. I told you about my shitty morning. He is now a bigger dumbass who wasn't paying attention and spilled beer on me."

"So, if he's such a dumbass, you won't mind if I hit on him, will you?"

"Really, Summer. You hit on everyone."

"Not if you're interested."

"You know I'm not interested. I'm focused on my future, and men are no longer on the to-do list."

"Well maybe you need to edit that to-do list. How long has it been since you stopped seeing Patrick? Time to move on to bigger and better things." Summer put her arm around my shoulder. "And Kai is much bigger and much better."

I shook my head, but I'd be blind if I couldn't see she was right. I needed to move on. It'd been months since I had been with Patrick. We weren't ever a big thing. When you grew up in a small town like Orlinda Valley, you tended to know everyone, and Patrick was on the newer side. At least he didn't go to high school with us. He came to town to work for the police department and became friends with Bryson through Trevor.

But Kai. He was sexy in a reckless, not Kora sort of way. "Maybe. But he isn't my type."

"Really? Maybe you need to change your guy type. If hot guys with gorgeous eyes who don't hesitate to stop and help stranded women on the side of the road aren't your type, what is your type?"

Hmm. Good question. I dated a couple guys in high school, Trevor for one, but high school didn't really count. I had one serious boyfriend in college, but that relationship only lasted a year, then just dates for formals. I dated Patrick for eight months; we were more friends than anything else. He was funny, focused, and ended up wanting more than I did which caught me off guard.

I shrugged. "Seems like I don't have a type. Every guy I've ever dated was a friend first before we dated. I guess my type will be someone I'm attracted to. Luckily all the guy friends I have are taken or married, so I don't need to worry about it right now."

"Yep. I guess you're right, but you can't get married if you don't date, and you're not getting any younger."

"Oh, please. I'm not interested in marriage. Anyway, why don't you take your own advice?"

"Please. There's no one in Orlinda Valley who can handle me. Not even that handsome, hot hunk. You, on the other hand, are perfect wife material."

I rolled my eyes. Summer was too much. "Again, I'm not interested in marriage. I'd just like a guy to date occasionally so I'm not always a third wheel."

"If you're a third wheel, what's that make me?"

"A colorful spoke." I smirked.

Summer pushed me playfully and opened the door. "Gotta come clean. I met Kai at the salon when he stopped in about the addition." Summer linked her arm through mine and weaved us through the crowd.

"Seriously? And you didn't say anything? I thought you were acting weird."

"What, weirder than normal?"

"Exactly."

Summer laughed, then nudged me. "Looks like you may need to get used to H cubed. Looks like he's making friends."

"H cubed?" I tilted my head and raised a brow, then followed her gaze. I stopped abruptly and caused Summer to stumble. The crystal-blue-eyed-beer-klutz slash tire-knight-in-shining-armor, Kai, was still at our table and as I stood frozen to the spot, he turned his head and the corner of his mouth ticked up.

Chapter 6

KAI

I pulled my gaze slowly down Kora's body, then back up as she approached the table. The sweater she was now wearing was slightly see-through, and I could make out a dark bra under it. My eyes stayed there for a beat and my crotch pulsed in response. I forced my eyes to continue their way up her body. She had sexy curves and was fit, yet not skinny. She was perfectly proportioned. I liked what I saw, and my gaze caught hers. Those deep brown eyes sucked me in, and I struggled to pull away. Even when they narrowed, like me still being here was not a happy surprise, my pull toward her was impossible to ignore.

Summer gave her a nudge.

"Sorry about making a mess," I said when she was next to me, the only place left around the tight high-top table.

A flash of irritation slid over her features, and she tilted her head to the side.

"Looks like you found something to wear," I continued.

"Yeah. I did." She slid onto the stool next to Darlene and turned her back to me.

Who could blame her? I did just douse her with beer, even though I was helpful earlier, but she did think I came across as rude. I shrugged. Women. You can't live with them, and . . . well, you can't live with them. That's why I was thirty-one and still single.

Darlene looked between me and Kora. "Do y'all know each other?"

"Yeah," I answered and took a pull from my beer. "I helped her change her tire this morning."

Darlene choked on her margarita.

"You weren't as helpful as you're trying to sound, then you poured your beer and our pitcher of margaritas all over me a bit ago," Kora answered. Her voice sounded a bit bitter. "You okay, Dar?"

Darlene nodded and wiped her mouth. "So, you helped Kora this morning? She told us about getting a flat tire."

"Did she? What else did she say?"

"Nothing of any importance." Kora gave Darlene a death stare. "He also dumped margaritas and beer on me."

Darlene shrugged one shoulder. "Fine. You owe us a pitcher of margs," she said. "We like them on the rocks." She held up the empty margarita pitcher and shook it in the air as their server came to the table. "Hey, Barb. Can you give us a refill? On the new guy."

Barb, a mid-forties server, turned toward me. "You're the only one new at this table, handsome. Is Darlene telling the truth, or just trying to get you to buy them a round?"

"Yep. I owe them." I smiled.

"Sexy dimple." Barb winked. "You got it, sugar."

"That's Barb," Bryson said. "She's a sweet single lady always looking for a good time, and I mean a *good time.* You better watch out. Age has never been a barrier for her, and she seems to be impressed with your dimple."

I chuckled. "Forty-something is a bit above my limit. I like them a little younger and a lot spunkier." My gaze darted to Kora, who was working hard to ignore me.

"Dammit." Bryson had looked at his phone. "Patrick won't be able to make it tonight." He glanced at me. "Please tell me you know how to play cornhole."

"I might've thrown a few bags in my time."

"Great. I need a partner and we're up." Bryson clapped me on the shoulder.

"I may be a bit rusty, but I'll give it a go." I followed Bryson to the tournament area, and it blew my mind how into the competition everyone seemed to be. The pub's outdoor area was filled with people. There was the cornhole area and a sand volleyball court, and tables were scattered everywhere. The music from inside played from speakers throughout the outdoor area. It was a great concept, and to keep with the fire department theme, there was a miniature fire truck for the kids to climb on.

We shook our competitor's hands, and the game started.

It didn't take long, and there were a lot of cheers and groans, but we emerged as the champs of the night and were headed to the championship round the following Saturday. "Kai, I think Patrick just got replaced. You're available next week I hope?"

"Sure am." Not that there was anything else for me to do. Not yet anyway.

"Looks like Triple H will be back with us again next week," Summer commented as she got up from her seat.

"Triple H?" Bryson questioned.

"Hot, handsome hunk. Not you, Bryson," Summer replied. She squeezed Kora's shoulders from behind. "See ya girls later. I gotta run. Triple H, it was a pleasure to see you again." she said. "You've improved the atmosphere around here a bit." She tipped her head to Bryson and left.

"Excuse her lack of manners," Bryson said. "She tends to hold grudges and doesn't like me much."

"It doesn't matter," Kora cut in. "Congratulations, guys. Now, Darlene, we're out of margs again." She shook their empty pitcher.

One thing was for sure, the women could drink. I watched Kora as she talked with Darlene. Her face was flushed which just added to her attractiveness. "Do you think you really need another pitcher?"

"What are you, the liquor police? Tomorrow's Sunday. All I must do is some grading. I have all day to recuperate. I'll get Trevor to refill us." She walked to the bar.

I felt compelled to follow. I couldn't explain why, but I had a desire to stay near her. I couldn't remember the last time I needed to be near a woman, except for when I had to protect my little sister.

Kora gestured to Trevor for a refill. He nodded and held up a finger.

I leaned on the bar next to her. Even though she was wearing a tequila-soaked bra, she smelled like vanilla and strawberries. Was it her shampoo, lotion, or perfume? I couldn't tell, but it smelled good enough to eat.

"You hoping to spill something else on me?" she asked.

I shook my head. "Nope. Just need some water." Trevor placed a new pitcher of margaritas in front of Kora. "Isn't that your third pitcher?" I asked as I waited for my water.

"Don't get in the way of her and Darlene and their margaritas. They've been putting them back since high school. They were my pretend customers before any of us were old enough to legally drink," replied Trevor as he placed a glass of water on the bar.

"Yeah, we were." Kora's words were only a little slurred.

"Here let me get that for you." I grabbed the pitcher and walked away. She'd follow without much complaint. I had her alcohol.

As the third pitcher of margaritas hit Kora's system, she relaxed, and the night became more fun. Bryson and I hit it off and made plans to practice a bit Friday night at his house. Yeah, it was just cornhole, but there was no point in competing if winning wasn't the goal, and Darlene and Kora were quite the entertainment once the tequila kicked in.

I learned all about what the girls were like in high school, and more about the town and the population than I really needed to know. Darlene and Kora went way back, and somewhere in there Bryson's brother, Rowan, came into play, and Trevor was his best friend. Kora even talked about Trevor. They dated for two years in high school. That bit of knowledge caused a flicker of jealousy to lodge in my chest, and I watched their interactions closer all night. I caught hints of Trevor flirting with her, but Kora didn't seem interested in any of his advances. That was good to know.

I pulled into the back lot of Shear Perfection after midnight and entered into the kitchen with the key I got from Diane. I was exhausted and wanted to hop in bed but unpacked first.

It was strange being at the hair salon alone. The quiet was deafening after the hours at the pub with the loud music and conversations. I put on some music, made the bed, and jumped under the covers, but sleep eluded me.

My brain was its typical hyper self and wouldn't let me get the night out of my mind, or more to the point, Kora. She invaded my thoughts. That bra that peeked through her sweater all night teased me now that I was alone. Was it black or navy blue? How did it look on her without the sweater? How smooth was her skin?

"Fuck." I raked my fingers through my hair. Sleep wasn't going to happen. I needed to either work or take a cold shower. I picked up the sledgehammer and slammed it into the wall. Demolition was a great substitute for what I wanted to do to, or with, Kora. It should get my mind relaxed and off the brown-eyed beauty with a body that left me horny as hell.

I turned on some heavy metal, perfect for destruction, and got to work knocking down walls. Between the heavy music and the rhythm of the demolition, my mind became busy, I got quite a bit accomplished, my muscles grew tired, and soon I was ready for sleep. The clean-up process could wait until morning.

Chapter 7

KAI

My hours this week were long and kept me busy. I usually didn't get back into Orlinda Valley until after dark, and Shear Perfection was always empty when I returned.

Part of the reason I worked later than I needed to was because I didn't want to interfere in the workday of the salon, and it was a little awkward being there in the small room when there were still customers.

I hoped to hear from the bank soon and get the acceptance I was expecting for the property I looked at. As soon as I did, my camper would be out of storage, hooked up, and I'd have a place of my own. The one good thing about staying at the hair salon was that it made working on the new addition easier, and I reached my goal of putting in the electricity when I got back from work Friday night.

Once I was done, I hopped in the shower with plenty of time to get to Bryson and Darlene's for dinner. I'd finish the electrical tomorrow, and Blake, the plumber, was coming over to get the new plumbing installed. Once that was all completed, the other steps would be easy.

Bryson and Darlene lived in a small subdivision just off the main square. Their house was brick, multi-story, and just about the same as all the ones surrounding them. It was a cute neighborhood if you didn't mind your neighbors having the same house as you and knowing all your business.

I lived in this type of subdivision for a while when I was a kid. The embarrassment and humiliation after a night of one of my parents' epic battles was legendary. The neighbors could hear every word they shouted, and the looks I got from the kids as we stood waiting for the bus boiled my blood to this day, and that was in elementary school.

No one ever talked about it or asked me any questions. Not even when I missed school for a couple days and finally showed up with sixteen stitches around my right eye. My mom was long gone by then, and we were living in a small three-bedroom apartment near Atlanta.

Glancing in the rearview mirror, I traced the half-moon scar, the remnant of those stitches. If I looked close enough, I could still make out the jagged edges made by the uneven break of my father's beer bottle after yet another one of our epic arguments. I still don't regret what caused the scar. It was either me or my younger siblings who would get the wrath of my father when he came home drunk and belligerent, and my goal was always to be the receiver of our fathers' drunken rages. As long as he had someone to take his anger out on, he was happy, and it wasn't going to be the twins if I could help it.

Got to go, Kai. I snapped the mirror shut and heaved my tired body from the car. This was not the time to go down shitty memory lane.

There were two other vehicles in the driveway. A large SUV, probably Bryson's. It looked like a family vehicle, and the other was a black Nissan Rogue. It looked vaguely familiar. Could be Kora's. The corner of my mouth ticked up. Bryson and Darlene, me and Kora. This could end up being a really good night.

"Hey, Kai. You're here." Darlene greeted me at the gate of their back yard with a one-armed hug. I gave her a slight hug back, even though I didn't really know her and was a bit uncomfortable.

I glanced around the small fenced-in yard. It was cute and well maintained. A long picnic table sat under a pergola which offered some shade, and a small raised vegetable garden and a wooden playset were out in the yard. Kora was pushing Bryson and Darlene's son on the swing. I tried to remember his name, but I couldn't. Oh, well.

"Thanks for inviting me," I answered, yet my eyes stayed on Kora across the yard.

"Of course. Bryson's a bit over-focused on cornhole, and winning the tournament is his ultimate goal, so this was an important night, at least where he's concerned."

Kora joined them with the little boy in her arms. "Hey, Kai. This is James."

I did a quick survey of her from head to toe and back again. James seemed to have the same thought as me, as he looked her up and down, then cuddled into her side. Lucky guy.

"We met at Shear Perfection last week," I said as James glanced at me with lowered eyes. He still didn't seem that sure of me. Not a big deal. If I had to be honest, I wasn't so sure of him either. I have never been that comfortable around kids, not that I'd been around many.

Bryson exited the house from sliding doors with his arms loaded with a tray of what looked like raw burgers and hot dogs. "Thank God you're here. I was getting concerned that you stood us up."

"See, told you he's a little over-focused on the tournament," Darlene whispered.

"There's no such thing as over-focused," Bryson replied, tending to the grill. "If you're going to do something, you need to make damn sure winning's a priority." He pointed his spatula in my direction. "Right man?"

"No other purpose to play."

"How about for fun?" Kora asked as she placed James on the ground, and he ran off to attempt to kick the soccer ball.

"Winning is fun," I replied.

"That's right!" Bryson agreed. I joined him at the grill and grabbed two beers from the cooler. I twisted off the caps and we clinked the bottles together.

"So, Kai, what brought you to Orlinda Valley?" Darlene asked when we were at the picnic table eating.

I shrugged. This was where I struggled around people. How much of my background was too much. Talking about construction—that was a safe topic. Personal stuff, not so much.

I decided to talk about my job. Ticks off the construction box and isn't too personal. "I was offered a job I found online for a construction company based outside of Nashville, Warren Construction. I moved my RV to a campground and lived at one for a while—it's cheaper than a hotel or renting—and I spent my free time driving around looking for a place that called out to me. I grew up near a city and always felt cramped, so I knew I wanted land. I drove through Orlinda Valley and loved the openness and the river. There's just something about it here." I took a big bite of the burger and caught Kora's gaze. Her brown eyes held surprise and something else I couldn't quite pinpoint. She sucked in her bottom lip and turned away.

"So, where's your family from?" Darlene asked.

I put a chip in my mouth and chewed before answering. "I grew up in Georgia, near Atlanta. My mom died years ago, my father and I don't talk, and my siblings are finally out living their lives."

I didn't miss the concerned look that passed between Kora and Darlene. I needed to squelch that. I hate being the receiver of pity. "Really. It's not a big deal. One thing that attracted me to Orlinda Valley was that everyone genuinely seems to care about each other."

"Hey, we're here." I turned and saw Tonya and Kaye, and a hoard of others. Thank you, God. The conversation will finally get off me.

I was introduced to Jamison, Bryson's older brother and his three-year-old daughter. I forget her name already, and Charles, Kaye's husband.

The chatter became loud, the laughter was prolific, and the fun began. After dinner was finished and desserts were shared, we all sat around the yard watching Jamison's daughter, Darcie—that's her name—chase James around the yard.

I sat back and observed life from a different perspective. This was what was missing in my family. Camaraderie. Friendship. Everyone here, blood related or not, was so close. This was what family should be. By the end of the night, my ribs hurt from laughing, my arm ached from tossing cornhole bags, and my stomach was full.

"Kai, we haven't seen you often at the salon, but everything's looking great." Kaye said as she drank sweet tea.

"Well, I'll be there tomorrow. I have Blake, the plumber, coming in to check on my plumbing skills. He should be there early, hopefully no later than seven thirty, and shouldn't be more than an hour. The water will be off when he's there, but as long as everything's good, I'll have it turned on before you open at nine."

"Blake's a great guy," replied Tonya.

"That's not what I recall you saying about him last year after he stood you up." Charles laughed and turned toward me. "Blake's one of my oldest friends and has had a crush on Tonya since middle school. She finally said yes to a date, then he ended up a no show."

Kaye broke in. "She was so angry. She ranted for days about never talking to him again."

Tonya shook her head.

"Mom," Bryson cut in. "You were rude to him for the longest time. Then you never apologized after you found out he didn't stand you up." He turned to Jamison. "Do you remember? We were at the house for Sunday breakfast when she got his call and found out he had been in the hospital with gallstones. He was scared to talk to her."

"Oh, yeah." Jamison laughed heartily. "Mom was so angry when she found out who it was, she threw the phone at you and made you talk to him."

Kaye laughed as she shook her head. "He apologized profusely, and T just totally ignored him. She refused to listen to a word he said."

"Not true," Tonya demanded. "I just expected him to call as soon as he could, but he never did."

"Yeah, because you had it all over town that he was a jerk and you wanted nothing to do with him," Kaye responded.

Tonya waved her hand through the air. "All that doesn't matter. He and I cleared the air and are back on speaking terms." She pointed her well-manicured finger at the boys who were bent over laughing heartily. "You two need to stop before you hear details of my night last Saturday with Joe."

Everyone's eyes went wide.

"Old Joe?" Kaye gasped.

Tonya winked at Kaye as Bryson and Jamison plugged their ears and yelled NO simultaneously.

That might be a story worth hearing one day, but I could tell this would not be that day. Kora stood up. "I'm sorry, but I've got to go." She pulled out her phone.

I was sitting next to her and noticed her pull up an Uber ap. "I thought that was your black Rogue in the driveway."

She glanced at me over her phone. Those brown eyes held nothing but contempt.

What had I done to consistently irritate her?

"That's Darlene's. We bought the same car."

"You know besties need to have the same everything," Darlene sang.

I looked back and forth. "I always knew girls tend to be close, but the same car?"

"It wasn't intentional," Bryson replied. "But it's a little frightening how alike these two are. It's like they have that twin clairvoyance, but they aren't twins."

"Nope." Darlene wrapped her arms around Kora. "Just besties since birth."

Kora blew her friend a kiss and looked back at her phone. "The closest Uber can't be here for over thirty minutes." She finally looked at me. "One issue with being so far in the middle of nowhere. No Uber."

I felt myself drowning in those rivers of brown. What was it about her? "Not a problem. I'll take you home. It can't be that far."

"You sure? It's about ten minutes, give or take, knowing the roads."

My brow ticked up. "Excuse me?"

"She means—if you don't know the roads it'll probably take you longer. She lives way out with nothing but cows, chickens, and goats as neighbors," Darlene answered.

"Not true." Kora hip-bumped Darlene. "I have Aunt Tonya. She can take me."

"Nope. Can't tonight, baby doll. I have places to go." Tonya wagged her brow.

The expressions of Jamison and Bryson were priceless, and I chose to act like I didn't hear that as quiet gasps filled the air. "Seriously. Not a big deal. I sort of owe you, anyway."

"How do you owe me?" Kora asked.

"I did spill beer over you. Let me make it up to you."

Kora looked me over, and I could feel her gaze stop on the scar. I've been told by many women that it makes me look a bit mysterious and sexy, and wondered what she thought.

She gave me a half shrug. "Fine. I've got to go, though. My animals need to be fed."

Time alone with Kora. What could be better?

Chapter 8

KORA

The truck looked much better on the inside than the outside. The seats were leather and didn't look anywhere near the age the truck had to be. There were no bells and whistles, and the windows even had manual cranks, but the radio was new. At least Kai had good sense when it came to music. "So, I know you came to Orlinda Valley because of work, but what made you settle here instead of somewhere else? There's a lot of small towns around if that's all you were looking for."

"I don't know. Being close to the interstate helped. Makes getting to work easier. And like I said, I love the openness, and the river is a major plus. I love kayaking and would love to start fishing." He glanced quickly at me and shrugged before getting his eyes back on the road. "I always dreamed of the quiet and peacefulness of a small town."

"Well, you'll get the peacefulness here, but quiet will all depend on what time of year it is and where you live. During baseball season, if you live near the city park, the noise and traffic of little league parents gets a bit much. If you live near the school, basketball season and football season are a racket." I pointed to the next right. "Turn right here."

We passed the school on the left. "This parking becomes packed to overflowing during football games. The entire town comes out on a Friday night. Football's a big thing."

Kai glanced out his window. "The parking lot and field look like they take up more space than the entire school."

"Well, you know. Orlinda Valley's got their priorities straight. Turn left here."

He hit the brakes hard, and I braced myself on the front.

"Sorry about that, but a little more warning would be nice," Kai said.

"Well, here's a warning. Slow down. The road is windy and bumpy, as you should remember." I gestured as we passed a stretch of road. Was it just last week I met him? Doesn't matter.

"The place we met." He slowed down a bit. "I guess I need to watch out for tire-eating potholes."

"Yeah, you do." I smiled at him without meaning to.

"You should do that more often."

I scrunched my face. *What was he talking about?* "What should I do more often?"

"Smile."

"I smile a lot." I sat up straight and scrunched my face up again. *How could he say that? I always smile.*

"Nope. You don't. Not for me at least. That scowl." He gestured with his head. "That's what I usually see."

I narrowed my eyes as he focused back on the road. *I've never been told that before. Maybe it's the company.* I really wanted to say that to him, but instead I faced forward and crossed my arms. "My house will be on the right about a mile up." I shot a quick glance in his direction. He focused hard on the road and had a concentrated squint going on which caused that scar under his eye to crease. "Answer something for me."

"I'll try." His concentration was still on the road.

"How'd you get that scar?"

He glanced quickly at me, and the corner of his mouth turned up. "Why, you think it's sexy?"

My eyes popped and I chuckled. "Have you been told it's sexy? Turn here. My driveway."

He slammed on the brakes—again—and caused my face to almost meet the dash. "Careful!"

"Sorry. Again, your directions," he answered as he turned the truck into the driveway and the gravel crunched under his tires. "It doesn't matter what I've been told. It matters what you think."

Why are all cute men egotistical idiots? Don't they know it takes away from their cuteness? "We just met. It matters not what I think."

"Now you sound like Yoda."

"I was trying for Shakespeare."

He glanced at me with a slight chuckle, then parked in front of the garage. He climbed out, and his gaze took in his surroundings. "How much of this is yours? It's awesome."

I tried to see my land from his eyes, or what I could make out in the glow of his headlights. My house was small. Just nine hundred square feet, yet cute. So cute—at least I thought so. It was an older brick ranch with a concrete patio. The patio was surrounded with bushes and pots which would be filled with flowers soon. Even though I couldn't see it well, the goat house and chicken coop were out in the pasture. I love my place. It's mine, and it's home.

"The house, right here"—I pointed to the left—"is mine. It's small but perfect. It used to be Tonya's guest house. Her house is over there." I pointed toward a tree line. "You can barely make out the outline of her house through the tree line during the day. She had twenty acres, but when my father moved to Florida last year and sold our house, she sold me this five acres and the guest house. I added that small barn and the fence. I have three goats and ten chickens, and a small garden. The shed we passed up by the road is my roadside stand where I sell eggs when I can, and extra veggies in the summer. It's not a lot, but it's mine and I love it."

I led him to the pasture. "She promised the boys land, but Bryson declined. He and Darlene enjoy being closer to town, and Jamison is building on the other side of her. Who knows what Rowan will decide."

I unlocked the gate, and a black and white goat came running up to us—Baby Goat. I laughed when Kai took a step back.

"He's not going to hurt you. This is Baby Goat." I crouched down and Baby Goat bleated and rubbed his head against me. "He's as friendly as a dog and about the same size."

Kai put out his hand and rubbed the goat's head. "He must be a baby. He's so tiny."

"Nope. He's a Nigerian Dwarf. That's the biggest he'll get. Come on. He'll follow."

I stopped at the chicken coop, and Kai leaned on the top rail. Two more goats, both white with black and brown spots came over to us. "Meet Percy and Jackson."

Kai chuckled. "Percy Jackson. Cute."

"My favorite books." I opened the door to the goat house and was followed by the three impatient goats pushing and shoving for both attention and food. I fed them quickly, gave them hay, checked their water, patted them all, and promised to spend time with them tomorrow before we left for the night.

"Won't Baby Goat get out again?" Kai asked.

"No." I latched the gate. "It's like he knows it's nighttime. He won't get out until he hears me close the back door tomorrow morning." I checked the chickens and gathered six eggs.

"Cool. I've never collected eggs before," Kai said. "Or had fresh eggs for that matter." He picked up one of the eggs and brushed my fingers as he did.

A tingle went up my arm. I glanced quickly at him. Did he notice that? Luckily, he was focused on the egg, so he didn't see how large my eyes got or the blush I was sure crept up my face.

"So how do you clean them?"

"What do you mean?" I was totally confused.

"The eggs. You know. How do you clean them so they're safe to eat?"

I chuckled. Was he serious? "You don't clean them. Just crack and eat." I watched him and cocked my head to the side as he turned the eggs over in his hand. "I've never thought about someone not knowing about fresh eggs. I've grown up with chickens. Eating our own eggs is a part of my life."

Kai shook his head and motioned toward all the land and the animals. "All this is just something I saw on TV or out my car window. I love it though. This is why I'm here."

I stared at him. This man. This hot man who irritated the shit out of me last week was now making my insides all muddled. I watched as a shadow crossed his features and he became closed off. But as quickly as the shadow appeared, it disappeared and was replaced by amazement as he looked out across the dark pasture.

I followed his gaze. It was beautiful and peaceful. There was the soft sound of crickets chirping, and somewhere off in the distance, a squirrel chattered, and a cow mooed lowly in the pasture across the street. "It's my favorite place. I couldn't wait to get out of college and get back home, teach in the elementary school I grew up in, find a husband, and raise my family right here in Orlinda Valley."

"So far you're living that life."

"Except for the husband. That's one bad thing about growing up in a small town. You know everyone, and all the good guys are taken, or we're in the friend zone. It'll take an outsider to get into my heart." My eyes met his, and my heart skipped a beat as our gazes held. I sucked on my bottom lip. A nervous habit. *Did I really just say that out loud?*

"No husband material in town yet?" Kai's voice was rough, yet quiet.

I'm so glad it's dark. He couldn't see the blush that again covered my cheeks. I really needed to get a grip on my feelings. One minute he was annoying the hell out of me and raising my blood pressure because he was the most irritating thing I'd ever met, and the next, my blood was pumping to other parts of my body, causing me to feel things I wasn't prepared for.

"I can't picture being so into the town I grew up in that I'd want to move back." Kai's words pulled me back to the now. "I couldn't wait until I was able to escape from my hometown and everything about it. Not that it ever felt like home." He shook his head. A mischievous grin filled his face. "So, do you consider anyone in town husband worthy?"

Those crystal eyes of his danced with amusement under the glow from my outdoor lights, and maybe a little heat as well. My voice eluded me, so I just shook my head. It was safer that way.

"Good to know." He responded as his eyes held mine.

The oxygen got sucked from my lungs as I melted into his gaze, and that tingling sensation—I was determined to ignore—sent my ovaries into overdrive and caused my desire for Kai to erupt like a volcano. I swallowed and took a large step away from him.

"Thanks for showing me around. I hope we can see each other again soon." He smiled and that dimple appeared.

God, I itched to reach out and brush my finger against that dimple. Instead, I shoved my hands in my back pockets, not wanting to give them the freedom they desired. If I touched that dimple, who knew where my hands would slide next. My eyes wandered down his body. I cleared my throat and averted my eyes to focus on a tree behind him. "I'd like that," I said. *Damn, I hope that didn't sound too desperate.* I watched Kai's ass as he walked back to his truck. The rear view looked as good as the front view.

"Hey, Kai?"

He opened his door and leaned on it with his brows raised.

"I never thanked you properly for the help with the tire. I really appreciate it. I know I was a bit . . ." I wiggled my shoulders up and down. I was never good at apologies. "Bitchy. I'm sorry. It amazes me how sweet I can be from seven thirty till three Monday through Friday, then as soon as I step out of the school, it all evaporates."

He nodded.

"And thanks for the ride home."

"Anytime you need anything, just let me know."

A shiver ran through me, and desire ignited within my core. *Good Lord, leave already, Kai.*

Chapter 9

KORA

This was a crazy week, and I was exhausted. If anything could go wrong, it had. There was a small fire in the cafeteria Tuesday, causing an impromptu fire alarm during the third grade's practice for our end of the year field day. Nothing like sixty third grade students needing to exit a school in an orderly manner in an area they weren't used to. It was chaos, but luckily the fire was a small grease fire and was contained easily and it wasn't serious.

Trevor and Patrick happened to be on duty and responded to the alarm. They ended up being guest speakers for Darlene's and my class. The kids loved it.

Then the zoo came in with some of the animals. Let's just say, third grade girls may not be the best choices to hold snakes. There was quite a bit of squealing and screaming. It wasn't good.

It was finally three-fifteen, and the last of my students had been picked up in the car-rider line, so I trudged back to my room. I was so ready to straighten up and start the weekend. I loved my job. I was living the dream. But I loved Fridays even more, and the day was finally over. I leaned heavily on the counter in my classroom and stared at nothing while thinking about everything—mostly not school related.

In between all the chaos of the week, Kai had popped into my mind at random times. When I was out feeding the goats, his face would be there. When I drove through town, I thought I saw him at the corner store. Just this morning, when I pulled into the parking lot at school, I saw a truck which I thought for sure was his, parked in the front row. Which was absolutely asinine. Why would he be at school?

His crystal-clear eyes crossed my mind randomly all week. The contrast between the lightness of his eyes and the darkness of his hair was captivating. That crescent-shaped scar by his right eye added mystery, yet a roughness to him which contradicted his kind, easy-going manners. And God, that body . . . that ass.

The sound of hands clapping shook me from my daze.

"Good lord, girlie. You've been out of it all week." Darlene jumped onto the counter and nudged me with her knee. "You look like you could use some girl time and margs. Do we need to have some sort of intervention? You've been by yourself all week and very quiet at school even during all the drama. It's so unlike you. What's going on?"

I ignored Darlene, pushed away from the counter, and went to my desk. I straightened it up and packed my bag. I always shared everything with Darlene, especially male related, but I wasn't ready to discuss Kai. Hell, I didn't even know what I'd discuss. One minute he was irritating the hell out of me, the next he was causing my heart to do weird movements and beat funny.

Margs were much needed. "What do you say we get out of here and drink early? Maybe by five I'll be five sheets to the wind and ready to have fun."

"That would be great, but first I need to go pick up James from daycare and drop him off at Shear Perfection. Kaye and Tonya are taking him to Diane's tonight. She's babysitting Skylar this weekend, so James and Skylar are having a little play date."

"Better watch out. That granddaughter of Diane's is adorable. James might fall in love at the ripe young age of four."

Darlene shrugged. "Could be worse. At least he'd be marrying money."

That was true. Diane's stepdaughter, Leila, was married to Adler Warfield. His family was loaded, and he'd adopted Skylar. "Money's not everything, Dar." I threw my bag over my shoulder, and we left. "How about if I leave my car at your house and go with you? If I get too drunk, I'll crash at your place." I'd spent many nights in Darlene and Bryson's spare bedroom over the years. There was a brief six-month stint where I lived with them after my father left for Florida and I was having my house renovated. Darlene's house has always been my second home.

"Sounds good." Darlene crossed the hall to her room and emerged just seconds later, her bag over her shoulder. "Let's blow this joint and enjoy our weekend."

James ran to the salon as soon as Darlene lifted him from the car. He knocked his tiny fist on the glass since he couldn't open the door, and Kaye let him in. "Well, hello cutie."

James ignored Kaye and made a beeline to Tonya. He flew into her arms and motioned immediately to the bowl of suckers. We chuckled as we followed Kaye through the door.

"Hey, Summer." I placed my purse and sunglasses on her station and plopped in her seat.

"Getting comfortable, Kora? I don't remember giving you permission to sit there." Summer swept her station of hair and wiped down the counter. "Why'd you even bring this in?" she said when she picked up my purse to wipe under it. "It's not like you're staying long."

I snatched it from her and plopped it back on the counter. "Because I knew it would irritate the shit out of you, and I live to irritate you."

Summer rolled her eyes. "Ain't that the truth."

"So, how's the addition going?" Darlene asked.

"Great," Kaye replied. "Kai has really worked hard all week. He finished the drywall and said he should be painting this weekend. Come on. You've got to see it."

Just the mention of Kai's name set butterflies free in my gut. I needed to get whatever these feelings were under control. Kai was annoying, yet frustratingly hot, and I didn't have time for that kind of confusion in my life. I puffed out a breath and followed Darlene and Kaye into what used to be just a large storage room. Now it was a room with waist-high walls separating stations with a sink and chair in each.

"This looks great," Darlene exclaimed.

She was right; it really did.

Just then, the back door shut and there he was with his arms bulging under the weight of paint cans. The veins in his arms popped under the strain, and my eyes popped at the mouthwatering sight. I swallowed hard to drown the nerves that the butterflies were determined to push out and put on display.

He looked fine as usual. He wore a gray T-shirt which made those sexy crystal eyes pop even more, and his dark hair was disheveled, making him look tastier than ever.

"Hey, ladies. Just bringing in the paint and materials I'll be needing. Didn't mean to bother you."

Good Lord, have mercy on my soul.

It must have been a long time since I had been with a guy because the nerve endings in my body were firing on every cylinder. I grabbed a magazine and fanned my face. It was getting warm in this room.

"No bother at all, Kai." Darlene gave me a questioning look then smirked.

I turned my head.

"You're not working tonight, are you? It's Friday," Darlene asked.

"Well, tomorrow I'm playing cornhole with Bryson. It's the finals, you know, so I need to get some work done tonight."

"Fine, get *some* work done but join us at the pub by eight. You and Bryson could get practice in. You don't need to stay late, but you can't miss the pub on a Friday," Darlene pointed out.

Kai placed the paint cans in the corner. "I need to get the walls taped and prepped for painting. Maybe when I'm done and cleaned up, I'll show up. I can paint this room tomorrow morning before Blake shows up." His gaze rested on Kora. "Are y'all heading there?"

No matter how hard I tried, I couldn't tear my gaze from him. I was transfixed by his biceps, and his shirt molded to his body and those eyes. Damn those eyes.

Darlene nudged me in the side, and I shot her a hard glare, then nodded. "We're heading there now. There's a pitcher of margaritas with our name on it."

"Then maybe I'll see you when I get things cleaned up here. Don't spill any margs without me." He smirked and that dimple appeared.

My heart thumped so loudly I was sure they all could hear it. I swallowed hard. "I don't think that's an issue I have. That's your wheelhouse." I hoped that jab sounded harsh. Darlene was giving me too many odd looks. "Let's go, Dar. I'm starving." I turned on my heels and high-tailed it out of that room. I needed to get some air and get out of there quickly before anyone noticed the flush I felt climbing my neck. Darlene gave James a hug and followed quickly behind. Thank God.

"Holy Shit." Darlene started laughing. "What the hell was that about?" We climbed into her car. "The heat between you two is scorching. Like able to burn down an entire forest hot."

I tried to ignore her and play it cool. "Don't know what you're talking about."

"Bull. Shit." Darlene turned left onto the road, then a quick right into the pub's parking lot. She put the car in park and shifted in her seat.

I shook my head, jumped from the car, and tried to escape into the pub, but Darlene blocked the door.

"No, you don't." She held up her hand to stop me from walking through the door. "I haven't seen you run from a guy that quickly since high school when you were stuck in the closet for seven minutes with Trevor."

"Yeah, well, Trevor's sweet and all, but that kiss was anything but exciting."

"Yeah, but he thought it was total heaven and you guys dated like, forever. He still gives you the eye."

I held Darlene's gaze and gestured to the door. We were not going to have this discussion.

"Fine," Darlene wined, and we walked into the pub and to the bar.

"Hey there, beautiful ladies. I'm guessing you two want the usual?" Trevor asked as he leaned on the bar.

"Please, Trevor," I answered.

He winked and went to fix our margaritas.

Good Lord, Trevor. You're just fueling the fire.

Darlene nudged my arm. "He's still got the hots for ya." She wagged her brows, and I raised my eyes to the ceiling. Darlene wasn't going to let any of this go.

He returned with a pitcher of margaritas. "Thanks." I smiled wide at him and leaned on the bar. "Trevor, it's been one hell of a week. Let's get started with some tequila shots and lemons."

"You got it." He placed two shot glasses on the bar and a plate of lemon slices dipped in sugar—Trevor's version of a lemon drop. "Shots are on me."

Darlene glanced at me from the side of her eyes. I ignored her and slid a shot glass in her direction.

She picked up the shot in one hand and a lemon slice in the other. "Here's to an awesome Friday night."

I toasted Darlene, and we took our shots and sucked on our lemon wedges dipped in sugar. The sour and sweet taste, mixed with tequila was always perfect.

Trevor filled our shot glasses again. "On the house, again."

"Thanks, Trevor. You're awesome," I said.

He winked as he strutted across the bar to take care of paying customers.

"Told ya," Darlene said as she cocked her head to the side and raised one brow.

God, I hated it when she acted all smug and for no good reason. "What's the big deal? We get a couple free shots out of him weekly. I don't think that's anything but friendship. We've known him forever."

"Keep thinking that, Kor." Darlene shot her tequila and sucked the lemon.

I did the same. "I better go slower, or he may just get what he wanted years ago. We might have dated for almost two years, but we never did the deed." I studied his profile as he served beers to a couple men down the bar. "He was sweet then. Now he looks much sweeter." I noticed. "He keeps in shape, that's for sure."

"As a fireman-slash-bartender, I'm sure it comes naturally," Darlene said.

"What comes naturally?" Trevor asked as he cleared away the shot glasses.

"Nothing," I said with a grin.

Trevor scrunched his eyes like he wanted to question me but luckily, he didn't. He shook his head instead. "Can I get you ladies anything else?" he asked.

Darlene poured our drinks. "Nope. I think we're good, Trev."

"Well then, have a good night." He smacked the bar twice and left to assist other customers.

Darlene held up her glass and grinned mischievously at me. "If he doesn't get lucky, maybe someone will. Here's to an amazing Friday night."

"Your toast lacks luster." I brushed her away and lifted my glass. "Here's to good drinks, amazing friends, and hot guys." I clinked my glass against Darlene's.

"Looks like they've already started." Bryson's arms wrapped around Darlene, and he kissed her neck.

"We're only two shots in and just started our margs," Darlene said. "You're earlier than usual." She gave Bryson a deep kiss.

"Come on, y'all," I said. "Don't get all mushy already. We've got a lot of drinks to get through, and if I have my way, Bryson, you won't get lucky tonight because she'll be passed out."

"Wouldn't be the first time. When she sent me a text that it was a Margarita Friday, I knew that would be a possibility," Bryson said. "Let's grab a table."

I grabbed my glass and the pitcher.

"Here, I'll get that."

Goosebumps crept across my skin at the sound of the deep, sultry voice behind me. I turned and there was Kai, his pants paint-splattered and his gray shirt tight against his chest. He wore a baseball hat backward, just like the first day I met him, and his face was smiling. My mouth suddenly went dry. Luckily, I had my margarita, and I took a big mouthful, then cleared my throat. "You sure you can handle that? If I remember correctly, carrying alcohol isn't one of your talents."

"Maybe not, but I do promise you there are many things I do well," Kai answered as he picked up the pitcher and walked toward the table Bryson claimed out on the patio.

My interest perked up—or was that my nipples? I glanced down to make sure my headlights weren't on, and surprisingly I got the all-clear. My eyes never left his ass as he led the way to the patio.

Yeah, I think I'd enjoy finding out what else he did well. Maybe the tequila was already taking effect.

I leaned against the table and looked up at him. "Why don't you share with us something else you do well? We hardly know anything about you?"

Our eyes met. "I'm great with a jack and can change a mean tire."

A smirk pulled at the corners of my lips, and I nodded. "I agree. But there's got to be something else we haven't seen yet. A *hidden* talent?"

He raised his brows. "Sweetheart, I have many hidden talents you haven't seen yet." His gaze held mine and was smoldering.

I sipped my margarita to put out the flames that erupted under my skin.

"I'm not sure what I missed, but it seems pretty intense." Bryson acknowledged as he leaned on the table.

Kai's brows raised in a flirty manner. He turned away, cutting off the oxygen, and the flames diminished. I sucked in a large breath.

"Kora just asked what it was I did well. I reminded her of my ability to change a tire and told her I have many other talents."

"Yeah, I heard that much," Bryson said.

"Like my amazing cornhole talents. My aim is spot on." He turned toward me. "And I can get it in the hole the first time, always."

Fuck me. Hopefully later. Heat crept up my neck, and I took another deep swallow of my drink. The cold, sour alcohol felt good going down and cooled me off. To bad there wasn't a breeze out here to help out.

Darlene leaned toward me and whispered. "You good?"

All I could do was nod.

Bryson smacked his hand on Kai's shoulders. "Well, let's go practice. Girls, you're our teammates." He grabbed Darlene's hand. "Come on, beautiful." He kissed the back of her hand as he pulled her to her feet.

Thank God. I needed some air and some space.

We moved to the grass and placed our drinks on the picnic table by the cornhole boards, Kai and Darlene on one end and Bryson and me on the other. It was a great game, not that I was any good, but with Kai's skills he all but made up for my lack of them.

"Again?" Bryson hollered as Kai's third bag slid into the hole. "Damn. You better be that on target tomorrow."

"Once I get warmed up, I hardly ever miss."

"You've already told us that. You got skills," Darlene answered and caught my attention across the grass. Her eyes were shining with amusement.

Either my mind was in the gutter, or we were all deliberately using sexual innuendos for everything related to cornhole tonight. I couldn't focus on the game any longer. My attention kept wandering to my sexy partner at the other end of the court who had that dimple stuck on his cheek. I was so focused on brushing my lips against it that my bag barely even landed on the board. Luckily, Kai was good enough on his own and finished the game. He didn't need my help.

"Good game," Bryson answered as we joined Kai and Darlene at the picnic table. "Should we play again?"

"I'm out. It's Friday night, and my margs are getting watered down," I said.

"I agree with Kora." Darlene answered. "That's fun but a lot of work, and I've done my share of work this week. Tonight's about chilling."

Another set of teams started a game at the cornhole pit, and Kai and Bryson agreed to play the winner. We relaxed at the table, Bryson next to Darlene and Kai next to me. He was so close, I could feel his body heat and smell his cologne. Maybe I was imagining it, but it seemed like he inadvertently sat close enough so our legs touched under the table. I thought of scooting away, but instead, leaned my leg against his.

His gaze caught mine, and I didn't miss the slight lift of his brow. I hid my smile in my margarita glass. Time to drown those butterflies and have some fun.

Almost two pitchers in and the sun had turned into a rainbow of colors behind the thin layer of clouds in the sky. It was a perfect night in mid-May. The pub had country music pouring from the speakers, and the smack of cornhole bags hitting the boards, along with a game of volleyball at the sand pit, filled the air. Summer joined us and helped us finish our second pitcher.

My favorite song started playing over the speakers. "Time to dance and get this party started," I yelled to Darlene.

"Yeah, well, I think you two have already done that," Summer replied as Darlene and I jumped up.

I pulled Summer up, but she pulled out of my grasp. "Nope. Not gonna happen. I have some catching up to do, and anyway, you're the two that like to dance. Me, I like to drink."

"Fine. Don't drink all the margs while we're gone." I danced my way onto a makeshift dance floor—basically just a square of grass—and Darlene followed. We were joined by others, mostly women. The night was still young, and the men weren't much for dancing until more beer entered their systems.

"Didn't know you had moves." A sultry voice sounded near my ear. I turned, and Kai was so close, if I wanted to kiss his lips, I just had to lean in. The music turned to a romantic slow dance. "May I?" He held his arms out.

Damn. Hot and manners. He should be illegal. I nodded, and he wrapped me in his arms. One of his arms slid around my waist, low on my hips, and the other clasped my hand. He pulled me closer, and we swayed to the slow rhythm.

The scent of his cologne and the warmth of his body seeped into mine as we moved effortlessly together.

"You good?" he asked, his smile concerned and his eyes clear and damn beautiful.

I nodded. I doubted things could get any better. "If someone asked you, what color would you say your eyes are?"

His brow raised.

"They're just so different. So clear. I can't tell if they're a light gray or a crystal light blue."

"My mother called them blue."

I didn't miss the past tense he used when talking about his mom, or the hushed tone his voice took on. My gaze lingered on his for a beat before moving down to his scar. His mouth ticked up, and I reached out and finally brushed my fingers against his dimple lightly. "Why do men always get the sexy dimples?"

Shit. Did I really just say that out loud? I needed to work on my diarrhea of the mouth. It was like I had to watch what I said all week, so when it was the weekend, and alcohol hit my system, if it was a thought, it became words.

His dimple became deeper. "You think it's sexy, huh?"

Again, I felt heat grow up my neck, but this time the temperature in my cheeks also rose.

"You're even more adorable when you blush," Kai said, his voice deeper than usual as he brushed his knuckles against my cheek.

A shock raced through me at his touch. Maybe it was the alcohol, but suddenly I really had the desire to kiss him. His lips were just inches away, and I could feel his warm breath.

"Our turn, Kai." Bryson patted his back.

The spell was broken. Kai's eyes held mine for a beat more. "We'll continue this later." He winked and followed Bryson to the cornhole boards, and I followed Darlene to the table. I don't know how my legs made it.

"I think you need a refill to cool off." Darlene filled our empty glasses.

I sat hard on the bench next to Summer. My heart was racing, and Kai's scent was everywhere.

"No shit," Summer agreed. "I could feel the heat between those two from here and was glad we're at a pub owned by a fireman. If they were going to combust, at least there are enough professionals around to put out the flames."

I ignored them and took a large swig of my drink. It tasted good. I needed that.

I downed the rest as I watched the game across the yard. Kai's body was in perfect form when he threw the bag. I don't know what Bryson said to him, but he laughed, and his eyes met mine. He winked. I blushed.

Even from across the yard, the pull between us was impossible to ignore. "I need a refill."

Darlene's eyes went up. "Kai's good looking."

"I second that," Summer agreed. "Those eyes are mesmerizing."

Their gazes were focused on me. Play it cool. "Really? I haven't noticed?"

"Oh, bull shit," Summer retorted. "You haven't taken your eyes off him since I've been here. And that dance you shared." She fanned herself. "Just admit you're attracted to him."

"I'm not," I said, staring off at nothing.

"Really? So, you wouldn't mind then if I make a move? I do see him more since he spends a lot of time at the salon . . . hammering . . . sawing . . . painting." Summer made a grunting noise.

I whipped my head in her direction.

Her eyes narrowed.

Mine copied hers. There was no way I was going to let her get in the way of whatever was going on with me and Kai—even though there was nothing going on between Kai and me.

"Down, girl," Summer remarked with a laugh.

Darlene echoed her. "No words needed. We know you, and you've got it bad."

Not true. I kept my thoughts to myself. Just because I wanted to know all about what his other talents were didn't mean I had it that bad.

Chapter 10

KAI

Bryson and I made a good cornhole team. I couldn't remember the last time I laughed and enjoyed myself so much. No matter how much I tried to fight it, though, I felt compelled to keep glancing at Kora. She'd intrigued me from that first day we met when she was yelling at that cow. The fire I noticed in her glare then was something that I now realized was her intense take-no-bullshit gaze and overall attitude that I really wanted to get to know more.

The brief dance we shared ignited feelings that hadn't been lit inside me for a long while, and from the reaction of my crotch when we were close, proved I needed to know her better. "Does Kora have a boyfriend?" I asked Bryson.

Bryson gave me a quick glance, then lined up his throw. It hit the board and landed near the hole. "Nope. Hasn't for a while." His points were countered by the opposing team. No change in score.

Good to know. I lined up my shot and let the bag fly. It landed in the hole with just enough force to push my other bag in with it.

"Damn, dude. You're good," the guy next to me replied.

I shrugged. "It's all about the aim." I glanced over at the girls and caught Kora rolling her eyes and mouthing off at Darlene and Summer. She did that a lot, roll her eyes. It was adorable.

"Hey, Romeo, we're almost finished. Keep your focus on the game," Bryson said from the other side of the court.

"What's the score?" I asked.

"We have eighteen," Bryson answered.

I nodded. I was over this game. I lined up my bag and aimed. *Swoosh.* Right in the hole. Three points. Game over. "That's game."

Bryson gave me a high five, and we shook the opposing team's hands, then I turned and walked away. I needed some water and to feel Kora beside me.

"Hey, we won. We can keep playing," Bryson yelled.

I put up my hand. "Sorry. I'm done. Need a drink." I got to the table and filled a glass from the pitcher of water and stood close to Kora. She made my testosterone rage. I always told myself that all women were good for was helping to release pent-up stress and extra energy. I'd never wanted anyone as much as I wanted Kora. It was a new sensation and one I wasn't sure I was okay with.

"Looks like you two ruled the game," Kora acknowledged.

I shrugged and downed the water. That tasted good. A beer would be great, but water was just fine.

Bryson's arm draped over my shoulder. "This guy's going to bring us the championship tomorrow night. He has amazing skills."

"I bet he does," Summer replied, glancing hard at Kai. "I'd like to see those skills sometime."

I laughed and lifted my brow. Summer was a blast. You never knew what would come from her mouth. "I don't know if I could handle you, Summer. You frighten me a little."

"Not the first time I heard that." Summer lifted her margarita and emptied the glass.

"Okay." Kora placed her empty drink on the table. "This was exactly what I needed tonight, but if I want to come back and watch you two become cornhole champions, I'm gonna have to call it a night. If I stay, I'll drink more, and if I drink more, I won't be back out tomorrow." She stood from the bench and wobbled a little. She reached out and grabbed hold of my arm and squeezed.

I put my arm around her waist to keep her from falling over. "You good? I don't think you should drive."

She nodded and patted me on the chest. She rubbed her hand up and down and sent a shock through my shirt, and the heat from her touch spread throughout my body. I glanced down at her, and our eyes met.

She bit her bottom lip.

My eyes fixed onto that lip.

"Well, I can't drive, anyway. I came here with Darlene."

"Well then, I can drive you home," I offered before I thought too much about it.

"I won't complain about that," Kora answered, and our gazes held.

"Take care of her, Kai. Make sure she gets home safely." Darlene wrapped me in a hug. "She's had quite a bit to drink."

"Whatever, Dar, I'm fine." Kora pulled Darlene away from me and hugged her, then Summer.

"Be good," Summer said. "But remember what I said, Kai. Take care of her, Lickalicious." She winked and chuckled.

I didn't miss the evil eye Kora shot in her direction. *Lickalicious? That's a new one.*

I led Kora from the pub with my hand on her lower back, pressed into her to keep her stable, and helped her into the truck. When she was situated, I hopped into the driver's seat.

I pulled away and was ready to turn toward her house when her hand landed on my arm, her nails digging into my skin. That heat was back, and my crotch woke up.

"I just remembered I don't have my purse. I left it at the hair salon today."

"Looks like we're stopping in to grab it. Good thing I've got a key." I turned the wheel to the left and drove across the street and to the back of the salon.

As soon as I unlocked the door, Kora went directly to the salon area. "Hey, do you want water? I have some bottles in the kitchen, or I can make some coffee," I said in a loud enough voice so Kora could hear.

"Water would be great," she answered.

I watched her as she checked Summer's station. She picked up some brushes and moved an iPad. My crotch was still reacting to her touch in the truck. This could end very badly. I needed to focus on getting her home quickly.

"Hey!" She hollered and held her debit card in the air and waved it back and forth, then wiggled her hips when she lifted her purse in the air. Her perky tits bounced under her tight shirt.

She really shouldn't have done that. My crotch seemed to like the show. *Remember—get her home quickly.*

"Here we go." She placed her card in her purse and walked into the kitchen and leaned against the counter. "When Darlene and I stopped by earlier, I put it on Summer's station."

"Glad you found it." I handed her water.

"Thank you." I watched as she downed half. Her eyes were closed like she hadn't drunk anything that delicious ever. Her eyes opened, and when they met mine, it was like the earth stopped rotating.

I moved closer, not able to tear my eyes off hers. The pull between us was impossible to ignore, and I was tired of trying.

She froze with the bottle near her lips, and I thought I might drown in her chocolate river.

"Is there something on my face?"

I shook my head and stared at a droplet of water that clung to her lips. I had an urge to lick it off but just pointed instead.

She wiped it from her mouth and brushed her hands through her hair. "My hair's a mess."

"No. It's perfect. You look amazing." My voice came out throaty and deep. I couldn't explain what was pulling me toward her, but slowly the space between us closed.

Her tongue wiped at her bottom lip and sucked it into her mouth. That slight movement made my crotch twitch and my mouth water. I wanted my mouth on those lips. Bullshit. I wanted more than that.

She kept staring at me, and I watched as her eyes wandered up my body, then down, then back up until they latched on to mine again. "Your eyes are so crystal clear. They're amazing. Sometimes when you look at me like you are right now, it's like they're seeing right into me." Her voice quivered and her eyes got wide as though she was surprised that came from her.

I brushed a lock of hair from her face, and my fingers lingered on her cheek. The heat from her skin seeped into me, and my heart started to beat hard and fast.

She lifted her hand and brushed against the scar under my eye.

The scar was still sensitive, even after all these years, but her touch made it seem even more so. I closed my eyes and enjoyed the touch of her fingers on my skin.

Even though women often thought the scar was sexy, to me, it was a deep reminder of why love seemed like an impossible dream. It reminded me daily of why I needed to keep my distance from people, that real relationships didn't exist.

Sex, sure. One-night stands, absolutely.

But I wasn't the kind of guy that women wanted long term, and the scar represented a history I couldn't involve anyone with and included skeletons I didn't want to unleash.

I backed away and involuntarily flinched.

"Kai, what's wrong?" There was concern in her voice.

"Nothing." I combed my fingers through my hair and shook my head. What was I doing? I came to Orlinda Valley to start a new life, but I don't need to involve anyone in my drama. My plan was to work and live alone. My feelings were all muddled up. Kora was a wrinkle in my plan. Things were becoming difficult.

She stepped closer and again reached up and brushed her finger over the scar. "What happened? How'd you get this?"

I grabbed her hand. This needed to stop. "Don't. It's not something I have any desire to discuss."

Kora's eyes filled with something I couldn't pinpoint. "Kai, I want to get to know you. I don't know what caused this scar, but it's intriguing and it can't be that bad, but even if it is, it doesn't matter."

She closed the little gap between us and licked her lips. "The scar's old. Whatever happened is in the past."

She was right. I couldn't let the past ruin my life forever. I promised my sister before she drove away that I would try and find happiness. That's why I came here, so far from home. To start over.

But finding a relationship? That wasn't the plan.

These feelings were definitely not part of the plan.

I reached out and brushed her hair off her shoulder. "Trust me. You may not like the answer you get. This scar is the remnant of a bad home life. A past I'd rather forget." I tried to clear the memories that invaded my consciousness. "Something you wouldn't understand."

"My life wasn't perfect. My parents got divorced when I was young. My mom left and I hardly ever saw her." Kora placed her hands on my chest. "My dad worked hard, and with my Aunt Tonya and the close community, yeah, I had a good life, but it wasn't perfect."

I rubbed my thumbs along her jawline. The air became thick with need, and electricity rippled between us.

I needed to do what I promised Darlene I would do. Get Kora home safely.

I hardly knew her. This wasn't a good idea. She wasn't someone to have a fling with. If I wanted that, I could go get Barb. I needed to ignore whatever this was and get my body under control.

Yet nothing in me could step away.

Her gaze burned into me, and the pull between us became stronger. Her lips looked delicious, and when she licked them again, I couldn't ignore her any longer. The desire I had been fighting since that first day on the side of the road became the focus. "I'm sorry. I know this is wrong." I placed my lips on hers. They were soft and warm just like I thought they would be.

The kiss started soft for a split second until the electricity between us exploded. I forced her lips open with my tongue and she readily obliged. Our tongues danced together. She tasted like the mint gum she had been chewing.

Her hands wrapped around my neck and gripped tightly in my hair as the kiss deepened. That's all the encouragement I needed.

I pulled her firmly against me and knew immediately that she could feel how badly I wanted her. I pushed her up against the newly built wall and lifted her. She wrapped her legs around my waist as I trailed kisses down her throat and dragged my tongue across her collar bone. She tasted like the sweetest dessert I had ever had. I pushed the strap of her tank top off her shoulder and brushed my hand down her arm. Her skin was as soft as silk.

"Kora." I broke our connection and made sure her feet were firmly on the floor. I needed to get control before this went any further. She'd had a lot to drink and may need to think this through.

"Kai, don't stop. I want you. I need you. Now. I cannot wait another second. Whatever this is between us is driving me crazy." She stared deep into my eyes, desire blazing from hers. Her chest raised and lowered quickly.

I couldn't believe the words that just came from her. This woman was so sexy, yet so out of my league. But God, I wanted her. "Are you sure?" I would not be the one to take advantage of a woman.

She nodded, and her mouth ticked up in a sexy-as-hell smile.

That smile sent heat right to my groin. "If at any time, you change your mind, just say the word, and I'll stop."

"Kai, shut the fuck up. I want you. If you want me, you can have me. You can have every fucking inch of me." She crushed her mouth to mine in the hottest kiss of my memory.

Things went from warm to hotter than an incinerator in less than the time it took for me to scoop her up and carry her through the kitchen to the back room that was my bedroom. I laid her on the bed as gently as I could muster and watched intently as she lifted her brow and bit her bottom lip—that sexy gesture made my crotch twitch. Then she lifted her shirt over her head and tossed it across the room.

Her breasts were amazing. "Damn, girl." My voice came out low and desperate.

She curled her finger in a come here motion. I straddled her, careful not to put my full weight on her legs, and stripped my shirt over my head, then crushed my lips to hers.

Chapter 11

KORA

I couldn't believe this was really happening. Maybe it was the alcohol keeping me from making the smart decision and leaving, but if I was drunk, I wouldn't be thinking of leaving. I wouldn't be thinking of anything at all.

When Kai stood, outside of feeling abandoned, I had a full view of him. I could easily see how worked up he was. Outside of the increase in his breathing, his crotch area appeared a bit full. I shimmied out of my bottoms and laid in front of him, naked and free. I motioned for him to do the same. "Come on, Kai. Show me what you've got."

He kicked off his shoes and shucked his pants quickly, then was back on the bed beside me. God, his body was amazing. I brushed my fingers down the ridges that were his abs. It was obvious that he worked in construction and carried heavy loads often. His body was perfectly sculpted and tanned from the sun.

He closed the space between us. His lips left a blazing trail from my shoulder to my neck and finally met my lips. I moaned in acceptance of his mouth while his fingers teased at the sensitive spot between my legs.

His mouth abandoned mine, and he kissed a trail down to my breast where his tongue played with my nipple, then sucked it hard into his mouth, causing a tingling sensation to travel all over my body. The feeling was intense. I couldn't moan. I couldn't cry out his name. I just sucked in my breath and prayed to God that this was not a dream. That this was real.

Suddenly, his mouth moved on and followed the tingle downward. I gripped his face in my hands. That would be amazing, but not now. "I want to feel you inside me right now. Nothing else." My voice was a whisper. Barely audible. I was high and didn't want to come down.

He licked his lips and peered at me with those crystal-blue eyes. "You sure? You'll be missing out on one of my talents."

I breathed out hard. "Damn, Kai." I paused as a throb started between my legs.

He smirked.

"You'll have to show me that talent another time."

"Sounds like a plan," he said as he kissed my breast again, then left for a brief moment—that felt like an eternity—then he was back with the condom he'd retrieved from his pocket.

Thank God he had a condom. Did he usually keep them? How often did he do this? The rational part of my mind told me this needed to stop, but I was never rational. I never thought things through. This was what I wanted. Kai was who I wanted. This was exactly where I wanted to be, and I wanted him now.

He kissed me deeply, and a moan escaped from deep in my throat. He moaned my name as he slipped inside me.

I gasped and grasped his ass. I wrapped my legs around his hips and pushed him deeper, accepting all of him, and he felt amazing.

He went slow at first. I moved my hips with his rhythm. He filled me and the feeling was pure perfection. I couldn't stop the moan that escaped.

Our hands were everywhere. Names were yelled. I was on cloud nine, and it was over with one final thrust of his hips as an amazing blast of heat exploded throughout my body. I worked hard to catch my breath as I held him close. I placed a kiss on his neck right below his ear, and he let out a final moan. My lips found his, and I kissed him softly.

Kai leaned up and brushed his hand across my face and tucked a lock of hair behind my ear. "That was amazing."

My entire body was numb and relaxed as he lay softly on top of me. "I agree." My voice was a whisper.

He laid on his back, still holding me close. I laid my head on his chest, my arm draped across him.

"That was better than I imagined." Kai's voice was soft.

I pushed up on my elbow and faced him. "You imagined sex with me?"

"Since that first day I heard you arguing with a cow." He smirked and that dimple popped.

I brushed my finger against it. "I've been wanting to do this." I brushed my lips over that dimple, then moved to his scar and kissed him there. I glanced at Kai, and his eyes were closed. He moaned softly. He looked more peaceful now than I'd ever seen him.

His eyes fluttered open.

I smiled. "I've been wanting to kiss your dimple and scar for a while."

"We've only known each other a week."

"Seriously?" I pursed my lips. Was it really only a week?

"Hard to believe, I know. It seems like we've been fighting whatever this is for a while."

I lay back on the pillow and pulled the sheet up to cover my breasts. Suddenly I felt a little self-conscious. I didn't do this. I hardly knew him.

He turned his face toward me and chuckled. "You are amazing. One minute you're throwing yourself at me, now you're covering up and look all shy. I hope this won't make things weird between us."

His chuckle had put me at ease, and I placed my hand on his chest and turned toward him. "We've known each other a week. You've changed my tire, drove me home, talked to my goats, and now we just had sex in my aunt's best friend's hair salon. No, nothing's weird about any of this."

He smiled wide and his dimple appeared. He pulled me on top of him and kissed me hard. That kiss sent an electric pulse throughout my body and caused some things to get wet and other things to get hard.

"Someone's ready for more," I said seductively. I Straddled his wide and strong body and went for round two.

The next morning, I awoke with a pounding headache. I draped my arm over my head, then cracked open my eyes. It took me a moment to remember I wasn't in my room and to remember where I was. It helped when memories of amazing sex came back. I closed my eyes and let the warm feelings of last night spread over me.

Noises from the other side of the bedroom door bombarded my consciousness. I was at the hair salon, and the sounds were coming from the kitchen. Kai must already be up, making us coffee.

I rolled over and stretched. My arm hit a body. I wasn't in bed alone. The noise in the kitchen wasn't Kai. He still snored lightly beside me.

My eyes popped wide, and I leaned on an elbow to focus harder on the noise in the kitchen. I recognized Diane and Tonya's voices immediately.

"Holy shit." My pulse jumped awake. "Wake up." I pushed on Kai's chest. "Kai." I hissed his name.

He rolled over, wrapped his arm around me, and nuzzled into my neck.

My insides turned into that familiar fluttering and my arm laced around his waist. I could easily ignore the issue on the other side of the door and get right back to what we were doing all night. His nuzzle turned to kisses, and my insides turned to mush.

"No, no, no." My eyes bulged and my pulse raced. Panic took over. I tried to lift his arm, but it wouldn't budge. Was he made of lead? Lord, his arm was heavy. It was like dead weight. But he had to get up. This was an emergency. "Kai. We can't do this right now."

"Yes, we can." His voice was thick with sleep. His kisses continued and closed in on my breast.

Good, God, I wanted to melt right into him, but a crash from the other side of the door made him freeze and reason return.

"They're here. They're here. They're gonna know." I untangled Kai's arms, jumped out of bed, and searched for my clothes. I found my bra hanging on a light, my panties over the chair, and my jeans were in a wad on the floor. I slipped into them and searched for my shirt. Where the hell was my shirt?

Kai's eyes opened and he pulled himself to a sitting position.

"Shit. I can't find my shirt."

Kai leaned back on the headboard with his hands behind his head and a smirk covered his face.

I couldn't believe him. "Seriously? You do realize how this looks, right? Fuck." I picked up his clothes thrown randomly everywhere and threw them on the bed, but still no shirt. "This is going to look so bad."

"I don't know. It looks pretty damn good from where I'm sitting." A smirk covered his face. A damn hot smirk.

Ignore him. Stay focused. I huffed out a breath and fastened my bra. At least now my breasts weren't hanging out for him to ogle. I finally found my shirt. *Hallelujah!* It ended up behind the chair in the corner. How did it get all the way back there? I didn't think I threw it that far.

"Hey?" Kai wrapped his arms around me, trapping my arms.

I hadn't even realized he had gotten out of bed.

"Relax. Last night was hot."

"Yes, but this doesn't make it any easier. What are they going to think?"

"It doesn't matter what they think. We are two consenting adults, and we both consented, and it was amazing." He kissed me lightly, then made his way to the bathroom.

I watched his sexy ass enter the bathroom. He looked just as good this morning as he did last night. *Maybe I wasn't as drunk as I thought.* And yes, the sex was great, but that didn't make this whole thing less awkward.

I paced the room. *How would I get to his truck without Kaye, Diane, and my nosey aunt knowing I spent the night?*

My pacing was interrupted when Kai blocked my path. My eyes slowly traveled from the floor to his strong thighs and stopped on his hips. He was clothed in basketball shorts which hung low on his hips. Those luscious, sexy hips. I blinked hard then forced my eyes to continue upward to his chest, where they hung out for a while and admired all the ridges of his six-pack abs and finally found their way to his eyes. Crystal clear and amazingly sexy. Desire churned deep within my gut, and the overly sensitive area between my legs yelled out with need. I squeezed my eyes tight. *Stop. This is not the time.*

His dimple appeared. "Having a hard time deciding if you should leave?" He took a step closer.

I took a step back and shook my head. *I'm leaving. Just push him away.*

Again, that dimple popped, and the space between the two of us shrunk until his body was pushed up against mine.

I took yet another step back, but the wall stopped my retreat, and his hands pressed on either side of my body. I was trapped, but not at all in a bad place. I placed my hands on his chest to keep some space between us, but as soon as I touched his skin a shock traveled downward, and that need returned.

Fuck. I closed my eyes. *Focus Kora.*

He brushed his hand along my face gently. "You know, we could just wait it out back under the covers. They can't be here all day." He kissed my neck softly.

I moaned.

"And it's Saturday. We have nothing to do until tonight." I felt a smile on his lips when he kissed my shoulder and scraped his teeth against my skin.

I blew out a long breath. "You're not making this easy," I whispered.

"Nope, not my goal. I think we could find a way to pass the time." He trailed his fingers up and down my right arm, causing goose bumps to appear on my flesh. "There's many things I still want to do to you. Like taste you," he said as he kissed the top of breast.

I took a sharp breast in.

"Take things slower," he said as he lowered my bra and kissed my nipple.

A breathy whimper escaped my throat.

"Make you say my name a bunch more times. Show you my other talents." He lifted his eyes to mine and winked.

My knees went weak. He was so sexy and so . . . Kai.

His mouth connected with mine in a tantalizingly sweet kiss that made it easy to imagine that climbing back under the covers with him was a good idea. A very good idea.

I moaned softly, then broke away. "I gotta go," I whispered. "We just gotta figure out how."

"Fine." Kai kissed the tip of my nose before he grabbed his keys off the dresser and walked to the door. "You might want to put that shirt on before you leave the room. I'm sure that would be a dead giveaway that we fucked like rabbits." He smirked, grabbed a shirt from off the chair, and reached for the doorknob.

I did what he suggested and slipped my tank top over my head just as he opened the door a crack. "It's clear." He stepped out into the kitchen.

I crossed the room, placed my hands on his back, and listened. I held my breath to make even less noise. Kaye's, Diane's, and Tonya's voices were in the main area. "I think we got this," I whispered as quietly as I could. "And if they catch us, we just act like I was drunk and we passed out together, but nothing happened."

"That sounds like a crystal clear, fail-proof plan. Let's do it." Kai led the way to the door, a smirk on his face.

I ran my fingers through my hair, tried to comb away the sex-hair evidence, and followed quietly behind him. *Okay, we can do this, not a big deal. Almost there. We got this.*

Kai unlocked the back door and opened it.

"Well, isn't this a surprise?"

Damn. We didn't make it. My heart dropped, and I ran into Kai and placed my hands on his back.

"Kora, honey. Why are you leaving the salon at this hour of the morning? Did you have a salon appointment?" Tonya asked.

"I'm sure she had some sort of appointment," Kaye agreed with Tonya.

I laid my head on Kai's back. "Fuck," I said under my breath.

"That's probably more like the appointment she had this morning," Tonya said, and peals of laughter came from the Orlinda Valley gossip channel.

Kai turned and glanced at me, his smile large and his dimple laughing.

I stood there and shook my head. *We only had a few more steps, and we would have been home free.*

Kai shrugged. "We tried."

"Look who it is," Diane said as she joined her friends. "Good morning, you two."

I turned slowly. "Look, it's not what it looks like. We were out at the pub last night, and I had a bit too much to drink. Kai offered to take me home, but I forgot my debit card here, so we came by so I could get it. He offered me some water, and I just passed out. Right, Kai?" I made eye contact and he shrugged again.

"Kai, don't answer that." Tonya raised her hand to stop all talking. "It's okay with us that you two had a hot night of sex… or fun."

"Or both," Kaye added.

"Oh, my God. Kaye! I expect this from my aunt, but you?" I could feel the heat rise in my face. I really needed to escape. I was not in the mood to listen to the book club gossipers. "Come on, Kai." I grabbed his arm and tried to pull him out the door, but he wasn't easy to move.

He chuckled. "We can't just leave." He addressed the women. "Good morning, ladies. I've got to get Kora to her car. I'll be back here soon to paint the room and meet Blake. See you in a bit."

"Oh, we can't wait to hear all about your night," Tonya said.

"Good Lord." I pushed the screen door open and about ran out to Kai's truck and climbed in.

"Hey, relax." He answered with laughter in his voice as he climbed behind the wheel.

"That was mortifying." I covered my face with my hands.

Kai started the truck, pulled out of the lot, and drove the short distance to Darlene and Bryson's. "It's all good. Don't worry so much about it."

"Don't worry?" I spun in my seat to face him. "You don't know them. They will make this part of book club lore forever. They will never let this go. You don't understand my Aunt Tonya. She's a lunatic and a sex fiend." I needed to calm down, but I was past embarrassed, and my mouth just wouldn't stop. "She's been telling me how hot you are and that I should try to get a piece of that ass, and here we are." I waved my hands. "And she was right. You are hot. And I did get a piece of that ass. And a very fine ass it is, I might add."

He pulled up in front of Bryson and Darlene's house and put the car in park before he turned toward me. "Thank you. Your ass ain't so bad either." He winked. "But is it so bad that we got together and had a great time? If I remember correctly, I was the one not sure about us last night, and you were all about it."

Shit. I was all over him. I'd never acted like that before. I'd never acted like a . . . I shook my head again and tried to cover my face, but he grabbed my hands and wouldn't let go. A blush crossed my cheeks, and I turned away.

That didn't help at all. Bryson and Darlene stood on their front porch. Bryson waved, and Darlene had a huge smirk glued on her face. "Dammit. Fuck. Shit."

Kai lifted his hand to return Bryson's greeting, then turned back to me. "Girl, you have one mean potty mouth." He made this odd growling noise. "I like it."

I narrowed my eyes at him and tried to look angry, but his voice was sultry. Sexy. Hot. I closed my eyes to gather myself. "I knew I should have moved. Nothing is ever private in this small-ass town."

"Look, I can't let you out without saying this. I know last night was unexpected, but I'm not sorry it happened. I'm glad you came on to me, and I'm glad you didn't let me turn you away." He moved my face toward his.

I got lost in those eyes—again—and let out a heavy sigh,

He chuckled. "It's all good, Kora. I promise." He brushed his lips softly against mine, then deepened it into a sweet lingering kiss.

I stayed there for a beat, enjoying the warmth that spread throughout my body.

He pulled slightly away, and our eyes met. "Now you can leave. I'll see you tonight."

Even in a whisper, his voice was sexy. My body perked up and became all hot and bothered. "Damn you, Kai." I grabbed his neck and pressed my lips against his again and deepened the kiss. I tasted him with my tongue, and my lips lingered on his before I pulled away. If my body wanted more and my bestie was going to watch, she might as well enjoy the show. "There. Now I can leave." I smiled and climbed out of his truck.

I watched him pull away and already couldn't wait to see him again.

I ignored the questions, sailing across the yard from Darlene. "Sorry. Can't talk. Gotta get to Percy and Jackson." I waved, blew Darlene a kiss, and climbed into my car. Tonight couldn't come soon enough.

Chapter 12

KORA

Percy and Jackson skipped and bounded along, filled with boundless energy as they frolicked in the pasture. They were excited to have me with them, their bleats of adoration echoing off the trees and openness of the pasture. I totally understood how they were feeling. If I were a goat, I'd be expressing myself the same way.

I also had boundless energy and felt I could face any challenge and win, which was a good thing because at the top of my to-do list this morning was finding a way to keep Baby Goat from roaming free. Luckily, right now he was off on his own but keeping me in his sights. He wasn't as interested in breaking free if there was someone to bother close by.

It was a perfect day to enjoy being outside, so I be-bopped my way out to the cherry tree with the goats. "Yes, I'm going to feed you some yummy cherry tree leaves, then clean your house and bowls and find a way to lock you in, you escape artist." I scratched Baby

Goat's head as he munched away on the delectable treats. Life really was good, and after last night, it had improved more than a bowl of vanilla ice cream with hot fudge and whipped topping.

I was laying down fresh straw in the goat house when the sound of gravel crunching under a tire caught the goats' attention and became more interesting than my job of cleaning their house.

I peeked out the door and a lump of disappointment lodged in my chest at the sight of Darlene's Rogue. Could I really have been hoping it was Kai? I just left him a few hours ago. "Damn, girl. Get a hold of yourself. It was one night, and you've only known him a week."

Darlene helped James out of the back of the car, and I could hear his little voice over the excited bleating of Percy, Jackson, and Baby Goat. They all knew that James meant they were going to have someone to run with and chase out in the pasture. Darlene's presence meant she wanted information about what she'd witnessed this morning.

I placed the rake back on the hook and wiped my hands on the butt of my jeans and walked out to join Darlene and James. *Guess I'll get the inquisition over with.*

Darlene opened the gate, and James came running in. "Kora!" He ran as fast as his little legs could take him, and the goats ran and hopped beside him.

His laughter warmed my heart, and a smile spread across my face. I caught him in midair as he leaped into my arms. "Hey there, JJ." I hugged him closely and spun him in a circle. "What brings you by?" I asked him.

"I need to see the goats." He wiggled out of my arms and ran off across the pasture with Percy and Jackson on his heels.

"Well, it's good to see someone so happy this morning," Darlene said as she wrapped me in a hug.

"It is. He loves those goats, and they're excited to have someone to run with. They were getting irritated with me."

Darlene shook her head and smirked. "I wasn't talking about James. He's four and almost always happy." She wrapped her arm around my shoulder, and we walked off toward the cherry tree where Percy and Jackson were once again busy trying to stretch for the branches that were just out of reach, and James jumped up to catch the lowest branch which was just out of his reach. "I was talking about you and the glow you're wearing."

I held back an eye roll. Darlene would jump on that and say it's a dead giveaway. I had to find another way to convince her that nothing amazing happened last night. Time to see if I could make it in Hollywood. "It's not a glow. It's called *perspiration*. I've been out here working for a while, taking advantage of the nice weather between rainy days. My goats were feeling neglected."

Darlene nudged me.

I struggled to keep my attention on the goats and ignore her inquisition but realized rather quickly that I would not make it in Hollywood.

"I don't believe you. That glow isn't from perspiration, at least not from the hard work from this morning. Maybe after the long night you had and from trying to sneak out of Shear Perfection at the crack of dawn."

"Seriously?" I stopped walking. Of course Darlene had already heard. "Who told you?"

"Oh, come on. Who do you think? My mother-in-law, a.k.a. your aunt, paid us a visit just a little while ago with her entourage and told Bryson and me that they caught you sneaking out the back door of the salon at eight this morning, which would explain why Kai dropped you off so early to get your car."

Again, I wished, though briefly, that I would have moved to a big city years ago. No one would care if a grown woman left a man's apartment at eight in the morning if they lived in a building surrounded by hundreds of other apartments. "That damn book club gossip channel really needs to get a life."

Darlene laughed. "Oh, please, they do. Their life revolves around the crazy things their families do, and since Bryson and I are a boring married couple with a child, Jamison is a single dad and never dates, and Rowan's not around, you and Kai are now the number one topic of conversation." Darlene stepped away and walked toward the tree. "So, did you have fun?"

"With what?" I pulled a branch down so the goats, standing on their hind legs, could stretch up and reach the leaves.

"Getting your hair colored." Darlene swatted at me. "What do you think?"

Percy leaned against my leg, and I petted the side of his neck. "James, why don't you pet them now. They're too busy eating to head butt you."

James clapped his hands quietly and stood next to me and petted Percy.

"You're ignoring me," Darlene observed.

"No kidding." I wished the ground would open and swallow me up. I really didn't want to discuss this. Out of everything I needed to do, this was not on the top of my to-do list. "Ok goats. That's enough." I let go of the branch, and it snapped up out of Percy and

Jackson's reach. They got down and wandered off to find something else to occupy them, and James followed.

"God, Kora." Darlene said as she followed James and me. But she wouldn't let up. "You're pretty and independent, with a lot to offer, and he's a hot man. You're attracted to each other. We can all see that. It's so obvious. The heat between the two of you could melt all the glaciers in the northern hemisphere. Hell, even Trevor had a hard time keeping his eyes off you and was shooting daggers at Kai all night long."

I snapped my attention toward Darlene. "You need to stop. Trevor and I were over a long time ago."

"Wrong. You were over. He's been pining after you ever since you broke things off with him years ago. When you and Kai danced last night, Trevor was collecting glasses, and if looks could kill, you wouldn't have had that amazing night with Kai. It's so obvious you're both into each other."

I rolled my eyes.

Darlene elbowed me. "Don't roll those eyes. Just say what you think. You do that eye rolling crap too much."

"Fine." I opened the gate. Darlene called for James, but he was still busy with the goats, so we leaned on the fence to watch. "Yes, we had an amazing night, and the gossip chain was there bright and early this morning. We tried to get me out before they saw but failed miserably." I blew out a breath and glanced sideways at Darlene, who had a shit-eating grin on her face. I elbowed her. "Take that grin off your face. It's not a big deal."

"And that's why we watched you kiss goodbye in his truck."

"Just saying bye. It's what you do after a date."

"That lasted all night and gave you a couple orgasms I hope." Her eyes went up with anticipation.

I tipped my head back and forth, and my face lit up like Nashville on the Fourth of July. I couldn't help it. Thinking of Kai and our night together made me feel things I hadn't felt in a long time, and I liked it. A lot.

Darlene let out a squeal. "I knew it!" She wrapped me in a death squeeze. "You deserve a good night of fun and amazing sex with a super-hot guy. I'm so happy for you." She rocked us back and forth, then stopped abruptly and held my arms in a death grip. "It was fun and amazing sex, right?" Darlene's eyes were wide with concern.

I laughed. How could I not? Her eyes were wide with shock and fear like the world would end if I told her anything but what she expected to hear. Thankfully, I didn't have to disappoint her. "Yeah, you could say we had fun. But the sex wasn't amazing."

Her eyes bulged wide, and her mouth dropped. "You can't be serious."

"Sorry, I am." I waited until I thought she might keel over. "It wasn't amazing. It was fucking life changing, emotionally fulfilling, hot, and dirty." I stopped and shrugged. "I can't think of any other adjectives that are fitting."

Darlene's squeal got the attention of the goats. "Thank God. You deserve it." The goats bleated in return.

"Gee, thanks, *Mom*. But you're not wrong. I do." His naked body flashed in my mind; my mouth watered and my insides tingled.

"I can't wait to see you together tonight. How exciting."

"It's not like that. Last night was a one-night thing." We didn't discuss anything more. I didn't want to make a big deal out of it. What if he thought it was just a one-night thing?

"Right. We'll see." She turned her attention to her son. "Come on, James. Time to go."

"Yeah, we will. I'll see you around five thirty. We can eat before the competition starts at six." I hugged them both.

"Yep. Sounds good." Darlene answered as she helped James into his car seat.

I waved as Darlene pulled away, then walked toward the house. Crystal eyes popped into my mind and my stomach rolled. I hoped I would be able to play it cool tonight. I didn't want to seem like that woman who, just because she had amazing sex with a hot guy, has to stick on him like Velcro.

Nope, that's not me. Last night wasn't the first time I had a one-night stand, and they weren't a big deal. This one wasn't a big deal either.

My stomach rolled again, then flipped like it was going downhill on a roller coaster. I froze and stared down the driveway but was focused on nothing.

What if he thought that's all it had been—a one-night stand? What if he acted like what happened last night wasn't a big deal?

What if he thought it was just sex?

I wiped my hands on my jeans, and my chest tightened. *Dammit.*

I blinked quickly to keep the tears at bay. *I don't want last night to be just a one-night stand. I like Kai.* I watched clouds float by. Where did these feelings even come from? How did he go from irritating the hell out of me to rocking my world?

Hell—I didn't even know his last name.

Well, there's one goal for tonight.

Chapter 13

Kai

I pulled in front of Jerry's Pub and noticed a black Rogue in the parking lot that looked a lot like Kora's. My mouth ticked up. I can't lie. It would make my night to be with her again. I spent the day painting and dodging the questions and comments thrown at me from the "Book Club gossips"—as Kora called them. Tonya tried her best to get information from me. She even used the tactic that Kora was her niece, and it was her job to keep tabs on her. But I held my tongue and gave them nothing. I'll be damned if I give them fuel for their gossip channel.

All afternoon, my mind kept recreating last night. How our bodies rocked perfectly in tune. The little moans she made. How beautiful she was in the moment. The memories were so vivid that my crotch kept getting in my way. I needed a cold shower before I left, and if I kept thinking this way, I'd need to take a minute before getting out of the truck, or I may not be able to take responsibility for my actions, and sex in a bathroom at the pub was not on my to-do list.

If I was being totally honest with myself, Kora had been on my mind since the moment I met her on the side of the road. I was immediately attracted to her spunk, her personality, her beauty.

And that mouth. Damn, that mouth. The words that came out of it—and the talent she had with it . . .

I puffed out a heavy breath. "You got this. Just act natural."

I climbed out of Matilda and combed my hands through my hair. Why did it feel like I was back in middle school, and this was our first date? Not that I went on any dates in middle school or had any friends for that matter.

Stop. Don't go there. Not tonight. I opened the door of the pub and my gaze fixed right on Kora like I was a compass, and she was magnetic north.

She was leaning against the bar laughing at something Trevor said. Her head tipped back a little, and her face sparkled. She was wearing a white button-up blouse tied at the waist and tight jeans which hugged her curves—all those perfect curves. She wasn't thin but was perfectly thick and muscular, and God, those hips.

I balled my hands into fists to keep from walking to her and filling them with her softness. My fingers itched to touch her. My eyes traveled to her face just as she glanced over. Her large deep brown eyes sparkled under the lights of the bar. I may not have come to Orlinda Valley expecting, or even wanting, to find a relationship, but when I see Kora, I can't think of anything else.

"Hey." I leaned against the bar beside her. A small smile climbed her face, and her eyes flicked around me and finally fell on mine. I lightly tucked a strand of hair off her face, and a tingle entered the tip of my thumb when it slid against her cheek before it rested again on the bar.

"Hey," she answered in a shy voice.

"What can I get you, man?" Trevor asked as he set the pitcher of margaritas and two glasses in front of Kora.

"Just a Coke, thanks," I answered, never taking my eyes off Kora. "How was your day?" My full attention was on this beautiful woman in front of me, and I nodded to Trevor in recognition of the drink he placed on the counter.

"It was good. I caught up on some work I needed to do with the goats and chicken enclosure."

"Good. Are Baby Goat's escape plans useless?"

"Should be. For now, anyway, though I'm sure he's already thinking of a new way to break out."

I took a drink of my Coke. "Should we join Bryson and Darlene?" I asked as I reached for the pitcher.

Kora nodded and grabbed the glasses. We walked to the same picnic table we sat at last night. Darlene and Bryson were already there.

I poured Kora and Darlene their drinks, then sat next to Kora. The vanilla and strawberry scent of her perfume and shampoo filled my nostrils. Damn, she smelled good enough to eat. I pulled my eyes from her and focused on the cornhole boards across the yard as I sipped my Coke.

"You don't drink much, do you?" Kora asked.

"Nope. Not really." She didn't need to know that with an alcoholic and abusive father, excessive drinking was something I tried my best to avoid. My past wasn't good, and I never made smart choices under the influence, so it was better not to partake. "But you go right ahead. I promise I won't take advantage of you, too much anyway." I winked at her jokingly, and a blush splashed across her face. She blushed a lot, and it was sexy.

"Don't worry. Nothing has ever stopped these two from enjoying their margaritas," Bryson said as he took a bite of a burger.

Kora and I ordered burgers and fries, and our conversation changed to the competition of the night. Bryson explained in detail who each team was and his thoughts on what our competition's strengths and weaknesses were.

"Good thing is," Bryson said between bites of his burger, "they don't have you on their team. None of them are as consistent. I think we've got the championship in the bag." Bryson's pun cracked him up. "Get it?" he asked Darlene.

She shook her head. "Yeah, we got it." She placed a kiss on his cheek, and I glanced at Kora. When our eyes met, she smiled shyly and turned away. That wasn't the first time she'd avoided eye contact. I placed my hand gently on her thigh under the table and gave it a light squeeze. I visibly saw her shoulders relax, and she leaned against me. A simple touch that could easily be seen as accidental shot a needle of electricity through my bloodstream. She seemed to feel it, too, and squeezed my hand. Good. She might be unsure how to act in front of her friends, but under the table, all was well.

"All right, ladies, make sure to cheer us on to victory." Bryson wrapped Darlene in a hug and placed a deep kiss on her lips.

"Good luck," Kora told me as she bumped her shoulder against mine and gave me the sweetest shy smile.

"Thanks." I took a deep drink of my Coke. "As long as my aim is on target, we should be good." I held her gaze a beat, then winked and gave her shoulder a squeeze. The competition would be a much-needed distraction and give my body time to relax as my mind got settled on the task at hand—winning.

Once we sweep the competition, I plan on spending the rest of the night making sure Kora remembered the feelings she experienced last night—all the feelings—enticing her to want more. Hopefully, it wouldn't be difficult.

We had to play three games before making it to the final round. It was a tough match which went into extra points, but Bryson and I finally pulled out the victory.

"Yeah, man." Bryson gave me a one-armed man-hug with a couple strong pats on the back as we thanked our opponents and celebrated our victory.

It felt good to be here. Making friends. Having fun. Winning a competition. I couldn't remember the last time I enjoyed myself with friends. I accepted the beer that was given to the finalists during the awards ceremony. Bryson accepted the trophy for us; since he had a permanent home, it made more sense. The music was turned up, and the dance floor quickly filled with bodies. Tonight, it wasn't just grass but an actual dance floor.

"Dance with me." A pretty brunette caught me off guard but didn't wait for my answer before she pulled me onto the floor. The music was upbeat, and I enjoyed dancing. I was a little hesitant, but what could one dance hurt?

"I'm Chloe, and you're Kai," Chloe stated as we danced.

"Yes, I am. And you know that how?" I asked as she danced closer. She had her arms in the air and wiggled her hips in a seductive manner. I took a step back.

"You're new in town, handsome, and I asked." She closed the gap between us, and another couple pushed me from behind. I had to place my arm around her to keep from knocking us over.

She winked and wrapped her arm around my neck and wiggled her ass in a seductive and sexy manner.

Any other time, I might have been interested in those moves, but tonight I was just interested in one person. I glanced at the table and my heart skidded. Kora was in a deep conversation with Summer and some guy I had never seen before. It was obvious, though, that Kora and the impostor knew each other well. She leaned into him and laughed.

Heat raged inside me—jealousy—a feeling I haven't felt often, but the few times I have, it never ended well.

I needed to go to the table and introduce myself, but Chloe held on tight and pulled me closer.

"So, how long have you been in town?" she shouted into my ear.

"I've been here two weeks."

She leaned away and raised her brow. "Well, newcomer, welcome to Orlinda Valley. Are you here to stay, or just passing through?"

Passing through and entering a cornhole competition at Jerry's Pub. What were the chances? "Does anyone just pass through Orlinda Valley?"

A slow song started, and Chloe put her body and voluptuous breasts against me. "Do you mind?" she asked as she started to sway to the slow twang of a Garth Brooks song.

I glanced at the table. Kora was no longer there. Shit. Where'd she go? The guy she was talking to was gone as well. I searched for her, but she was nowhere.

Shit. I pulled away from Chloe. "I'm going to go sit back down." I gestured to the table. "Thanks for the dance."

"Anytime, sugar."

I let out a breath as I hightailed it to Bryson and Darlene. I still couldn't find Kora. "Congratulations," Darlene said as I sat down. "You two are naturals. Maybe you should take it to the professional Cornhole League of America."

I laughed. "I think we'll keep it local, but thanks." This was crazy. Where did she go?

"Hey, Kai. What's got your attention?" They were joined by Summer and the guy Kora had been talking with. He seemed older than the rest of them. He was broad-shouldered with brown hair and blue eyes.

Summer's hair, which was black with blue tips yesterday, seemed to be a more natural brown with burgundy highlights throughout today.

"Kai. Are you the one doing the renovations at Shear Perfection?" the broad-shouldered guy asked.

"I am." Who was this guy, and where was Kora?

He put out his hand. "I'm Lance. My mom, Kaye, told me all about you." A sheepish grin appeared on his face.

My brow ticked up. What exactly did Kaye say? There was no telling. I shook his hand. "Nice to meet you. Your mom's been great. She and Diane are letting me stay at the salon. It makes working on the room much easier."

"I heard," he said as he opened a beer from the ice bucket in the middle of the table. "I've also heard that you had a sleepover."

Darlene choked on her margarita.

"Holy shit," Summer shot as she busted out laughing.

Bryson pushed Lance playfully. "Don't be a dick. Kai was just taking care of Kora because *'she had one too many margaritas'* last night." He did air quotes.

"Yeah, okay. Is that really the bullshit she ejaculated in the salon this morning?" Lance retorted.

"Yeah, it is," Bryson answered. "That's what *she* ejaculated this morning, but I'm not sure that's exactly what was getting ejaculated last night."

"Guys. Enough. Don't you dare say that word again," Darlene interrupted, then placed her hand on my arm across the table. "Ignore them. They always have to act a fool when they're around each other. It's worse when Jamison and Rowan are around also."

"Except that Rowan would get irritated and would kick both their asses," Summer added.

"Whatever, Summer," Bryson said. "You've always gone to the baby's rescue."

Summer shook her head and took a drink.

I watched Summer intently. I'm not sure what the deal was with her and Bryson, but I didn't miss the death stare she gave him and the eyebrow raise from Darlene.

I didn't know, and I didn't care. I had more pressing matters to discuss, and since it seemed like Kora and me weren't a secret, I might as well just ask. "Where'd Kora get to?"

"She got a call from Tonya and told me to let you know she had to go. Percy and Jackson escaped, and she had to go get them corralled back in before they ate Mrs. Jenning's garden," Darlene answered. "She didn't want to bother you."

"Unlike last night when she bothered you at the salon all night long." Lance peered at Kai over his beer bottle.

"Yeah, I wonder what they were doing all night." Bryson raised his brows and stared at me across the table. I made sure my gaze didn't falter and stared right back.

"I think she was getting a manicure and a body massage," Lance said.

"Maybe she was getting a deep moisturizing scalp treatment," Bryson answered back.

"Or a facial," Lance added.

Darlene spurted her mouthful of margarita across the table as Summer squealed with laughter.

"Could be," Bryson answered. "I hear all the above are quite rejuvenating and relaxing."

"Unfortunately, when Kai dropped her off this morning at our house for her car, I didn't have a chance to ask. She barely waved before she hopped in and drove off," Darlene added.

She had to get into it now?

Lance nodded and pursed his lips. "Interesting."

"All of you leave Kai alone," Summer interjected. "If he wanted to tell us why Kora was leaving the salon at eight this morning, I'm sure he would." Summer turned to me. "Don't worry, Kai. I've got your back. I won't let these dumbasses give you shit for getting laid. Lance's just jealous because it's been a while. And Bryson, well, Bryson's just a jerk."

Lance and Bryson chuckled.

I just shook my head. "Is nothing private in this town?"

"Not when the book club's a part of it," Darlene said as she finished her margarita.

"Or it's about Orlinda Valley's golden child," Lance added.

"Don't worry. The book club only talks about those they like," Summer said.

"Same's true for Orlinda Valley," Bryson said.

"You sure about that?" Darlene asked.

"Probably not," Summer said. "Orlinda Valley will talk about anyone who is entertaining enough or drama filled."

Lance and Bryson started talking football, and Darlene and Summer headed to the bathroom together.

Why women couldn't go alone, I'd never understand. I took a sip of my beer and pulled up Kora's number. Maybe she was home and would invite me over.

Kai: I got back to the table, and you were gone. I was hoping to get at least a dance.

It took a while, but finally, my phone vibrated.

Kora: Sorry. You were busy on the dance floor, and I had a small emergency at the farm.

Kai: I heard. How's Mrs. Jenning's garden? I wasn't busy.

Kora: I saved it and now have to fix a part of the fence. Those goats are amazing escape artists. Saw you with Chloe. You've got some moves.

Kai: Maybe I can stop by tomorrow and help you with the fence? And you know all about my moves.

I watched as dots appeared and went away, then appeared again, then went away.

"Kai, you good?" Bryson got my attention and tapped on his beer bottle.

"I'm good." I held my hand over my beer. No way did I need another beer. Especially if I got an answer I'd love. Something like why wait for tomorrow? No time like the present.

Finally, a text came through.

Kora: Sure. Come over tomorrow about ten.

My face fell. Tomorrow. I'd have to wait until tomorrow.

"Is Kora good?" Darlene asked quietly across the table as Bryson and Lance talked loudly about the local football team and weren't paying us any attention.

"Yep. All's good. The goats are back in safe and sound." I pocketed my phone. "I'm going to stop over tomorrow to help her out."

"I'm sure you will," Bryson said.

"Sometimes it's difficult to corral that girl's goats," Lance said.

The men glanced at each other and rolled with laughter.

What a clever metaphor. I knew they were right. I could already tell that Kora would be as big a challenge to corral as her goats, but I sure couldn't wait to try.

I pulled into the hair salon parking lot after leaving the pub and tried hard to fight the urge to stop over Kora's. The pull to see her and start a round two was intense, but I was determined not to do anything about it. If she'd wanted to see me, she would have invited me over.

I leaned heavily on Matilda's steering wheel. "Do I leave it alone, or just go to her?" I asked the truck. I liked talking to Matilda. She was never judgmental and always told me what I wanted to hear.

I forced myself through the door of the hair salon, and a picture of Kora in my arms with her legs wrapped around my waist while I pushed her against the wall flashed into my mind. The thought of her kiss seared a flame of hunger in my chest.

The need and desperation in those kisses. The desire in her eyes. I leaned hard against the kitchen counter as my jeans became uncomfortably tight. I took several deep breaths to control the throbbing in my crotch.

Ten o'clock wouldn't come soon enough.

Chapter 14

Kora

"What the flying fuck are you doing, Percy?" Percy was on top of the trash can that held their food, and I had to nudge him to get him off so I could feed them. I finally succeeded, but before I could open the can, he jumped back up. "You're being a pain in my ass today." I patted his neck and then gave him a hard shove, causing him to jump off. *Thank God.*

"Baaa," Percy retorted.

"Whatever. Be mad at me all you want. I can't feed you if you're standing on top of your food. Now go." I shooed him away and was able to scoop goat feed from the container and latched down the lid.

"Baa," Percy said again before he munched away on the food I poured into his feed trough.

"See, I told you. I can get things done so much quicker if you don't help me. Be more like Jackson. He stays out of the way."

"Baa," Percy answered.

"Dumbass goat. It's a good thing I love you."

"Arguing with farm animals is a thing with you. First a cow, now a goat. What did the goat do?"

Kai. My heart did a flutter thing as I turned away from the goats, and there he was, leaning on the gate, one arm draped on the top rung and the other in his back pocket. That man was a picture of perfection.

"Mind if I come in?"

I shook my head, and he unlatched the gate.

My gaze swept over him, and I liked what I saw.

Damn. Just looking at him made me weak in the knees and warm in the belly. He was built just enough, but not overly buff. Then that face with a couple days of scruff, and those eyes and the way they popped underneath the halo of his black hair.

Yeah, well, I could just stare at him forever, and that was just what I was doing.

He walked with a swagger to his hips and slipped his thumb into his front pockets. "You left before I could say goodbye last night."

I wrung my hands, not sure what to do with them, then slid them into my back pockets. "You were busy, and there was an emergency."

"I wasn't that busy. It was just a dance."

"But it was Chloe. She has a way of getting her nails in a man and not letting go."

"Only one woman has had her nails in me recently, and I'd love to get them to dig into me again."

My eyes went wide, and my stomach flopped massively "Well, you seemed really into Chloe, and we didn't say anything about last night being a date, so I didn't want to push you if you weren't interested.

And . . ." I stopped because Kai had closed the space between us and placed his hand on my arm. Heat seeped into my skin.

He tipped my chin up, and our eyes met. He was serious. "I wasn't interested in Chloe at all. I wanted to spend time with you last night. I would have come over last night—I wanted to come over last night—if you would've asked."

I took a deep breath in and blew it out slowly. It had been a long while since a man made my insides melt. Maybe even never, but they melted under his gaze, and I swallowed hard. "I didn't want to bother you."

"I don't know what's going on between us, but I know I've thought of you a lot since I changed your tire." He held my face in his hands and forced me to gaze into those eyes. Those eyes. I swallowed the lump that had lodged in my throat. "I had a lot of fun Friday night. I'd really like to get to know you more, but I need to know that's what you want also."

He smelled so good, like aftershave and outdoors. I lifted my hands to his arms. Was this what I wanted?

Yes, it was.

I wanted to get to know him as much as a bear wanted honey. I nodded, not sure if my voice would work.

His mouth ticked up and that dimple appeared.

"I love that dimple," I whispered.

"You told me that Friday night."

"Yeah, well, Friday night I was a little drunk. Words tend to spew from my mouth without thought. I wanted to make sure you knew I meant it."

He pulled me into his arms. "How much of what you said Friday night was because you were drunk?"

A feeling of intoxication came over me when I looked into his eyes. I swallowed, and my voice came out as a whisper. "I wasn't that drunk."

Our lips touched lightly. The kiss was soft, warm, and sweet.

I wanted to feel this last night, but seeing him dance with Chloe got me upset, and that phone call about the escaped goats was a great excuse to not have to face my feelings.

Now, though, was another issue. My body reacted immediately as a tingle rushed from my lips to between my thighs. My body knew exactly what it wanted even if my heart wasn't sure. How could I want him this badly when I hardly even knew him?

My mind flew backward and sifted through my memories like a filing cabinet. Where did he come from? Why was he here?

My mind sorted through the chaos going on inside it when he broke the kiss. That was probably a good thing.

"What's wrong?" Kai asked as he brushed my hair behind my neck.

When his fingers touched my skin, an electric pulse sent the throbbing between my legs into overdrive. This was crazy. I needed to get a hold of these feelings. "We hardly know each other." I put some much-needed space between us.

"Then, I guess we need to get to know each other. What can we do for fun around here?"

I guessed I was getting what I wanted.

It was a perfect May day, pleasantly warm and sunny with a very slight breeze. I stared across the field. "We could go kayaking down the Red River," I said with excitement. Nothing was better than the relaxing current of the river on a day like today.

"Sounds fun," he replied and gave me a wicked grin.

That grin. I shook my head. I'd love to show him Orlinda Valley from the river. It was so pretty and peaceful, but being that close and alone...

Maybe going into town and spending some time window shopping on Main Street and stopping for a hot dog and shake at Orlinda Valley Pharmacy would be a better choice. Or even a walk in the park. With little league going on, we would be alone, yet not in total privacy. "Or, even better, I could show you around my little town. Let you get to know more than Shear Perfection and Jerry's Pub. We can save kayaking down the Red River for another time."

"Whatever you want. I'm game as long as I get to spend time with you."

I watched him and shook my head. Hot, handsome, and uber sweet. He was the entire package. "First, help me fix the hole in the fence so these goats will stay put, then we'll go get lunch in town. Orlinda Valley Pharmacy has amazing hot dogs and milkshakes. There are more places in this town to eat outside of Jerry's Pub. Then we can walk around the square and see what stores are open on Sunday."

We worked well together, and soon the gate was fixed—again—and we headed for town. Kai parked Matilda in a spot in the lot next to city hall.

As we walked across the square, he held my hand, and our fingers curled together perfectly. When we entered the pharmacy, eyes turned. I knew most people in town, and seeing me with a man was big news, and I'm sure Tonya was going to hear about it soon enough. I nodded and smiled at some of the customers I knew and led Kai to the counter. If we were eating at an old-fashioned soda fountain, we were going to eat at the counter.

"Hi, Ms. Mitchell. What can I get you?" Eileen, the teenage server, turned shyly toward Kai, her brows raised in question.

"Hi, Eileen." My gaze went from Eileen, who was staring at Kai, to Kai, who was biting the inside of his cheek. "I think I'll take a sweet tea. Kai, what do you want?"

"Sweet tea sounds good." When his dimple popped, Eileen blushed and hurried away.

"Seems as if you make all the females blush," I said, not bothering to hide the amusement in my voice.

"Yes, *Ms. Mitchell*." Kai swept my hair from my shoulder. "That was sweet, but she couldn't have been one of your students. You haven't been teaching that long."

Eileen placed our sweet teas in front of us. "My first class was fourth grade, and Eileen was one of my students. You're finishing up your junior year, aren't you Eileen?"

"Yes, ma'am," she answered. "Are you ready to order?"

"You want a hot dog, fries, and a shake? It's the best ever." I raised my brow. Nothing judged a person's character like a hot dog and shake from the pharmacy. If he refused, there was nothing more I could do here.

"So, you say." Kai turned toward Eileen. "What do you think? Are they the best ever?"

Eileen's eyes went wide. "Uh, yes, sir?" Her words raised in a question, and she still wouldn't make eye contact with him.

"Sounds good," Kai concluded. "I'll take a hot dog, fries, and chocolate shake."

"And I'll take the same. Thank you, Eileen."

Eileen nodded and walked away.

Kai sipped his iced tea. "So, you've been teaching, what? Seven years?"

"Yep," I answered. "I spent five years in college, got my master's, and came home to teach. I taught fourth grade my first year before moving to third grade, and I've been teaching third grade ever since."

"Did you ever want to teach anywhere else?" he asked.

I thought about that. Yes, I did consider getting a job in Clarksville, where I went to college, but that was a much bigger town than Orlinda Valley. I loved it here. I stirred my shake. "I thought about it and considered other places, but Darlene got hired to teach fifth grade at OV Elementary and called me about an available position. Working at the school I went to *and* with my best friend was a dream come true. I applied and was hired."

Eileen dropped off their food and smiled shyly at Kai before walking away.

We became quiet while we ate.

This was, hands down, the best hot dog ever. They were so good that Jerry's didn't bother putting hot dogs on their menu. I wasn't sure what kind the pharmacy used or how they were cooked, but they were always plump and juicy, and with the fries and a shake, this could easily rank right up there with the best meal ever.

"How about you?" I asked as I swallowed a mouthful of hot dog. "What did you want to do after you graduated? Did you go to college or anything?" I wanted to know more about this man who grabbed hold of my heart so quickly. It amazed me that it had been only two weeks since I first met him. In that short time, he'd already rocked my world in a way that I really hoped would happen again.

Kai shook his head and took another bite of his hot dog. The muscle in his jaw ticked, and a faraway look clouded his features.

"Kai?" My heart sped up with concern. I wiped my hands on a napkin and reached out to touch his arm. "Hey, is everything okay?" My voice was soft. My concerned teacher voice is what Darlene called it.

His tight-lipped smile was forced. "Let's just say getting out of high school was a challenge due to a far from perfect home life. I wanted to go to college, but I needed to stay close to keep an eye on my younger siblings, so I took a construction job and have been working construction ever since. No college for me." Kai took a sip of his shake, and some light entered his eyes. "Damn, you were right. This shake's amazing."

I couldn't tell if that's what he really thought or he was just trying to change the subject, but he wasn't lying about one thing. The shake was amazing.

Chapter 15

Kai

What the hell was going on with me? How did my life change so quickly in two weeks? It seemed like yesterday I pulled Matilda into Orlinda Valley, with nothing but one suitcase of clothes and a full bank account. My brother and sister were settled and living their lives. It was finally time for me to be selfish.

Leaving Georgia to work in middle Tennessee with Warren Construction was a good upward move. I finally had a job that could lead somewhere positive, and my boss, Christian Warren, was a good family man.

As soon as I found the land I wanted, I paid for it in cash and put my fifth wheel on it. Once the septic was in and a line was tapped, I'd move out of Shear Perfection and into my own place. My place. My rules. Everything I always wanted, with a life I enjoyed. It was time to put the past in the past.

Add in Kora, and an unexpected bonus was added to my plans.

My gaze fell over her as she ate. She was the epitome of small-town life. She loved everything about this town. Our morning together had proven that. She knew everyone and enjoyed showing me around the town and the stores. She could be the Orlinda Valley welcome committee. Her dark auburn hair fell over her shoulders, and her large brown eyes shone with excitement as she talked about her job and her students. She was breathtaking. Everything about her was beautiful.

I know so much about her. It's time I share a little about me. I finished my hot dog and fries and wiped my mouth. "I have a younger brother and sister. They're twins. My brother just graduated from basic training. He's in the Army, stationed at Fort Wainwright in Fairbanks, Alaska. You remind me a lot of my sister. She's a teacher and loves life."

I had Kora's undivided attention, *Keep it simple. Now's not the time to divulge too much.* "They're twenty-four. My brother and I worked to get our sister, Susie, through college. We knew she wouldn't complete her classes if we weren't there for her. As soon as she graduated, she got a job in South Dakota. Her roommate was from there, so she went to live out there with her. Sebastian, my brother, felt his duty to her was finished, and joined the Army. Once they were both situated, I could finally focus on me, and here I am."

I *never* talked about myself or my life. I hadn't had any intention of sharing any of this with her. I usually kept to myself, but Kora was so easy to talk to and was focused on every word I said.

Hell, I've come this far. I might as well tell her everything, or almost everything. "I was seven when my mom had the twins. My dad had been out of work for a while and instead of searching for a job, he took up drinking. I'm sure it wasn't a pregnancy either of them anticipated or wanted. As soon as the twins were born, Dad's drinking increased, and his meanness intensified. Mom took care of us the best she could, and I took some of the load off her by helping with the twins. I'd bathe them and make sure they were fed." I paused and sipped my shake, then took a deep breath. "My first memory of him beating my mother was when I was eight. He beat her so badly I had to doctor her because he wouldn't allow her to get medical attention. After that, when Dad came home drunk, I'd do anything I could to make sure he took his anger out on me instead."

This was harder than I thought. I hadn't talked about all these details in a long time. "Sometimes Dad would be gone for nights on end. Those were the good days. Finally, the twins were old enough to start kindergarten. I'd always pick them up from the elementary school and walk home with them. I was twelve and in middle school which was directly across from the elementary. It was chilly one day when we were walking home, so it must have been January. Mom wasn't home when we got there. I didn't think too much about it and fed the twins. But after a week of her being gone, I realized she left us."

I froze. *What was I doing?* I glanced up and couldn't miss the concern that shrouded Kora's gaze.

I always hated people's pity. That's why I kept all this to myself, but with Kora I couldn't. "Yes, it sucked. But I learned to move on. The twins needed me, and I knew I had to be their role model. I became a mom, dad, and older brother to them that day. I did whatever I could to make sure they had anything they needed, and I took the old man's money when he passed out so I could put food on the table. After Mom left, he still drank, but his anger dissipated. He became someone to pity. Not to fear." I shrugged. "I can't complain about my upbringing because it made me strong. I took care of my brother and sister, and they both turned out great."

Kora's eyes glistened, and her lips pressed into a thin line. *Great way to kill the awesome afternoon. This was not okay.* "Enough about me." We needed to get out of here. I cleaned the counter and held out my hand. "Where to now?"

She pulled me to the door and down the road and into a small alleyway.

She wrapped her arms around my neck and pulled my head down to her. Her lips crashed into mine, and our tongues tangled. My breath caught, and I swear all my blood went south.

This woman could kiss. The softness of her lips caused my blood to pool in one area, and all the concerns I had earlier about telling her too much evaporated instantly. I wrapped my arms around her and brushed my hands over her silky hair.

This was exactly what I needed. Kora grounded me.

She pulled away, and I wasn't prepared for the emptiness I felt.

"You're amazing, Kai." Her gaze blazed into me. "That story totally explains what I've noticed. You are such a helpful and genuinely kind person. It seems that you've been that way since you were seven. Your brother and sister were so lucky to have you to support them."

"Thanks." My voice was gruff. I've never been good with compliments. "I didn't tell you all that for your pity. Honestly, I don't know why I told you that. It's my life and not something I usually spill to anyone. It's a past I've tried to leave in the past."

"Well, thank you for sharing with me." Kora brushed her hand against my chest. Then her eyes met mine. "Have you ever heard anything from your mom?"

I breathed out heavily. "I did look for her." I hated a lot of my life story, but this was at the top of my list of all-time shitty tales. "When I got a job and started earning more money, I did some research and hired a private investigator to find her, and he was successful. He found some death records." I ran my hands down her arm and intertwined our fingers. My eyes stayed on our hands. "She died of an apparent drug overdose five years after she left. She was living in Atlanta."

"Kai. I'm so sorry."

I shrugged and waited for the heaviness that always sat on my chest to show up, but it didn't come. Guess I'd finally moved on. "What can I do? I spent most of my life wondering why she left. When I found this out, it hurt, but over the years I've learned to live with it. Three years ago, Sebastian, Susie, and I gave money in her memory to a battered woman's shelter. I still donate to them every year, and I've done some volunteer work for them as well. It's my way of remembering a mother I only knew for twelve years and was stuck in a bad situation."

I kissed Kora again and my heart lightened. "One day, I plan on doing more for the shelter, but right now, I want to do something else with you. What else can we get into?"

The cutest smile came to her face.

God, that smile was luscious.

"Want to kayak?" she asked.

Within an hour, we had stopped at the salon so I could change, then went to Kora's. She came out of her back door dressed in black swim shorts, a bikini top with a short button-up shirt tied in the front, and a pair of water shoes. I wanted to strip her naked and lick her from head to toe. "Girl, you are hot as hell." I raised my brows and took my hat off to brush back my hair and placed my hat back on my head.

Kora let out a hard breath. "You need to stop looking at me that way."

"I have no clue what you're talking about?" I said as I sauntered up to her and placed my arms around her waist.

She grabbed my shirt. "I can't," was all she said as she stood on her tiptoes, pulled my shirt toward her, and crushed her lips to mine. "If we don't leave soon, I'm going to take you into my house and leave the river for another day."

"That's an idea." My voice was deep, and my hands traveled up her back. I held her body tight and replaced my lips on hers.

She rested her head against mine. "I really want to show you the river. I know you'll love it," she whispered almost inaudibly.

"I'm sure I will, but you're making it really difficult to leave," I answered.

Our gazes locked.

She rubbed her palms along my neck and played with the few hairs sticking out the back of my hat. "I know, but if you weren't so damn sexy, or didn't taste so delicious, it wouldn't be so difficult." Her voice was seductive.

"Well . . ." I slid my hands into hers. We needed to go now, or we wouldn't make it to the river. "I totally agree with you. Let's get these kayaks into Matilda and get going before I change my mind."

"Are you sure Matilda will make it to the back of the property?" She gestured to a grassy dirt path beside the fencing. "That path leads back behind those trees. The Red River flows through there. We can drive up to it. There's an easy put-in."

"Matilda can do many amazing things."

A wicked grin filled Kora's face. "Just like her owner."

"Woman, you need to walk away."

Kora laughed and jumped into the front seat as I loaded up the truck and headed down the road.

Chapter 16

Kora

We floated lazily down the river. The easy-moving current carrying us effortlessly through the water. It was always peaceful on the river, and today was no different. I floated along, enjoying the peace and quiet and the surrounding scenery. It wasn't just nature that held my attention, but Kai. His shirt billowed in the light breeze as he focused on the scene in front of him.

I pulled my kayak up to the left side of his but made sure to stay behind him a bit. I took in his profile as he rowed gently down the river. The concern that had covered his face back at the pharmacy was gone. He seemed uninhibited, and his features softened as he immersed himself in the peacefulness of nature. His face, which was once tense and stressed, now seemed relaxed, and the lines that once creased his forehead had faded away.

The sunlight played across his skin and highlighted the contours of his face and the strength of his jawline. His crystal-clear eyes now sparkled with an inner light. Maybe I'm crazy, but this man seemed to grow more handsome, more alive, the farther we drifted down the river.

He turned toward me and gave me a lazy, crooked smile. I knew I had a goofy grin glued on my face but didn't care at all.

"It's beautiful out here, and so quiet," Kai said, his voice hushed. He reached over, grabbed my boat to pull it next to his, and laid his oar across both our boats. I grasped his oar to lock us together as we continued to float in silence with the calm current.

"It is." I agreed with him but wasn't only talking about the river. "When I was younger, my dad and I kayaked every Sunday afternoon when the weather was nice. Then, when I got older and was too cool to hang with him as much, we still made time for a trip down the river." I pointed up ahead. "There's a great beach right down a bit and around the bend. We would stop there to eat lunch before we turned around and headed for home. If it was a warm day, it was a great place to wade in the river, and just a bit from the beach is a swimming hole, complete with a rope swing. As I got older, I realized it's where all the high schoolers went to drink and have fun."

I laughed as a memory popped into my mind. "One time, I guess I was around twelve, there was a fire pit with beer cans in it. I asked why the cans were there. Dad said he guessed the wildlife had a party. It was our job to clean up after them since they couldn't do it on their own. I thought he meant the raccoons and deer. I pictured them all huddled around the fire drinking. I didn't realize he meant teenagers were the wildlife." I shook my head. "It wasn't until I was in high school and at a party, sitting around the fire pit, drinking a beer with my friends, that it became clear what he meant."

Kai's face lit up.

Damn. How can someone be that handsome? My heart fluttered until he turned his gaze away.

"High school Kora, partying on the bank of a river around a fire pit." Kai nodded. "I bet you were hot then, also, and had all the guys all over you."

I chuckled. "Not all the guys, but I did date one for all junior year and most of senior."

"Really? Have I met him yet?"

I nodded and scrunched my face. "Yeah. You have."

Kai became thoughtful. "I haven't met many guys our age except Bryson. But I doubt that's who you meant since he's your cousin and all," he glanced at me with raised brows.

I rolled my eyes and laughed. "Nope. Not Bryson. We're not kissing cousins."

"Well then, I guess that leaves Trevor."

I nodded.

"Dang. That would explain the evil eye he gave me the other night. I think he still has the hots for you." He pushed my kayak away from his and started rowing slowly.

"You and Darlene both." I rowed to catch up. "The beach is right around this bend."

"Did I tell you I purchased land on the river?" asked Kai.

I sat up taller. "No, you didn't. Where? Is it close by?"

"Honestly, from this view, I have no idea, but my property has a pebbly beach area that leads down to the water. It seems like it's used often, as there's a rough fire pit near the water's edge."

"No shit." I raised my brow and rowed faster. "It's not the land off Johnson's Path Lane, is it?"

"Yeah, it's ten acres off Johnson's Path."

"Damn. That's your beach we always partied on. That property's been for sale for a while. We heard someone purchased it but didn't know who. You are planning on staying a while, aren't you?"

"I've got nowhere else to go. Orlinda Valley caught my attention the first time I drove through, and it's getting better and better every day." His eyes didn't leave mine, and my breath caught.

I sucked in my bottom lip and bit down. My nervous habit. "I always thought Orlinda Valley was perfect, but I was wrong." My voice was a whisper. Barely audible over the singing of the birds and chattering of squirrels in the trees. My insides were doing all types of gymnastics. Darlene was right. I had feelings for this guy, and I still didn't know his last name.

Kai's gaze narrowed, and the temperature seemed to climb a couple notches.

"Come on." He broke the spell as he paddled away toward the shore.

We were approaching Kai's property. My kayak hit land, and he pulled me from the kayak like I weighed nothing. My arms automatically wrapped around his neck as his lips locked on mine.

The kiss was deep and intense. I curled my fingers in the hair at the nape of his neck and allowed my tongue to dance with his.

When our lips finally parted, we hovered within millimeters of each other, and my eyes slowly fluttered open.

"Welcome to my home." He smiled wickedly. "I want to show you something." He pulled me up the slight incline to the flat acreage just above the water's edge.

It was a beautiful view. I had stood here before, many times, actually, as we'd partied up here in high school after floating down the river like we just did. We knew no one would ever find us here. "I've always loved this land."

"You've been here before? Not just on the beach then?" He laughed.

"Most high schoolers have," I joked.

"Well, I don't want to hear who you've been here with, or what you've done. But come on," he said and pulled me along.

We made it to the line of trees, and there was a camper parked on the grass, the slides open and the awning out. There were two Adirondack chairs with a table between them under the awning. Out, away from the camper, was a fire pit.

It was quaint, yet homey. My mouth dropped open and I turned toward Kai. "Is this camper yours?"

"Technically it's called a fifth wheel not just a camper." Mischief filled his gaze. "Come on."

We entered the camper, or fifth wheel. It was an older model, yet still in great condition. I swiped my hand over the granite countertop in the galley kitchen and turned a slow circle in front of the flat screen television. "This is great. When did you put this here?"

"Thursday night when I finished work." He leaned on the counter. "I spent the night last night. Water's an issue, but it's a place to sleep, and it's my own." His hand brushed up my arm and sent goose bumps popping on my skin.

My eyes followed his fingers as they traveled to my shoulder, and I tilted my head to the side, exposing my neck. I didn't want him to think I was an easy lay, yet after the day we had, after he had opened up and trusted me with his story, there was nothing I wanted more than him—well, there was one more thing. I covered his hand with mine and placed it around my waist. He got the message and wrapped me in his arms.

I held his neck and rubbed my fingers against the scruff on his chin. "Kai, what's your last name?"

His gaze burned into me. That molten feeling I experienced Friday night returned, and my heart fluttered madly. His eyes smoldered and glowed in the dim light of the sun coming through the windows.

"How do you know that someone bought this land but haven't heard my last name? Your aunt and her book club buddies know it."

I shrugged. "It never came up. Past couple weeks have been busy."

He gazed away quickly then wrapped his arms tighter. "I guess so. It's Lawson." His voice was deep, throaty, and damn sexy.

Lawson. Now I knew everything I needed to know. I knew how sweet and wonderful he was. I finally knew his last name. Those things mixed with his voice and his rugged good looks, and damn, those eyes, caused me to throw caution to the wind. The heat in my gut exploded. I wanted him. I wanted him badly, and I covered his mouth with mine.

It was all me and intense need. I deepened the kiss, and my tongue tangled with his. I slid his shirt from his shoulders, and it fell onto the floor.

I separated our lips, and my gaze progressed down his front. Everything about him was perfect. My hands traveled up his hard chest, and he sucked air into his lungs as I ran my fingers over his six-pack. My pulse raced. I placed my lips on his nipple and played with it with my tongue and nibbled it lightly.

A deep, throaty moan escaped him.

I smiled against his skin and continued to trail my kisses southward. His breathing increased, and I could feel his heartbeat thump against his chest. I slipped my hand into the elastic of his shorts and around to his tight ass. His skin was warm and so soft. I gave it a squeeze.

"Kora." His voice was deep, and he clasped my arms.

A need deeper than any I'd ever felt before filled me. I wanted to taste all of this man. Feel him inside me again.

No, I didn't want to. I needed to.

I walked him back and pushed him gently to the couch. He sat, shirtless, his shorts low on his hips, his chest moving up and down, his pupils dilated and drunk with desire. He was pure perfection. I took his hat off his head and ran my fingers through his dark thick hair. The contrast of his dark hair and light eyes made him so damn irresistible. So desirable. So hot, and completely sexy.

I got on my knees between his legs and brushed my hands up his muscular thighs to his manly chest. I gave him a sly smile.

He traced his tongue across his bottom lips and his breaths became rapid.

"Lie back, Kai. Relax." I kissed just below his belly button, at the small patch of dark hair that disappeared under his shorts. When I glanced up, his head was back, and those crystal eyes were slits of desire and followed my every move. His chest raised and lowered quickly,

I tugged on his shorts, and he lifted his hips slightly to help. I freed his hardness from captivity. It stood at attention. Ready for me. Waiting.

I felt empowered. I did this to him. He wanted me, it was evident. I licked my lips and lowered my mouth to indulge my desire and his need.

I had his full attention.

Groans almost as deep as a growl came from his chest.

I continued to lick and suck and became turned on by his groans.

"Kora." My name came out as a long deep moan.

I took him one last time, then unhooked my bikini top. I held it out and dropped it to the floor.

He puffed out a breath and stretched his arms toward my breasts, but I shook my head and stood. I was just out of his reach. Slowly, I stepped out of my shorts. He quickly followed my lead and deposited his shorts on the floor.

"Kora." He held his arms out and gestured me toward him.

I licked my bottom lip and straddled his lap. My mouth found his immediately as his hands slid down my bare back and cupped my ass. The warmth of his hands made me shiver. I shifted to my knees and placed him right at my opening.

"Kora, I don't have anything."

I met his gaze. "I'm on the pill and am religious about taking it."

"If you're okay, I'm not going to stop this." It sounded like he had run a marathon.

I smiled against his mouth. "Good, because I'm not either." I lowered onto him slowly.

I sucked in a breath as he filled me, and closed my mouth on his as a moan of satisfaction escaped my throat.

Sex with Kai was a marathon I enjoyed running. We moved together effortlessly, and his fingers found my sensitive area. He knew exactly what I wanted, and just when I thought I was going to die from all the built-up tension, my body trembled and contracted as warmth exploded from my core to my toes, and I moaned his name.

He brought his mouth to mine and maneuvered us to the floor. "My turn." His voice was hoarse and husky.

His mouth found my breasts and sucked long and hard on my nipples.

I gasped for breath.

He then slowly kissed his way down my stomach. Teasing me, taking forever to get where I wanted him. "God, Kai. Please," I begged. I needed to feel the warmth of his lips between my thighs. I wiggled under him as he continued to tease me and circled his tongue closer and closer.

Finally, he reached the promised land. And yes, he had a talented tongue. I moaned his name again and again.

We lay cuddled on the floor when we finally finished, both fighting to catch our breath. Kai put a pillow from the couch under his head and covered us with a blanket. I was warm, relaxed, satisfied, and spent. I napped, wrapped in his arms.

Chapter 17

KAI

My back was slightly uncomfortable from being in one position for so long. I needed to get up, not only because of the discomfort but because I had to take a piss. But combing my fingers through Kora's hair and feeling her breath light on my skin, was the most relaxed I'd been in a while, and I didn't want to bother her. Not yet.

Part of me couldn't believe that I, Kai Lawson, was lucky enough to be here with her. Kora was a small-town girl and was so well-loved in this town that she adored. She grew up around family and extended family and had friends that went back years.

I couldn't picture what that would be like. Since my mother left, and we were left with our father, a loving family was something I only experienced in books and on television. My goal was to make sure the twins didn't realize what they missed out on. It seemed to have worked. They were both doing well and living their lives to the fullest. Once I found Orlinda Valley, I immediately fell in love with the openness, and now here was Kora. Everything seemed to be fitting into place.

I continued to comb my fingers lightly through her hair as she slept steadily with her head on my chest. She was a natural beauty, both inside and out, and had a light about her that brightened every place she was. Whether it was at the pub hanging with friends, taking care of her animals on her farm, or enjoying nature on the river, her eyes shone with excitement. Even when she was pissed and hot on the side of the road, with no phone service, a flat tire, and a vocabulary colorful enough that a sailor would have been embarrassed, she was a natural beauty.

Her students were lucky to have a teacher as wonderful as she was. If she had been my teacher, I'm sure I would have had my first crush.

A moan broke through my thoughts, and Kora kissed my chest lightly.

"Mmm." The warmth of her lips seared into my skin and caused my heart to beat a little faster. "Well, sleeping beauty. Did you have a nice nap?" I placed a soft kiss on her head.

"Yes," she said in a sleepy, relaxed voice. She pushed up on her arm.

I grabbed the chance to roll over and push myself up and kissed her lightly on the lips before standing. "Excuse the view. I've got to pee."

She laughed. "Don't worry. The view is amazing."

When I came back to the living area with shorts on, she was up and dressed.

"I guess we need to be heading back up the river," Kora said.

Yeah, we needed to go if we wanted to get off the river before it got dark, but I needed to feel her against me again. I sat on the couch and pulled her onto my lap. "I agree, but first I want to say thank you."

"For what?" she asked as she wrapped one arm around my neck and her other hand caressed my face.

I closed my eyes briefly. I loved the feel of her hand touching me. I opened my eyes, and her face was filled with a beautiful glow. Never had I imagined I could be with someone as wonderful and beautiful as Kora. "Are you real?" I asked.

"What?" Her face became a question. "Of course I'm real."

"Good. Because a part of me was afraid you were a dream, and if you were, I'd hope I'd never wake up."

"Kai, why would you say something like that? You're an amazing, thoughtful man. I'm sure you've had better women than me in your life."

That made me chuckle, and I shook my head. I'd never had anyone like her. "Nope. Sorry to disappoint you, but you are unique. There's no one like you." My lips met hers and I kissed her deeply, almost desperately.

My heart beat wildly, and I held her tighter. I was almost scared to let her go, like if she slipped from my grasp, I may never get to hold her again.

It was overwhelming. I needed to understand these feelings which churned in my gut and caused my heart to falter at her touch. I was caught off guard at how quickly they developed. It was so surprising, so unexpected.

Our faces stayed inches from each other when we broke the kiss, but I couldn't take my eyes off hers. A huge part of me wanted to carry her back into my room and stay with her the rest of the night and into tomorrow. Hide away from the world. Just the two of us.

But I couldn't. We needed to get going. "Kayaks are waiting. We might need to race back to your place to beat the dark."

"That wouldn't be fair. I know the current's light, but it's harder than it looks paddling against it."

The trip up the river was relatively easy. At least Kora didn't complain any, and I enjoyed paddling behind her, watching her work. Watching her body move with the oar. Pure perfection. Pure beauty. Pure . . .

I pulled my eyes from her quickly and adjusted my hard-on. *Don't think it. Get your thoughts together.*

We finally pulled the kayaks onto land and loaded them into the back of Matilda. I climbed behind the wheel and pulled Kora across the seat next to me. She placed her hand on my thigh as I drove back up the grassy gravel path.

"That was a wonderful day, Kai. Thank you so much."

"Why are you thanking me? You invited me and treated me. Many times, I might add."

The glow that had been a permanent fixture on Kora's face turned scarlet.

"God, you're adorable when you blush." I kissed her briefly, trying to keep my eyes on the windy path. Between her hand on my leg and the hotness of her blush, blood was gathering again in my shorts. Maybe I could get a tour of her bedroom.

"Shit," I said under my breath. So much for that tour.

"What's wrong?" Kora asked as she followed my gaze.

We weren't alone. As soon as we pulled up and got out, we were greeted by three goats, Tonya, Kaye, and Charles. "I think you have company."

"I'm sure they're here to check on me and seeing us together will make their day." The smile Kora gave me was filled with mischief.

She kissed me and curled her fingers into the hair at the nape of my neck, and that's all it took. I wasn't going anywhere anytime soon. "Dammit, woman. I'm not going to be able to get out of the truck any time soon."

"Really?" Her gaze smoldered into mine, and she rubbed her hand lightly up and down on my crotch. "Mmm. You're right. Feels like someone's worked up." She gave me a slight squeeze.

A grunt escaped from deep within my gut. "So unfair. Now you really need to give me a minute." I squeezed my eyes shut and whispered under my breath all the grossest things I could think of.

"What are you doing?" Kora asked. She sounded appalled.

"Trying to calm my thoughts and think of the most disgusting things I can. I can't stay in the truck all night. I need to get out and say hi."

Kora laughed and climbed out.

My mental disgust game seemed to do the trick. I resituated my junk just in time to meet Kora and go see the guests while everyone was still standing there.

"Well, we heard y'all spent the day together." Tonya greeted us with a smile.

"How? We intentionally avoided all the book club hangouts today," Kora answered while squeezing her aunt in a hug.

Kaye playfully swatted Kora's arm as she, too, wrapped her in a hug. "If you really wanted to keep your date secret, you wouldn't have drug this handsome man all around town." Kaye put her arm around Kai's shoulder.

"Hey now, don't steal Kora's man and leave me all alone," Charles said as he joined the group.

Kaye laughed and hugged Charles. "Don't you worry handsome. These eyes are only interested in you." She gave him a quick kiss.

Charles's billowing laugh echoed around the pasture. "Good to know beautiful. Hey there, Kai." He turned to me and shook my hand with a cobra-like grip. "It's great to see you again. I've been by the salon and checked out your work, but you haven't been there. I've heard you've been busy with our Kora, and I guess the rumors were right." He pulled Kora into a squeeze.

"Charles, I can't breathe," she whispered.

"You're fine, baby girl." He patted her on the back. "Gotta watch out for this one, Kai. She's a wild one. I think we need to tell you some stories about high school Kora that are so entertaining." He squeezed Kora to his side, and a blush crept across her face.

"Don't you dare." She pointed a finger at him.

"Your dad expects me to keep an eye on you. He'll be interested in finding out all about this fine young man who is taking up his daughter's day."

Kora rolled her eyes and turned toward me. "Charles and my dad have been friends since the dinosaurs roamed the earth."

"Not quite that long. But almost," Charles bellowed as he released Kora.

I met Charles before, but we didn't talk much. He and Kaye made a cute couple, and he adored Kora. At least we had something in common. How could I not like him?

We all sat on Kora's patio, and they did exactly what Charles said they would. They told lots of great stories of high school Kora and college Kora. I laughed so hard my side was hurting. I also learned that Kora had a killer gaze and didn't like that I was amused by all the stories. Luckily, gazes couldn't really kill, or I would have been dead on the ground a couple times.

This was what I always pictured family and extended family to be like. Joking and laughing together and sharing memories of the past as if it was just yesterday. I hoped Kora realized how lucky she was to have these people in her life.

"I don't know about y'all, but I'm hungry and I don't think anyone has planned dinner." Tonya grabbed her phone and started dialing. "I'm going to order pizza. Is everyone good with pepperoni and mushroom?"

"Please order one with pepperoni only," Kaye said. "You know I can't stand mushrooms, T."

"Kaye, hon, I still have hopes that you'll grow up one day," Tonya said. She winked and ordered the pizzas.

"While we wait, do you want to help me settle in the animals for the night? These goats will only go to bed if they get fed." Kora stood, and Percy's head popped up.

The goats had been lying around like a bunch of dogs the entire time we were talking. Percy at Kora's feet, Baby Goat next to Tonya, and Jackson off on his own munching on the grass.

"Of course." I followed Kora, and the goats fell into step behind us.

"You were quiet," she said as she wrapped her arm around my waist and leaned her head on my shoulder. I could really get used to this.

I kissed the top of her head and let go of her to open the gate. The goats bounded ahead.

I chuckled. They were so entertaining. "I was just taking it all in. I loved the stories." I pulled her to a stop and turned her toward me.

The light breeze blew strands of her hair around her face, and I brushed it back into a ponytail. "This is all exactly what I pictured a family would be." I placed a light kiss on the tip of her nose. Her eyes were closed when I pulled away, and I just watched her. Took her in.

It was twilight, and the sun fell behind the hills in the distance. There was little light, but the moon was full, giving me just enough light to see all her perfect features.

Her eyes fluttered open, and she tilted her head to the side. "This is why I came back here after college. This is home to me. Everything about it. I'm lucky; I know that. But things have become even better recently."

She wrapped her arms around my neck and weaved her fingers into my hair, sending chills down my spine. The feeling of her touch seemed to always have that effect on me. I held her face. "Things *have* become much better recently," I agreed with her.

Her dark brown eyes smiled. Our eye color was as opposite as our upbringing, but we seemed to both want the same things: family, friends, and love. But they were all easier for her to express since she'd experienced the positive side of all those things. Our lips touched, and she pulled me closer to her. We might have grown up differently, but when we were together, none of that mattered. I moaned her name as the kiss intensified.

"Baa." My thigh was rammed by a hard head.

"Ouch." I broke away.

Baby Goat jumped up, his front hooves on my thigh. "Baa."

I released Kora and patted Baby Goat's head. "I think someone wants to eat."

Kora's laugh rang like a bell. "Yeah, they won't leave us alone until they're fed." She walked off at a quick pace and patted her thigh. "Come on, goats."

They hopped and skipped after her, bleating their excitement.

Chapter 18

KORA

What a great night. I waved as Kaye and Charles pulled out of the driveway and joined Kai and Tonya at the head of the walkway which led to Tonya's. As I approached, their conversation quickly ended.

"Okay, what were you two talking about?" I bumped into my aunt. "It got mysteriously quiet. What secrets are you telling him?"

Tonya winked. "Our secret. None of your business." She kissed my cheek. "You two kids be good and make good choices." She blew a kiss at Kai and walked down the path toward her property.

We watched her in silence for a beat before Kai spoke. "Will she be okay walking by herself? It's pretty dark."

"Trust me, we could both walk that path in our sleep." I crossed my arms. "So, what were you two so involved with over here?"

He shook his head and pursed his lips. "Honestly, nothing at all. She was telling about how she and your dad grew up in this house and she and her husband built the one she's in now after Jamison was born." Kai wrapped my hands in his. The warmth of his skin was familiar, and I squeezed his hand in return. "You really have a great family," he added.

"I know I do." I tugged on him, and he followed me. "But now I don't want to talk about them. Help me clean up."

We entered my tiny kitchen. My house wasn't large, but I loved it. It was homey and comfortable. The kitchen and living room were one large room separated by a counter. I picked up some empty Coke cans and placed them in the trash and started to wipe down the counters. Kai wandered around the room.

I liked him here. It felt natural to have him in my house.

As soon as the kitchen was clean, I joined him in front of the fireplace mantle. He was looking at a picture of my family. Both blood and extended. "I love that picture. It was taken right before my dad moved to Florida. You know almost everyone in it. Bryson and Jamison, Tonya, Kaye, and Charles. That's my dad." My dad has the same dark hair and dark eyes as me and an amazing smile.

"I know Kaye, Charles, and Lance, but who's this?" Kai pointed to a brown-haired girl between Charles and Lance.

"That's Kaye and Charles's daughter, Lilly. She lives in New York City with her husband."

Kai nodded like he was taking it all in. "So, why'd your dad move to Florida?"

"It's something he always talked about. We vacationed in a small town outside of Tallahassee every year. He bought a house there about three years ago, and after he retired, he took the plunge. He spends his days golfing and fishing." I placed the picture back on the mantel. "I'm going down to visit in June. That's one of the perks of teaching. I have all summer free to do what I want." I turned to Kai and wrapped my arms around his waist. "And right now, I'd like some of you." I squeezed his ass and gave him what I hoped was a sexy smirk.

Kai laid his arms on my shoulders. "Do you always get whatever you want?" he asked in a husky whisper.

"Usually." I raised my brows and pushed up on my tiptoes so I could press my lips against his. The kiss was sweet and tender and caused my stomach to flutter. I broke away and stared deep into his eyes. "Stay with me tonight. I want to wake up next to you."

He brushed his hand across my face and pulled my hair back.

Chills raced down my spine.

"I have to work in the morning and don't have a change of clothes."

"We both have to work. We can wake up extra early, hop in the shower—you don't have water at your place anyway—then you'll be early enough to run home to change." I rubbed my hands on his chest and swallowed. "Please?" Was I begging? Yes, and I probably sounded desperate, but I didn't care at all. All I cared about was having a night of fun with this incredible man and waking up with him beside me. "I'm going to be busy with my last week of school, so we won't be able to see each other much this week if at all. So, what do you say?" I traced my nails along the scruff of beard on his face, then peered up at him.

He sucked in his bottom lip as the corners of his mouth ticked up.

His dimple appeared and stole my breath. "God, I love that sexy as hell dimple." I placed a soft kiss there, then one on his chin, then moved my lips down to his neck. I stayed there and sucked in some skin and nibbled his neck.

I held his gaze as I pulled him into my bedroom. I pushed him against the door. It clicked shut, and I slowly lifted his shirt above his head. I brushed my hands down his chest and over his hard abs. "If you want to go, you can. I won't stop you." I circled his nipple with my tongue and sucked it into my mouth.

A moan escaped him.

"Thought you wanted to leave," I teased, my lips not far from his skin.

He grabbed my head and pulled me up to his lips and pressed them against mine, hard and desperate.

My pulse raced. He swept me into his arms and deposited me on the bed before I could object—though I wouldn't have. He stripped off my tank top and my pants. My body was so ready for him, and as his eyes raked over me, anticipation filled me with excitement.

"I'm staying tonight." His voice was thick and so masculine. He brushed his hand over my breast and down my body.

My skin tingled at his touch.

"I want you, Kora," he said, his eyes filled with desire. "Do you want me?"

My heart strummed hard against my chest. "Yes, Kai. I'm yours. I'm all yours." I melted into his kiss.

Chapter 19

KAI

Damn, life was good. It had been a long day, and I was finally on my way back to the hair salon. They were planning on moving into the space tomorrow, so one last coat of paint, and I could call it a night.

I was exhausted but had nothing to complain about. My boss, Christian Warren, gave me an on-site promotion. I heard from Sebastian—he had been promoted too—and Susie sent me a text. She was asked to work summer school for the reading program. Everything was good, and when I added in the weekend with Kora, life seemed about perfect.

Kora and I texted occasionally throughout the day, which was new for me. I couldn't remember the last time I anticipated talking with a woman. Kora had a lot planned this week with a field day Thursday and only teachers at school Friday. Then she wouldn't have any excuses to not spend time with me. She'd have nothing but time all summer. Maybe I could take some time off. Go visit her father with her.

I shook my head to get these crazy thoughts to go away. But then, last night popped into my head, and my blood started pooling in my crotch. The things she did to me and the way she felt and tasted . . .

Enough. This wasn't the time for those thoughts. I needed to get the walls painted, not hop in a cold shower as soon as I got back to the salon. *Think of something else.* I turned the radio up and sang at the top of my lungs to classic rock.

It was late when I pulled off the interstate and entered the Orlinda Valley city limits. Most things were closed, and even Jerry's Pub was empty. It was Monday night. Nothing to do. I turned right into the back of the salon's lot and was greeted by a police car. "What the hell?"

I jumped out. "Can I help you?"

The policeman held out his hand. His badge said Pierson. I shook his hand.

"Kai, correct?" Officer Pierson asked.

I was on guard. I'd never had a good rapport with the law. In my experience, they never seemed to be very helpful when I needed their services. I nodded, reserved.

"I'm Patrick. It seems as if you took my place in the cornhole tournament."

Patrick, Bryson's friend. my shoulders relaxed. "Yes. Patrick. I haven't had the privilege of meeting you yet. No one mentioned you were an officer."

"Yeah, well, one negative thing about working in a small town, you're not taken very seriously by friends." He hooked his fingers through his belt loops. "Anyway, we picked up an older gentleman for public intoxication and disturbing the peace, and he said he knew you."

My brows lifted. Why would anyone say they knew me? I shook my head, totally confused. "I've only been here a few weeks. I don't know why someone would say they knew me." Then it hit me. Like a slug to the gut. He found me. I couldn't run far enough. But it can't be.

"Does the name Terry Lawson mean anything to you?"

Holy fuck. I closed my eyes and dipped my head. *How did he find me?* I puffed out a deep breath and linked my hands behind my head. *Relax and breathe.* "Yeah. Why?" I didn't want to hear what Patrick had to say. There was no possible way my father followed me here. I made sure to cover my tracks. Orlinda Valley was to be my hiding place. My refuge. A place no one would find me unless I wanted them to.

"We have him down at the station. He didn't know your number but told us your name. He knew you were here somewhere."

I lifted my face to the sky. The stars were out in abundance. It wasn't something I would have noticed in Atlanta, but here, where there weren't as many lights as in a city, it was easy to see. I wished I could have enjoyed it. "What do I need to do?" I said under my breath. My shoulders already seemed heavy with the extra burden Terry always brought.

"We'd like to keep him for the night, but if you could come by the station in the morning, you could pick him up and post bail."

"Dammit!" I breathed out hard and paced. *It's happening again. I just got a promotion and need to take time off work to deal with my father.* This was not okay. "What if I don't? What if I choose not to post bail or acknowledge his presence?"

"He'll have to stay. Trevor's going to press charges. He did some damage at the pub."

"Shit. Of course, he did." I could feel my blood pressure rising. I clenched my fists tight. I had to relax. I couldn't let him affect me this way. I wanted nothing more than to ignore the entire situation but couldn't. He was my father, even though he never did anything but cause my life to be a mess. "Let him sit there all day. I just got a promotion and need to be at work. I'll get off as early as possible and be by then. I work in the city, so won't be able to get by there tomorrow until at least seven."

"That's fine. His bail is one hundred and fifty dollars."

I nodded. "Not a problem. Sorry for the inconvenience."

"No inconvenience." Patrick stuck out his hand again, and I shook it. "It was good to finally meet the guy who replaced me in cornhole—and other places." Patrick walked to his squad car. "Talk to ya later."

I watched as he pulled out of the lot. My brow raised. *What did that mean?*

Patrick—I heard that name before—but where? It wasn't just that he was Bryson's original cornhole partner.

Then it hit me. Patrick and Kora dated for a while until she broke up with him.

I gritted my teeth and unlocked the back door of the salon and let myself in. I slammed the door in frustration and leaned heavily against it. "I'm not your replacement. You fucking dick." I had to get these feelings in check. With Terry here, shit could go south quickly.

My father's here in Orlinda Valley, I just met Kora's ex, and not under good circumstances.

I glanced across the room. Painting was just the thing I needed.

The next day ended up being a total shitshow.

My first day being in charge, and I couldn't focus, and it was obvious. I also got snippy with Kora on the phone. It seemed as if she heard about Terry being arrested—yet another issue about a small town. I'm sure Patrick wasted no time letting her know. Nothing was confidential. She called to see if I was okay. That was it. She was concerned. I was always the one to deal with family issues and I did it alone. Never had anyone to help, and when it was offered, I never really knew what to do with it. She insisted, and I finally told her it was none of her business.

The interstate passed outside my truck windows, and my exact words came to mind. "Kora, it's none of your fucking business. Stay out of my family issues."

That was smart—dumbass. I sighed deeply and flipped the turn signal to merge onto the exit ramp. "Great way to mess up the one good thing you've ever had."

Her voice was quiet and oozed with hurt when she said fine.

I hurt her and it sucked. But I shouldn't be surprised. That's the only way I knew to treat those I care about. I had learned from the best. Well, it didn't matter at that minute. I'd have to deal with it later. I pulled into the police station. *I don't have the time to worry about it now.*

I slammed the truck door, trudged heavily into the station and up to the counter.

An older lady with big red hair sat there. "Hey, sugar plum. How can I help you today?" Her voice had a strong southern twang.

I cleared my throat and glued a grin on my face. "I'm here to pay the bail for Terry Lawson." I reached into my pocket and pulled out my wallet.

"Yep. You're Kai, ain't cha? The hunk doing the work over at Shear Perfection?" the big-haired woman asked.

I forced my eyes not to roll. I didn't have time for this. "Yes, ma'am, I am. And you are . . . ?" I made eye contact and tilted my head. Hopefully, I seemed genuinely interested.

"Aww, sugar plum, how rude of me. I'm Ethel. Tonya told me all about you and that you and that sweet niece of hers, Kora, have been spending all kinds of time together." She gave me an exaggerated wink as she continued to type on the computer in front of her. "That'll be one hundred and fifty for bail."

I placed the money on the counter. Ethel typed more and a receipt printed out, then she picked up the phone next to her desk. "Kai Lawson is here to pick up Terry." Ethel agreed to whatever was said, then typed more. "Patrick will bring him up here shortly." She typed some more, then folded her hands under her chin. "That Kora is so adorable. She's my grandson's teacher, and he has the biggest crush on her."

I chuckled. *Smart kid.* "Well, I can tell you, she loves her job. If every teacher had that much enthusiasm, school might be a good place to be."

"You didn't like school much?"

"No. Not really." A loud bang from behind a door got my attention.

"That would be Patrick and your dad." Ethel slid some papers through another window as a scruffy and aged man appeared at the window. Patrick told him to sign and slid a ziplock bag toward him. I heard beeps, then a click, and the door next to the counter opened, and there he was.

A boulder lodged in my gut.

I shook my head, and my eyebrows lowered. Last time I saw my old man, he looked rough. Now he was just old. The sad thing was, he was only fifty-five but looked almost seventy. His skin was dehydrated and extra wrinkled like crepe paper, and his bald head had age spots. I had no resemblance to this man that I could make out, and for that I was forever grateful.

"Well, lookee here. My son tried to run, but I found him anyway."

My eyes narrowed. What the hell was I going to do with him?

"Kai, Terry has a court date next week. We're releasing him into your custody. Please make sure he shows up to his hearing. If he misses his court date, he'll be found and arrested," Patrick said.

Terry smiled. "You and me, kid. And you thought you could get away."

"Thought nothing, Terry. Hoped." I never called my father Dad. He wasn't a dad. I was the one who'd done all the fatherly things. I took care of the twins and fed them dinner. Heck, I even had to take their food card and purchase groceries with it. If it wasn't for me, they would have been placed in foster care and separated long ago.

"Don't worry, Patrick. He'll be there." I turned and opened the door. "Come on."

Terry sauntered through the door. I turned to Ethel. "Ethel it was nice to meet you." I nodded to Patrick and followed behind Terry.

"So, I see you still have this shitty ass truck working." Terry opened the door. "Where do you live in this Podunk town?"

A black Murano pulled into the parking lot. Shit. Not now. "Terry, hop in. I'll be right there." My attention was on the car as it parked, and Kora got out. I walked to her. I needed to keep her as far from Terry as possible.

"Kai, I heard . . ." She glanced toward the truck.

I caught her arm. "Hey, I need to apologize for how I spoke to you earlier. I'm surprised you're here."

Her expression was filled with concern. It melted my heart. What did I ever do to deserve her? Nothing. That's exactly what. She was so far out of my league.

"Of course, I'm here." She leaned her head toward the truck. "Is that your dad?"

I nodded. "Yep. That's Terry. Seems like he's going to be with me until his court hearing next week." I shrugged. "I'm going to have to talk with Trevor. It seems that he damaged some things at the pub." I rubbed her arm. "I'm so sorry for how I talked to you."

She opened her mouth to say something, but I placed my hand over her lips. "It is not okay, Kora. I had no right to talk to you like that. To treat you like that. It sounded like something he"—I gestured my head toward the truck—"would've said to my mom." Guilt filled my gut, and I felt bile rise to my throat.

Footsteps crunched on gravel and reached my ears. Kora and I turned. *Could he not listen?* I removed my hand from Kora's arm and scrubbed it down my face. "I told you to stay in the truck." Frustration cut into my words.

"That you did, boy, but then I'd miss meeting your friend here." Terry stuck out his hand. "I'm Terry, Kai's father."

Kora hesitantly shook his hand and nodded. "I'm Kora. A . . . friend . . . of Kai's."

Terry glanced from Kora to me and back to Kora. "Yeah, I'm sure that's what you are." He gave a creepy smile. "Come on, boy. I'm starving. Buy your old man something to eat, and let's get out of here."

"Go back to the truck. I'll be right there." I gave Terry a focused and steady glare. He better listen. I didn't want to show Kora what a tense situation was like between us.

Terry held his hands in the air and walked away. He chuckled and muttered to himself. I blew out a breath and rolled my eyes to the sky. I needed a minute to gain control. My pulse was racing, and I could punch something. I took a few steps away and focused on the quiet of the night. The crickets and the light breeze.

Finally, I was calm. "I'm sorry about that." I was still facing away from Kora. Terry brought out everything I hated about myself, and I needed it to go away, quickly.

"Hey," Kora placed her hand on my back and pulled me toward her. Her fingers rubbed my cheek, and a smile broke across her face. "I like it when you have day-old scruff. It's really sexy."

I laughed, and my shoulders lightened. I wrapped my arms around her waist. I didn't want to give Terry a show, but being with Kora made everything better. She lit up even the worst moments, and I hoped it would stay that way because, with Terry around, there were sure to be many more bad moments. "Then I'll keep it."

She wrapped her hands around my neck. "Please do." She brushed her lips against mine lightly and quickly. I wished I could take her home and lose myself in her body. Forget about the nightmare in my truck.

"So, what are you going to do about him?" she asked.

"I'm going to take him to eat, stop by the grocery and get him food for tomorrow, and take him back to the fifth wheel. There's enough water there for a couple days, and on my way home tomorrow, I'll fill the water barrel. I guess I need to get the water tapped sooner than I was planning." I soaked in everything that was Kora. Her porcelain skin, dark auburn hair that fell just below her shoulder, the brown slacks she wore, with the white short-sleeve shirt tucked in. She was the hottest teacher I ever saw. "You look amazing. I wish we could play school, and I could be your misbehaving student. I'd love you to punish me right now."

Kora's head fell back as she rolled with laughter and swatted me. "Kai, that's awful. I would never punish a student. I'd send them to the principal's office."

I shrugged and a wicked grin filled my face. "Then I guess you'll need to play two parts. Teacher and principal."

"Kai." She held my face with her hands. "You're too much." She kissed me deeply. "Figure out what to do with him, and maybe Friday night we can attend the kick-off-to-summer night at Jerry's Pub and end the night at my house."

Being at Jerry's after this week would be great. Being with Kora would make it even better. My eyes traveled down her body, and I pictured what I knew that body could do and how that soft skin tasted. I maneuvered to relieve the tightening that had occurred in my pants, and my lips tipped skyward. "Can't wait."

She brushed her finger over my dimple. "Good. See you Friday."

One more quick kiss and she was on her way. The warmth that filled me when she was around dissipated immediately as soon as I climbed into the truck.

"Now I know why you're here. Shooting a little high, ain't ya, kid?"

I shot Terry a harsh drop-dead glare. *Maybe I'll get lucky, and he'll shut up.* I turned the key. "You smell like a cesspool. I'll run into the grocery store. You stay in here."

Chapter 20

KAI

It had been the most god-awful week, and it wasn't over yet. Work was long, the addition at Shear Perfection wasn't as straight forward as I had hoped, and add in the unforeseen addition to my life—my father—and my stress level was through the roof.

I was totally exhausted by the time I got home from work every night and checked on Terry, that I fell behind on my work at Shear Perfection and had to put in extra hours at night. Somehow, I managed to work through fatigue and exhaustion. There was nothing quite like the satisfaction of finishing a job and being able to step back and admire it, and the salon was something to admire. It looked damn good.

I pulled into my rocky and hole-filled driveway late Thursday night. I couldn't wait to relax in front of my television, in my bed. Terry had the couch in the living area, and spending time with him was not on my agenda.

As I bumped and jostled up my driveway, I was reminded of the next item on my list: focus on my own place—number one priority—the driveway.

I pulled up in front of the fifth wheel, and my heart sank. "What the hell?" I shook my head and climbed begrudgingly out of Matilda and stalked to the fire pit. There was a pile of beer cans on the grass next to a lawn chair. *Great. Just what I needed. To deal with my drunk ass father.*

How did beer get out here? He didn't have a vehicle, and I didn't have any beer on the property.

I stormed in the door. "Terry, what the hell? You have a mess out there." I froze. He was passed out on the kitchen table, and the small living area was a wreck and smelled like a dump. It seemed like Terry had a party while I was at work. Memories of my childhood accosted me, but I fought them off.

This was not the shithole I grew up in. This was my place. My castle—well, my fifth wheel—but still. I grabbed a trash bag and started tossing all the paper plates, empty bags, and cans into it. I made as much excess noise as possible in the process.

Once the trash was picked up, I grabbed the spray cleaner and sprayed and wiped down the counters and even the floor. It smelled like stale beer, and I wasn't having my childhood life brought into my house, even if it wasn't really a house yet.

I was done with his bullshit, and it had only been two days.

"Terry," I shouted. Nothing. No sign of life. I nodded. Maybe he finally drank himself to death. That would make my life much easier and would end the crap I had to deal with.

I sighed heavily. *I guess I should make sure he's alive.* I whacked him on the back. Hard. "Terry!" I bellowed.

"What the fuck?" he yelled as he sat up swinging.

"Chill." I placed a bottle of water in front of him. "What the hell were you doing here while I was gone, and where did you get all this beer?

"Simple," Terry answered as he took a sip of water and scrubbed his hands down his face. "I was bored off my ass, so I decided to go for a walk. Noise down by the river caught my attention and I followed my ears. I ran into a group of kids kayaking and drinking. They were having a last day of school dardy."

"Dardy? What the hell's a dardy?" I asked. Where did my father come up with this stuff?

"That's what I asked." Terry gestured agreement with his hand. "I was told it's a daytime party. A dardy. Anyway, I offered them money for beer. We started talking, and they came back here. I fed them sandwiches—peanut butter and jelly was all you had, by the way. A little embarrassing."

My jaw dropped. *Was this idiot for real?*

"Doesn't matter. They were teenagers. They didn't care. It was free food. Anyway, I gave them money and they left two cases of beer behind."

"You had money?" I placed my hands on my hips. I was tired and didn't want to deal with this bull shit. But where the hell did he get money?

"Nope. You did. I found it in the coffee container in the closet."

"You what?" Anger sliced through me. I swiped my hands over my face and stalked to the closet. I took out the coffee container that had cash in it. The cash I was saving was for work around here.

Or had been saving. The container was empty.

My blood boiled. If I took my blood pressure right now, it wouldn't be good. "That was my money." I needed to hit something. "I've been saving that, and there was more in there than a couple cases of beer would have cost. What else did you do with it?"

"Oh, they door dashed food and needed some for pot. They got some good weed out here."

Terry was so not good for my health. My blood pressure was sky high, and a dull ache started in my temple. A headache. Just what I needed. "You got high with a bunch of high school kids. Seriously?"

I paced the small living area and gripped my neck with my hands. "This is a small town. I'm trying to make a home here, and your stupid choices better not mess things up for me. *Again*." This was ridiculous. I really needed to punch something, or better yet, someone. "And that money you used was for my driveway. You had no right to use it. That's stealing, old man."

"You're my son. It's not stealing. I helped you out while you were growing up. It was about time you did the same."

"You were my father. I was your son. It was your job." I placed my hands on the counter and leaned heavily on them. "Once I was old enough to make some money, I took over all the responsibilities. We ate because of me. We had lights on because of me. The twins had everything they needed Because. Of. Me."

"Oh, yeah, I remember. You made some good money on the side. Don't you dare judge me, *son*. I'm sure your pretty piece of ass would love to know your history."

I froze and held his glare. He wouldn't say a word, would he? I hadn't planned on things with Kora going as far as they had. She needed to know everything, but I wasn't sure how to let her know.

I wasn't happy with the choices I made, or what happened because of them, but it was for clothes, food, survival.

A sneer appeared on Terry's face. "She doesn't know, does she?"

I started to pace again. *I can't do this. I came here to get away from the crazy that was Terry Lawson. Now here he is, trashing my place, stealing my money, and threatening to ruin my life—again.* "Terry, I can't do this."

"It's Dad."

The tone of Terry's voice froze me in place. How dare he talk to me like he deserved the respect the term dad held. How dare he talk to me in my house like he had any authority over me.

The rubber band that was holding my anger in check stretched to the max. "You aren't a dad." I sneered. "The term *dad* is for the men who work hard and take care of their families so their teenage son doesn't have to take matters into his own uneducated, immature hands. You are a stranger and a loser. And your name, Terry, fits you perfectly. You are a Terry."

Terry's fist caught me off guard as it slammed into my jaw. I stumbled back, held up by the counter.

"I'm your father, and you'll start respecting me as such." Terry's words slurred slightly.

I wasn't the skinny teenager he could bully around and use as a punching bag anymore. I was thirty-one and had the body of someone who worked hard all day lugging heavy material around a construction site. Terry was no match, and there was no way in hell I was going to back down. "Fuck you and your respect," I spat as I rubbed my aching jaw. "You're in *my* house. You will respect me. While you're here, you will *not* drink. If that's going to be an issue, I'll kick you out on your ass.

"I can see what you're doing here, boy." Terry took a small step in my direction. "You think you can come to a small town, find a job, get to know the locals, and start fucking the cute little brunette, and your life will become a storybook romance? Don't forget who you are, you *dumb fuck*. You are Kai Lawson. You're a useless piece of shit who has a record, whose mother didn't even love you enough to stick around—or even better yet, take you and your brother and sister with her." Terry took another step closer. "What mother would leave a kid who was worth anything?"

I was dumbstruck. A part of me had always thought those very things Terry just said. What kind of mother left her children behind? What type of person made the stupid decisions I did and spent time in jail? I felt the familiar heaviness in my chest settle in and make itself at home like it did when I was younger.

"If your own mother couldn't love you, what makes you think a pretty little thing like that Kora could ever want anything to do with you? You are just a pity case for her," Terry spat with venom.

Anger and hatred rose from deep within my chest.

The anger turned to rage, and the rubber band snapped.

Broke.

Exploded.

Before I could stop myself, I punched Terry in the gut, then punched him again with an uppercut to the jaw. He flew backward and landed on the chair he just got out of. He didn't move. He was knocked out. Good.

I fled from the fifth wheel and stalked across the yard to my truck. Terry couldn't stay here. This wasn't a good thing at all.

I climbed into Matilda and tore down the dirt and gravel drive and back onto the road. The clock on the dash read eight o'clock. Had

I really only been home an hour? It was amazing how time stopped when Terry was around.

I shook my hand as I drove. It throbbed. I didn't feel it at the time, but now, I felt it. It throbbed, and it sucked. It was my right hand. I needed it to work. Luckily, I was in charge now and didn't do much manual labor, and the work at the salon was completed.

I pulled up in front of Jerry's Pub. The parking lot was about empty, and I didn't recognize any of the cars. I laid my head on the steering wheel for a beat and tried to get control of my breathing.

What Terry said was true. If Kora found out the truth about me, she wouldn't waste another second. She was too good, too perfect, to allow the chaos and negativity that was my past into her life.

If Terry had just stayed away, I could have left this crap in the past and took my time telling Kora. I couldn't put it past him to let it out. He'd do anything to ruin my happiness. He'd done it plenty of times in the past.

My breathing calmed. I considered leaving and driving around for a bit. I could find somewhere else to stay for the night. I still had the salon key. Kaye and Diane wouldn't mind if I crashed one more night. Or I could call Kora.

No. Just go in, get something to eat and drink, and calm the fuck down. I entered the pub and sat heavily on one of the bar stools at the counter.

"Hey, man," Trevor greeted me in his usual jovial manner, then stopped when he saw the expression on my face. "What the hell happened to you? You look like shit."

I shook my head. I didn't want to talk about it. "I need a beer and a bag of ice," I whispered the words, then wiggled my jaw to make sure it wasn't broken. Now that my adrenaline had dissipated, pain started to settle in.

Trevor didn't say anything but returned quickly with one beer and two bags of ice. He placed one on my knuckles and gestured with the other toward my jaw.

I held the bag on my face. "That bad?"

"Like you had a fist meet your face. But from the look of your hand, seems like you got a good jab or two in yourself."

I put the ice down and took a swig of beer. "Father-son bonding."

Trevor's brow ticked up.

"How much do I owe you for the damages?"

Trevor stood straight. "Won't take your money. You didn't do anything. Your dipshit dad owes me."

I laughed. If Trevor waited for Terry to pay up . . . "Hell will freeze over before that useless asshole pays you anything. I need him out of here, and if I pay it, he might just be allowed to go on his way next week after his court date."

"Dude, I'm sorry. I shouldn't have called your dad names. Even if it is true. Let me get Nico to make you some jalapeño poppers. Be right back." Trevor slapped the bar quieter than usual.

I tipped my beer toward Trevor in thanks and took another swallow. It tasted stale and sat heavy in my stomach. I stared behind the bar at nothing in particular.

Terry's words reverberated in my mind. What kind of mother left her kids? That question had haunted me my entire life. I spent my teen years wondering what more I could have done to make her stay. To make her love us enough so she wouldn't leave.

Trevor placed the jalapeño poppers on the counter. "On the house."

"Thanks." I took a bite of a popper and chewed slowly as the spicy, cheesy goodness filled my mouth. I finished the beer and held it up.

Trevor acknowledged and placed a fresh cold beer on the counter. "You good, man?" He raised his brows.

I stared at him and tipped up the beer, taking a good long swallow, and gave him a short nod. Maybe if I didn't use words, Trevor wouldn't feel the need to stay and hover. I downed the rest of the beer. This one went down like water, and I gestured for another.

Trevor sighed heavily before placing a new bottle on the counter along with a glass of water. We held each other's glare, then he finally left me alone.

It was about time.

Soon the poppers were gone, and so was my third beer, then my fourth. I had no clue how long it had been since I drank four beers in such a short time. Did it matter?

Suddenly I felt someone near me. I only had to inhale to know it was Kora. Her scent of flowers and vanilla filled my olfactory nerve and sent my pulse racing.

I lowered my face, not wanting her to see me like this.

Monday night it was at the police station, now four beers in, and I had no clue what my face looked like, but it throbbed like hell.

"Hey." Her voice was soft and sweet. I felt the pressure of her hand on my back. The heat from her touch radiated through my shirt and calmed my racing pulse. She rubbed her hand in a circular motion. It felt good. It helped me relax.

I sat up straight and took a large mouthful of water and emptied the glass. "I'm guessing Trevor called you." I turned my head just enough so I could see her from the corners of my eyes. I tried my best to hide the other side of my face.

"Texted me, but same difference." She gently turned my face toward her and brushed the tender area on my cheek. "What the hell happened?" Her voice was still soft and now concerned.

Which made me smile. Only Kora could cuss and be sweet in one breath.

She reached for my hand, which had already started to bruise and swell, and gently picked it up. "Kai?"

"Don't."

She let go of my hand, and I attempted to flex my fingers, which sent shock waves through my nerves. I sucked in a breath.

"Tell me what happened." Her voice was stern and direct. This was probably her teacher voice she reserved for behavior issues. "You've had four beers, and you look like you got in a fight." She tipped my head up and held my gaze.

I could be as stubborn as the next man, or in this instance, woman, and I glared right back into those large brown eyes.

Those sexy, large brown eyes, which glared directly at me. Focused and intense.

Shit. my resolve melted. "You win. I can't stare in your eyes and be all tough. Those brown eyes turn me into a pile of nothing. The only thing that has the ability to think is my little man, and you've got his full attention."

Her mouth ticked up at the corner. "Oh, your man is anything but little."

I let out a slow breath. "Fuck me."

"I'm game. My house is empty."

God, this woman. She was inches away. Her lips were so tantalizing. I brushed my good hand against her cheek. She was so soft.

Her lips brushed against mine.

She tasted amazing. "What are we waiting for?" I reached for my wallet and pulled out a pile of bills. It was at least three hundred dollars. My driveway would have to wait. "Trevor." I held up the bills and threw them on the counter. "This should get some repairs started. Let me know if you need any help fixing things up."

I pushed up from the stool just as Trevor came over to us. "You good, man?"

"Yeah." I nodded. "Thanks for calling her."

"No problem." He scooped up the money and gestured his thanks.

I wrapped my arm around Kora. "My little man needs a stern talking to."

"Don't you worry, I'll take care of him, and you." Kora placed a gentle kiss on my bruised cheek.

I flinched. "Does it look as bad as it feels?"

"It makes you even sexier, if that's possible, and makes me want to nurse you back to health." She wiggled her brows.

"Woman, you're bad."

"And you love it." She winked.

I smiled wide. Yeah, I undeniably did.

Chapter 21

KORA

It was noon when I closed the door of my classroom and ended year number seven of my teaching career. It had been another successful year, and I couldn't wait for the summer and the chance to have time to relax and rejuvenate before I had to do it all again.

My phone pinged, and I pulled it from my pocket. I smiled wide as I read the text from Kai.

Be Ready to celebrate tonight. I'll be over by 8.

"So, does that smile on your face have to do with a handsome, dark-haired, crystal-eyed stud?"

I glanced up from my phone as Darlene closed her classroom door. I fell into step beside her and answered Kai's text.

"You going to fill me in? You've been lost in your thoughts today." Darlene nudged me with her shoulder.

I gave her a wicked grin. "I don't kiss and tell."

"Since when?" Her eyes were wide with amusement. "You've always kissed and told me everything."

"That's when I was young."

"That was last year. You've not matured that much in a year."

"Kai makes me feel more mature." Our twin cars were parked next to each other as usual. "I'll meet you at the pub."

I climbed in and pulled away, leaving Darlene staring. *You're going to have to keep stewing, Dar. I have no clue what I can tell you. He's a mystery with a spotty past and family life but is surprisingly sweet, affectionate, hot, and we have amazing sex, probably the best of my life.* Yeah, until I could figure out exactly what was happening between us, how I felt about him and vice versa, I was better off not saying much of anything.

Darlene and I were meeting a few other teachers for our end-of-the-year celebration at the pub. One perk of being a teacher is the long summer break, and we always celebrated the beginning of the two months of vacation with margaritas and fried goodness. I had a hair and nail appointment at two, but that gave me two hours of celebrating the beginning of summer with my coworkers.

I climbed out of my car just as Darlene pulled in. We entered the pub together, and Bryson had seats saved for us. Darlene sat next to him, and I took the seat across from her. The long table was one-half men, the other half women. Another great thing about a small town was that even though there was an elementary and high school, you worked closely together. The elementary school went through sixth grade, with seventh grade going to the high school.

It was always a great time. Bryson—a history teacher and offensive line coach of the football team, and Lance—the head football coach and PE teacher, led a discussion of the future of the football team.

There was lots of laughing, eating, and drinking. I needed a break and got up to refill our margaritas and took a seat at the bar.

"Looks like y'all are ready for summer." Trevor laid a full pitcher on the counter.

"Of course," I smiled. "I love my summers."

"You still planning on going to visit your dad and need me to stay at your place to take care of the animals?"

"Absolutely. Why do you ask?" I had been planning on leaving soon after school was out and spending a couple weeks in Florida. Trevor was always happy to take care of my menagerie.

He shook his head. "Just wondering, with Kai and everything. Speaking of Kai, how did things go last night?"

"He's good. Thanks for calling me." I smiled. So much for relaxing at the bar. I picked up the pitcher. "I'll let you know the dates after the weekend."

"Sounds good. As long as it's before July. I've got plans, remember."

"I know. It'll be soon." I went back to the table. I had been planning on heading straight to Florida once school was out, but now I didn't know if I wanted to leave Kai and whatever this was. Maybe I should ask him to go. Seeing him in trunks with no shirt for days in a row at the beach and splashing in the water with him . . .

"What's that smile for?" Lance asked.

"None of your business." I didn't want to discuss this with him, though I was sure he knew more than I'd like. Sometimes the oldest friends are the nosiest. I needed to get focused before people asked too many questions I wouldn't be able to answer.

"Her mind has been preoccupied lately," Bryson said.

"That's right," Lance said. "I heard you've been spotted all over town with Kai." A sneaky grin crossed his features.

"Who told you that?"

"I have my sources," he said.

Damn book club gossips. It wouldn't surprise me at all if they told him everything they knew about me and Kai. And honestly, I don't care if the entire town finds out I had amazing, hot sex with him. It wouldn't be the first time I was a part of the gossip channel.

"We're still trying to figure out what appointment she had early Saturday morning at Shear Perfection. She's not talking. Maybe Kai gave her painting lessons," Bryson said.

"Stop." Darlene slapped Bryson's arm. "You've been messing with Kora too much about her night with Kai. She's an adult and is entitled to some fun once in a while."

"Thanks." I gave her a half smile. "I think?" Luckily, it was one thirty, so I needed to wrap up here and end this discussion. Maybe I did care if they knew my business. Getting to the hair salon early wouldn't be so bad. I could use a talk with my aunt. "I'll talk to you later, Dar. I gotta go. I've got a meeting with Summer."

"Well, there she is. We were just talking about you." Diane welcomed me with a hug.

"What a surprise." I raised a brow and held Diane at arm's length. "What could I have done now that would have merited y'all's attention?"

"Oh, nothing serious."

"Nope, nothing at all serious. Just . . . you know," Kaye answered.

"You are both up to no good. Oh, Kaye, I saw Lance at Jerry's. Thanks for talking about me with him." I sat in Summer's chair.

"You're welcome, sweety. He likes to be kept up to date with happenings in the romance department."

"I'm sure he does. When are you going to set him up so y'all can talk about his love life?"

"He's not ready to go there." Kaye motioned for the woman whose hair she permed to get under the dryer.

Thankfully, Summer entered the area with a bowl of color and a cape she wrapped around my shoulders. "Okay, ladies, let me talk with my customer. Y'all have been talking about her enough today. Give her a break."

Relationships were always the main topic at Shear Perfection, and I couldn't stand it when it was about mine. This was why being in one was overwhelming, and I refuse to allow what Kai and I have going on to be called that. It was too soon. "What's been said now, Summer?"

"Nothing different than all those nosy women wondering about details of your and Kai's relationship. Too bad you couldn't have kept things under wraps."

"No shit." I should have tried harder or just stayed locked in the room until the salon had closed for the day before sneaking out. I also shouldn't have been holding his hand while I took him on a tour of the town. If I would have just gone kayaking, this talk wouldn't be a thing. I lowered my voice. "Just think what they would say if they knew we have spent multiple nights together."

Summer pursed her lips and nodded. "Nice."

"I agree. Anyway, have you seen my aunt at all today?" Even though she worked, she often stopped in during her lunch break. She worked at city hall, and it was within a short walking distance. A perfect situation to spread the daily gossip to her friends before she forgot all the juicy details.

"Yeah, it's Friday. She was here with some stories, but I wasn't paying attention. I actually have to stay busy. I have bills to pay."

Soon, my hair was in foil, and my feet soaked in a bath. Nothing like starting summer off with new hair and pretty nails. "This area is nice. Kai really knows what he's doing." The newly completed area had three pedicure bath chairs and a manicure station with two seats. It was a nice addition to the salon. They'd been talking about it for a long time, it was finally good to see it completed.

"From what I hear, he's professional in other ways as well." Summer glanced up from her stool.

"I won't complain," I said with a smile.

Just then, the door to the salon opened, and a male voice filled the room.

"Speak of the devil." Summer gestured toward the door with her head.

I didn't need to turn my head to see who Summer was gesturing to. I recognized Kai's voice. My eyes popped wide. Holy shit! He couldn't see me with foil in my hair. I looked ridiculous. "Summer, hide me," I whispered.

But it was too late.

"Kora's back getting a pedicure, Kai. What a coincidence her being here and you walking in," Kaye greeted him. "But I'm sure you knew that didn't you?"

Damn Kaye. I pulled my foot from Summer's grasp.

"Hey." Summer jerked my foot back on the footrest. "Don't move. I'll end up painting your entire foot. Not just your nails."

"No, ma'am. I'm just here to meet Blake. He needs to do the final plumbing inspection. But Kora being here sure is a bonus." Kai's voice floated in from the front but was getting closer.

"Hey, Summer. Kora?" My name ended in a question.

Of course it did. I looked like I was preparing for an alien invasion with all this tin foil on my head. Maybe an alien ship could show up right then and beam me up. Heat crept up my neck, and I lifted my eyes slowly.

"Hey." My heart thumped hard in my chest from a combination of absolute embarrassment and this amazing hunk standing in front of me. A sky-blue T-shirt, jeans, and boots were all he was wearing, but with the typical scruff on his face, he was breathtaking, and when he smiled and that dimple popped, he took my breath away and stole my heart.

"There. Toes complete." My toes were a bubble gum pink. I liked the color and planned on having my fingernails match. Summer slipped my flip-flops carefully on my feet. "I think you have about ten minutes before we need to check your color, so you're free. Just stay out of that now empty bedroom." Summer winked and started to clean up the pedicure station.

I stood carefully with Kai's help, and a spark shot from his hand through my entire body.

"Your toes are cute. Pink's your color."

"Thanks."

He kept his hand on my arm as we walked into the kitchen. "I thought you were meeting Blake," I said as I filled a cup with water.

"I am, eventually." He ran his fingers across one of the pieces of foil in my hair. "Sexy." His grin was crooked. His eyes glowed.

I was totally embarrassed, but my stomach fluttered and a tingle shot all the way through my body to my groin. I held his gaze. Even though I resembled a crazy lady, his eyes were totally into me, and I melted.

"So are you ready for a fun summer filled with . . . well, whatever you want, I guess. What do teachers do all summer, anyway?" His arms wrapped around my waist.

I shrugged, my hands on his chest. "Usually, I do odd jobs around town, volunteer at the civic center, do an art and craft class for kids, help around here, take care of my animals, kayak down the river or tube and drink." I brushed my hand in a circular pattern on his chest. "This year, though, I'm thinking I'll find some new hobbies to keep me occupied."

"Really?" His eyes were smoldering, and I became lost in his gaze.

"Hey, Cinderella, we need to get your hair washed out," Summer interrupted. "You can continue this little . . . whatever . . . later on. Oh, and Blake's here, anyway."

"What time are you planning on being finished with all this?" Kai gestured.

"She needs to be finished by six, as I have another customer, but if you don't set her free, she'll be here longer than that," Summer yelled from the other room.

I chuckled. "I guess I should go. The last time I pissed her off, my hair became a bit shorter and a really interesting shade of blue." I stood on my tiptoes and kissed him. I planned on a quick simple kiss, but my lips had a different idea and a quick peck turned into a deep, hot, tongue-dancing kiss that made me want to leave with him right then, tin foil hair and all.

"Your hair is going to be fried. Get a move on!" Summer yelled.

"She has some amazing customer service skills," Kai whispered with a smile.

"No shit. Now you know why she got Miss Congeniality for our class superlative."

"I hope you're kidding."

My eyes went to the ceiling. "Of course." I batted at his arm. "I'll see all of you later." I glanced down at his crotch, wiggled my brow, and sauntered off, putting a little more wiggle in my ass.

Chapter 22

KAI

"Word around town is that you and Kora are a thing." Blake crossed his beefy arms across his chest. "I guess it's not just gossip."

"Excuse me?" I inwardly shook my head. Blake knew his stuff and had been a great help, but could use some cleaning up. He was quite a hefty man. At least six feet four and, I would guess, two hundred twenty-five pounds. With a bald head and a full beard, he screamed plumber. But from what I could tell, he was a good guy. He was in his forties, married, and had a couple kids in middle school.

My eyes rolled—maybe Kora was wearing off on me. There'd be worse things that could happen. "Why don't you go check out the plumbing and whatever else you need to do. Get done so we can get out of here."

It didn't take long, and Blake completed his work.

Thank God. I wanted to find Kora. I should probably not make such a big thing about whatever we are, but I couldn't help it. I was drawn to her like bees to honey. Knowing she was in the same building kept me from being able to focus on anything else.

"Well, here comes Mr. Stud now," Summer said as she filed Kora's nails.

"Keep them long, Summer. I enjoy the feel of those nails as they scratch down my back."

Summer stopped her filing and shot daggers at me. "T.M.I.," she said and let out a heavy sigh, then got back to work.

Kora laughed

Damn, she was gorgeous. I combed my fingers through her hair. The lights of the salon made her hair dance with color. A couple shades of blonde and different shades of red and copper highlighted her dark auburn hair. It was beautiful, like her. "Your hair looks amazing. And it's so soft." I kissed her cheek. "Seriously Summer, you do some great work."

"Thanks. Just what I needed. Your appreciation."

I shook my head and smirked. "You're such a joy. I hope your bedside manner is a bit different with your other customers."

"You need to go away. We've got to focus here, and you're bothering us."

"Summer, seriously? I think you need to get laid." Kora's statement caught me off guard, and I laughed heartily. Summer's expression was priceless. If looks could kill—thankfully, they don't.

"Okay. I'll leave you two alone." I kissed Kora's cheek. "Take care—of her, Summer."

"Leave now." Summer didn't even glance up.

"See ya at eight?" Kora winked.

"Can't wait."

"Hi, Kai honey," Tonya said as I passed her. She was dressed in long, black flowing slacks and a white blouse.

"Hi, Tonya. You look nice today." I was engulfed in her arms and hugged her back easily. For someone who didn't get much affection growing up, I was surprised at how easily I returned hugs and other friendly affirmations with the people of Orlinda Valley. The only ones who showed me affection growing up after my mom left were the twins, and I always made sure they knew I cared.

"Aren't you a sweetheart." She held me at arm's length. "If you weren't interested in my niece and were twenty years older, I'd be fighting off the woman to be next in line."

"T. Leave the poor guy alone," Diane said.

"Oh, whatever," Tonya said. "Anyway, Kai, we're having a big dinner with our families Sunday. I hope you'll come with Kora. We'd love to have you."

"Kai, that would be wonderful," Diane agreed. "You'll meet my husband, Tom, our granddaughter Skylar, and our daughter and her husband. Well, my stepdaughter, but blood doesn't make a family."

"True, and Kai, we see you as family," Kaye answered.

"We sure do, even if you weren't with my niece, you'd still be family." Tonya patted my cheek.

They see me and Kora as a couple already. I'm not complaining, but it's a bit quick. But even if Kora and I weren't a thing, I would still love to be there. "Thanks. I'd love to come. See you then."

I left the salon and climbed into Matilda. As I drove through town, I waved to the old gentlemen who hung out in front of city hall. I honked at Trevor who was getting gas at the corner station. I didn't think I'd ever seen him outside of the pub before. Bit strange to think he had a life. It had only been a month, but I already saw Orlinda Valley as a place that felt like home.

With the purchase of my land and the house I planned to build someday, and with Bryson and Trevor, whom I started to see as friends, things were going well. I had a great job, I was able to put money away, I'd finally started to put down roots, and it felt good.

Then there was Kora. A girl like her might have been out of reach during high school, but now, as adults, things were different. So much different and so damn good. Life was more perfect—if that was a thing—than I could ever remember. I was on cloud nine, and I felt that nothing could bring me down.

I thought too soon.

As soon as I pulled down my driveway, life smacked me hard across the face. In reality, it was more like a punch. A hard, direct sucker punch to the gut.

Terry had made a fire in the fire pit, and if the pile of beer cans scattered all around him were any indication, he had been drinking for a while. Shit. How did he get more beer out here? I thought I got rid of all the alcohol. Having a drunk Terry on my property was not good for my sanity.

I jammed my foot on the brake and slammed the truck door.

"Terry!" My heart pounded, and my blood boiled. I stomped with my hands clenched into fists until I was directly in front of him. He didn't hear me when I yelled his name the first time, so I hollered with my voice deep to be heard above the obnoxiously loud music that was playing. "What. The. Hell. Are. You. Doing. Now?" I gestured to the mountain of beer cans.

Terry glanced up and turned down the radio. "Sorry. I couldn't hear you. The music was too loud."

Is he serious right now? God, I wanted to punch him—again. Instead, I took in a deep breath to calm my nerves. "Ya think?" I had nothing else to say. There wasn't a point.

"You need to relax—have a beer." He held a beer toward me.

The last thing I wanted right now was anything that would put me one step closer to being like him.

"I figured with that sweet piece of ass you were with, you'd be nice and relaxed. Sex usually does that to a man." Terry glanced over his beer can. "Is she not giving it up?"

"Holy shit!" My insides were as hot as that fire. "You really need to watch what you're saying, old man. Have some respect."

Terry shook his head slowly. "You've got it bad." He tipped up his beer, emptied it, and threw it on the fire. He leaned his elbows on his knees. "You work construction. You're from a small town even less interesting than this hole in the wall. You barely finished high school and have never amounted to anything. Do you really think a small-town hottie and favorite elementary teacher could ever be interested in someone the likes of you?" Terry popped the tab on another can of beer. "You're in over your head, kid. Just like usual. You need to come back down to earth before you do something stupid." He offered me the beer he just opened. "Take the beer, sit down with your old man, and let's drink together like father and son."

Damn. *Don't hit him, don't hit him, don't hit him.* Maybe if I said it enough, it would evaporate from my mind. I flexed my hand. The fingers were still sore and tight from our last bout, and anyway, I was a bigger man than him. Even though I was itching to beat the shit out of him—again—I wouldn't stoop to his level. It didn't solve anything, but damn it felt good. Instead, I ignored him.

He waved the beer in the air. "Just take it. One beer won't make you an alcoholic. You've always been so scared of turning out like me. If you would just stop fighting the inevitable, you could finally settle down and stop running from the truth."

I snatched the beer from his hand. "What truth is that?"

"That's something you need to figure out for yourself." Terry leaned back in his chair and stretched his legs toward the fire.

Life hadn't been easy on him. I sloshed the beer around in the can and watched my old man. Time hadn't been kind to him either, and that was no surprise. He had abused his body, both inside and out, for as long as I could remember. There was no way I would turn out like him. That was one thing I was sure of.

I tipped the beer over and watched as the liquid soaked into the ground. When it was empty, I crushed it in my hand and tossed it in the fire. "Kora will be home soon, so I'm going to clean up this shithole, then head to see her." It was just before eight. I didn't know how much cleaning I would get around to in the little time I had before I left, but I'd be damned if I let this useless man bring my property down to his level.

I left him by the fire and went inside, prepared to face the chaos I was sure was going to great me. Thankfully, Terry hadn't done much damage—on the inside at least. There was only a coffee cup and cereal bowl in the sink. I washed them quickly and wiped down the counter and table. The fifth wheel was clean, so I grabbed clothes before joining Terry back at the fire.

"Don't wait up. The RV's yours for the night." I walked with a heavy step to Matilda.

"You better get some before she realizes she's slumming and dumps your sorry ass."

I froze and my stomach fell. My hands curled into fists, and I closed his eyes. *Breathe and don't react. That's what he wants. He'll be out of your hair soon enough.* I calmed. I hadn't had to do so many relaxation exercises since I left Atlanta. Terry was certainly not good for my health.

Thank God I had Kora to run to.

I rolled my windows down and turned the radio up as I drove down the road. Fresh air relaxed me, but it didn't work that night. I was too wound up and couldn't get Terry's words out of my mind. *Don't let him get to you. You know what he's like. His goal is to get under your skin. Don't let him.* Unfortunately, I did. He was under my skin and dug himself in farther.

Orlinda Valley's fields passed by the windows, and the town came into view. I turned onto the long windy road toward Kora's and slowed as I came to the spot we first met. Who knew that a simple thing like helping a woman with a flat tire on the side of the road would rock my world?

She was breathtakingly hot, loud, vivacious, and stubborn. I stared out over the fields. The cows grazed in the pasture in the moonlight. I could see why Kora loved it here—it was so serene.

I watched the cows a bit longer until my pulse slowed. I was finally relaxed enough and more than ready to face Kora.

I pulled into her driveway a few minutes later and my breath caught when the beam of my headlights fell on her. I parked and put the truck in gear and watched her close as she latched the gate to the goat pasture.

Terry's words came to the top of my mind. She *was* too beautiful, too good. He was right. I was beneath her, and it would only be a matter of time until she found out the truth about me. A rock seemed to wedge in my chest. I hoisted myself out of the truck and trudged quickly up to her. My pulse, which was relaxed just a moment ago, now throbbed wildly.

I wanted us to work. I wanted Kora.

But we don't always get to have what we want.

"Hey." She wrapped her arms around my neck and pressed her soft, warm lips on mine. I gave in to her kiss with desperation. She tasted like sweet tea and smelled of honeysuckle and hay.

My breath was heavy when I pulled away. I held her head in my hands and ran my thumbs over her jaw.

"Kai, what's wrong?" She grasped my wrists.

"What are we doing, Kora?" The beat of my pulse escalated. I shook my head. I was exasperated. "This won't work. We can't work."

"What?" Kora backed slightly away as confusion flashed in her eyes.

My heart cracked a bit.

"I thought everything was going well between us. What are you talking about?" she asked.

"Kora. This. Us. It's not possible. It doesn't even make sense."

She raised her brow, and her eyes were on fire. "What happened?"

"Just listen." I backed away. I had to. I couldn't think clearly when she was so close. She clouded my judgment and made what had to happen more difficult. "Listen to what I'm telling you. I'm not interested in . . ." I hesitated, then gestured between us. "Whatever it is you think is between us. This is not what we need to do. I'm not someone you need." My frustration was building, and if I didn't contain it, I would explode like a cannon.

"What the hell are you talking about?" she asked. "You aren't making a lick of sense, and you sure weren't thinking like this earlier or the other night." Her voice was getting louder. Not surprising. "You sure as hell wanted this the other night. You sure as hell loved this the other night."

"That was then; this is now. You don't understand." This was so much harder than I expected. Not that I thought I'd be ending things like this.

Kora laid her hands on my chest, and her eyes held that spitfire determination I was so attracted to. "Then make me understand, Kai. Because with what's going on, and with what I feel between us. With what I know you feel between us. I don't understand." Her voice was harsh and demanding. Her voice cracked, and she cleared it. "One minute you're flirting with me and giving me your sexy-as-hell look. Next, you're throwing me in bed and having your way with me, and a damn good way it is." She brushed her nails over the scruff on my face. "Then you're kissing me everywhere, sucking everywhere, and making me feel all types of feelings everywhere." Her hands met behind my neck, and she held me tight. "So, no. I don't know what's going on. You need to explain it to me."

I peeled her hands from my neck. "I'm not okay with things. You're so different from me. We're so different."

Kora's hands went up in frustration. "Yes, Kai. You're right. We are different. That's not a bad thing. It's a good thing. I promise you, it's okay." She turned and put some space between us. When she spoke again, her voice was softer. Calmer. "I know there's some skeletons in your past you need to deal with, and I'm sure they have something to do with your father. You don't get a scar like that because you've had a good homelife."

She touched the scar and rubbed her finger across it. It sent a shiver through me.

"Stop, Kora." I'd had enough. She wasn't going to see things my way. I had to make her understand. "This is the right thing to do. You're from this town. You're important. You could have any guy in Orlinda Valley you want. You don't need me."

"Trust me, I've had about all the guys in this town I can handle. That's the one downside of living in a small town. Eventually, you know everybody. Sometimes you know them too well.. And I think I'm old enough to decide what I want."

I stepped backward. I needed to put as much space between us as possible. "Kora, I'm sorry, but we can't do this anymore. Something came up, and I can't have you be a part of it."

"Don't, Kai." Her gaze was hard and determined. "Let me decide what I can and can't be a part of."

I walked backward and shook my head. My heart shattered—this was a new feeling for me, and I didn't like it at all.

"Don't you dare walk away from me, Kai." Her voice was thick.

"Kora, I have to. I'm sorry." I had to get out of here. If I didn't go soon, I didn't know if I would ever be able to leave, and for Kora's sake, I needed to. I jumped in Matilda and tore away, but I had no clue where the hell I was going.

•

Chapter 23

KORA

What the hell just happened? I stood with my mouth hanging open as I watched Kai pull out of the driveway at breakneck speed. My vision became blurry as his taillights got smaller and smaller until I could no longer see them. "Dammit, Kai," I yelled out into the night as tears fell down my cheeks.

"Kora?" Tonya's voice broke through the dark.

I wiped my face and turned toward my aunt.

Kaye, Diane, and Ruth were with her. Of course they were. It was Friday night—book club. They each had a glass of wine, and Ruth carried the bottle.

Just what I needed—an audience, but they came bearing wine. Things could be worse—well . . .

"Come here." Ruth poured me a glass, and we all sat around on my patio furniture. "I'd like to say we were giving y'all privacy, but as you know, these ladies aren't much for ignoring drama."

I laughed softly and took a sip of my wine. My favorite chardonnay from the local winery. Diane, Kaye, and Tonya's expressions were way too innocent. I knew better. "Don't act like Ruth isn't right. Y'all couldn't stay out of drama if you were offered a million dollars."

"You're probably right, sweety," Kaye said.

"I'll blame your aunt," Diane replied. "She's corrupted us when it comes to needing to know everything about this town."

"Seriously. Y'all are some shitty friends. Always throwing me under the bus. When we were on my back patio, I didn't see any of you suggesting we leave Kora alone. Hell, Ruth, you snatched up the bottle of wine, and Kaye, you grabbed a glass for Kora."

"If her heart's broken, nothing's better than a glass of wine," Kaye answered. "So, sweet girl, what happened?"

"Kora, honey." Ruth reached out and placed her hand on my thigh. "Don't you listen to them. If you don't want to talk, you don't need to. You can keep your thoughts and feelings private."

Bless Ruth. She was always the sweet one. The one who thought of everyone else's feelings all the time. The world needed more Ruths in it.

I shook my head and took another sip of my wine and shrugged. "I really don't know. I mean, Kai and I never said we were an item, but it seemed like there was something more than just sex between us."

"See, they did have sex," Kaye exclaimed and slapped her thigh.

"No shit, Sherlock. They didn't just have a sleepover at the salon. A little sexy time was quite apparent," Tonya said.

"Which was why she was attempting to sneak out." Diane nodded once and lifted her glass toward me in a salute.

Wow. The book club. Her aunt's oldest friends. Women I had known since birth. Why did I think getting advice from them was a good thing?

"Kora, don't say another word. These harlots are just nosy busybodies," Ruth said.

"Ruth, enough. She can't keep her feelings bottled up. She'll explode like a bottle of cheap champagne." Tonya slapped Ruth on the shoulder, then turned toward Kora "Not that you're cheap, honey."

"Of course, she's not cheap." Ruth's voice was going up a little. It was the angriest I'd ever heard her.

"T didn't say she was cheap," Kaye said.

"Ruth . . ." Diane started to intervene.

I put up my hands in the air. "Stop. All of you." I needed to stop this craziness before it got out of control. "I love y'all and am thankful that you care so much. But to get back to the item at hand—me and Kai." My gaze landed on each woman's and held a bit. "Y'all know his father's in town and has already gotten into trouble. Kai and his dad don't get along well at all, and I also know some things about his past that aren't pleasant. His mother left them when he was seven. His father was an abusive alcoholic. Kai was left to raise his brother and sister, and because of his shitty past, he doesn't think he's good enough for me." Kora emptied her glass. "That's a quick summary of what I know." I held out my empty glass, and Ruth filled it. I took another sip. "There's something else bothering him, but I don't know what it is. He's not telling me."

The book club became quiet and thoughtful. Gazes met and brows were raised. Sometimes it was like they had telepathy and could speak to each other with their thoughts. It was so creepy.

Darlene and I often wondered if we would one day be able to speak without words as well. I doubted it because we could never keep our mouths closed long enough. "What should I do?" I asked apprehensively. Enlisting the book club's help wasn't always a smart thing, but what did I have to lose?

"You just leave it to us, sweety. Go and promise us that you'll get some sleep, and we will take care of everything," Kaye answered.

"Absolutely we will. If he never felt like he had a family, we'll make sure he knows that we consider him part of our family already," Tonya said.

"Absolutely," Ruth and Diane agreed simultaneously.

"Here's to the book club and our desire to always help when people need our assistance!" Tonya held her glass up.

"To book club!" Diane said.

"Book club!" Kaye and Ruth clinked their glasses against Diane's and Tonya's

"Woo-hoo!" they all yelled in unison and downed the rest of their wine.

I rolled my eyes but clinked my glass to theirs anyway. I couldn't lie. I was a little scared. I guess I was desperate if I wasn't going to stop the book club from butting into my business. There's no telling what they were planning, but some help wouldn't be a bad thing.

And that quickly, the party was over. Everyone gave me a hug before they started down the path toward Tonya's.

"Okay, sweety," Kaye said. She was the last one to give me a hug goodnight. "Come by the house Sunday around two. Everyone will be there. Charles is grilling, and we're going to have our annual celebration to welcome summer."

That sounded like fun, or as much fun as I could handle right now. Everyone meant all of us. Everyone included Bryson and Jamison, so Darlene and all the kids would be there as well. "Of course, I'll be there, and I'll bring some deviled eggs."

"I love your deviled eggs." Kaye squeezed my arms. "Try to get some sleep, and don't let the situation with Kai stress you any."

I smiled and watched as the book club ladies followed the path back to Tonya's. As soon as they were out of earshot, I sighed. The quiet was instantly overwhelming. Being alone was not how I pictured spending my first night of summer break, especially after spending last night with Kai. "Oh, well." I went into the house, filled the wine glass with some wine from the fridge, and sat on the couch with a book.

I stared at the page and read the words but got nothing out of it. I picked up my phone and opened it to Kai's name.

Should I text him? Tell him we need to talk? I typed a few words but deleted them. What would I say? Whatever his deal was, it wasn't my fault.

I turned the phone over and over in my hand. *What the hell. I'll just send him one text.*

Hey—I don't know what happened, but I wish we could talk.

I clicked send.

There. Now the ball was in his court.

Three dots popped up.

My heart jumped. Then they disappeared. "Shit."

Then they popped up again. My eyes went wide.

I waited and stared, but nothing came through. "Whatever. Kai, you're being ridiculous." I placed my phone upside down and turned it on silent. I couldn't wait for him all night.

I turned off the light and prepared for a hard night's sleep.

Chapter 24

Kai

Terry was passed out on the couch, and the RV smelled like a combination of nasty feet and stale beer. I needed to get my house back under control and out of the grip of Terry. I spent Saturday working outside, clearing and staking out where I'd be laying the foundation for the house. I let Terry do whatever he wanted, and now here it was Sunday, and I was left to clean up after him. I opened the curtain and lifted the windows. I cranked open the vents and opened the door wide. Fresh air would help clear out the funk that was built up inside the fifth wheel, and my mind also.

"Close the curtain. A guy needs to get his sleep." Terry slapped the pillow over his head and rolled over on the tight couch.

How could he sleep on that couch? It wasn't made for people six feet tall to use as a bed, but here Terry was every night, passed out, and every morning, he slept in.

"Get over it and get off your ass. I'm cleaning, and this place needs airing out. You need a long hot shower with lots of soap. I filled the water last night. Use it all if you need to, but this laziness is going to stop. You've got to get yourself moving and put together. Your court date is Tuesday. You look like hell." I scrubbed the kitchen counter, using more bleach than probably safe for human inhalation, but bleach smelled clean, and right now, it was needed.

Terry pushed himself off the couch and mumbled something about dumb shit and fuck off.

It didn't matter. He was gone, and I had a chance to dust, sweep, and mop the small area.

Eventually, the RV was shining and clean and no longer smelled like stale beer and feet. If Terry was going to stay here, things would have to be ultra-organized, and I needed to get things started.

He appeared in clean clothes, and his hair was wet. Finally. "All right. You're clean and are somewhat respectable. I'm heading into town for lunch. Why don't you come with me? It wouldn't hurt for you to talk with Trevor at Jerry's Pub and apologize. Maybe you could do some work there and work off what you owe him."

Terry narrowed his gaze and opened his mouth but closed it quickly and pushed his feet in his shoes. "Fine, let's go. I'd like something to eat outside of a turkey sandwich. I think I'm going to start strutting around and gobbling."

I chuckled and closed the door behind me.

It didn't take long for us to get to Jerry's, and when we walked into the pub, Trevor's brow shot up and Terry wiped his hands on the legs of his pants, a nervous habit he'd always had, but it didn't show itself unless he was sober.

So, in a way, that was good.

Trevor walked toward us and placed two glasses of water on the counter. "So, what brings you by?"

I took a sip of the cold liquid. "Well, we're hungry, and I think Terry has something he needs to say to you."

Trevor leaned on the bar, his hands clasped together, and stared at Terry like a father waiting for a guilty admission from their child.

Terry took a drink, placed the glass on the counter, turned it in his hands, and played with the water droplet that escaped down the side. I let out a breath and elbowed him. "What was that for?" Terry rubbed his side. "Fine." He turned toward Trevor. "I was a bit drunk and belligerent the other night. I owe you a new television and whatever else I may have broken. What can I do to help pay it back?"

Trevor drummed his fingers on the counter and glanced back and forth between me and Terry. I shot my brow up and continued to sip my water.

"Tell ya what," Trevor said. "If you're willing to work for free, I think you can work off some of the broken cups, liquor, plates, and odds and ends. We can discuss the television and table and chairs after your court date."

"Sounds great." I said and sat up tall, very interested in Trevor's deal for Terry. It gave him something to keep him busy, and most important of all—he'll be out of my camper for a few hours every day. "What are you thinking?"

Trevor lifted his face toward the ceiling and wobbled his head. "Well . . . Nico could use a dish washer in the kitchen. You could work today and tomorrow all day. We can see how that goes and readjust from there."

"Perfect." I thumped Terry on the back. "Get to washing, old man."

Terry sat up. "What? Now?"

"No time like the present. You made a mistake and have a chance to make things better, so might as well get started. I'll pick you up later. Just call me when you're almost ready to go."

Terry glanced between me and Trevor and stood slowly. "Fine. How about I eat a bacon, lettuce, and tomato sandwich with fries, then I'll get to work?"

"Sure. What do you want, Kai?"

"Cheeseburger with the works and fries would be great."

Trevor slapped the counter twice, then made his way to the kitchen. It didn't take long until we were finished eating, and then Trevor took Terry to the back to begin his work detail.

I sloshed the ice in my glass, and my mind wandered to Kora and me and our last conversation. I don't know why I said I wasn't good enough for her. We worked well together in every way. Yes, she was from a different background than me, and I didn't understand what a family unit was meant to be like, but I knew what I wanted. I always wanted what Kora had.

"Kai."

It was Patrick. The last time I talked to him he irritated the fuck out of me. With how things ended with Kora last night, it probably wasn't a great time to talk with him now, but as he walked to the other side of the counter and helped himself to a beer, it didn't seem like I was going to have a choice.

Patrick leaned on the counter. "Can I get you anything?"

"Do you work here now?" I finished my water and continued to pick at the fries as I eyed Patrick.

"I don't necessarily work here, but I am part owner." He popped the top off a beer and placed the bottle on the bar.

"Thanks." I took a sip. One beer wouldn't hurt.

Trevor joined us and pounded Patrick on the back in greeting. "Your dad is settled in, and he and Nico are getting along well," he said to me. "Just so you know, Nico attends Alcoholics Anonymous meetings at the church on Sunday nights. He'd be a perfect sponsor."

I laughed. That was a joke. To go to AA, you needed to admit first that you had a problem. Terry didn't think he did. AA wouldn't happen. People have tried many times over the years, and it did nothing. "It would take a miracle. Terry's been told to go to AA multiple times in his life, but he has yet to step foot into a meeting. He doesn't think he has a drinking problem. He thinks everyone else is the problem." I took a sip of beer, then set it down. Nothing like talking about my alcoholic father to have me do a double-take at my own habits.

I pushed the beer away. "How about a Coke instead?"

Trevor filled a glass and pushed it toward me.

"So." Patrick leaned back and crossed his legs in front of him. "Why aren't you at the beginning of summer bash held by the book club every year? I figured with you and Kora an item, you'd be there as her date."

The beginning of summer bash was today. I totally forgot. With everything I was doing yesterday and this morning, it totally slipped my mind. Tonya and Kaye invited me, and it was almost two o'clock.

Patrick watched me, and there was something in the man's gaze which wasn't just pure interest. It was something else, but I couldn't put my finger on it.

I dipped a fry in ketchup and chewed before talking. "Is there something I need to know?"

Patrick nodded. "She's a great person. Loved by the community. Everyone's favorite third-grade teacher. I don't want to see her hurt."

I cocked my head to the side and felt my blood pressure rise a notch. *Be careful. Choose your words wisely, and don't jump to conclusions.* "Why the interest? You're not dating her anymore."

There was a noticeable tick in Patrick's jaw, and his face grew red. Seemed as if I wasn't the only one with blood pressure issues.

"Okay, guys," Trevor interrupted. "I think all of us are concerned about Kora's well-being. In case you forgot, I did date her in high school. Like you both, I care for her also, but now she's one of my best friends. But . . ." Trevor laid a hand on Patrick's shoulder. "Patrick here is still getting over her."

The glare Patrick shot in Trevor's direction was classic. I chuckled.

"And, Kai, you're her recent interest. And from what I've noticed when you've both been here, there is definitely something going on between you two. I haven't seen her give anyone that much attention probably ever." He shrugged at Patrick. "Sorry, man, you haven't seen them together."

Patrick held up his hand. "Believe it or not, I'm over Kora. She's a sweet girl and a friend, but like I was saying, I don't want to see her hurt. I thought you and her had something going, and I'm just curious as to why you're here and not at the book club summer gathering. I'm even going later. Bryson's best friend and all. I'm still part of the family."

I puffed out a breath. My issue wasn't with Patrick or Trevor. This small town loved Kora. Heck, they'd taken me in, and I'd only been there a month.

I couldn't deny my feelings for Kora, yet sometimes feelings weren't enough. "Yes, there's something between us. What, exactly, I don't know. I came to Orlinda Valley to get away from my past life. Once things with me got straightened out, my brother was situated in his first duty station, and my sister was in her job and happy in South Dakota, it was my turn to get away from Terry and focus on me. I got a job, found Orlinda Valley, purchased land, and hoped to start my life and set down roots, far from Georgia and the misery that was my past."

I swirled the ice around in my glass. "I thought it would work out. Terry didn't know where I was, my siblings were finally happy, and I had a plan to build my house by the Red River and start over. Then, out of nowhere, I pulled over on my way to town and met this auburn-haired spitfire, fell in . . . well, something . . . and things seemed to be going amazingly well with us. Until Terry showed up, and shit's been going downhill since then. And to make matters worse, here I am talking with you two instead of being with Kora at the book club summer party."

I sighed. Would shit ever work out? "Terry made me remember who I am and that you can't run away and hide from your past no matter how much you may want to. So, now I'm double guessing if Kora needs to be with someone like me." I shrugged and watched the ice slide around my glass. "One thing I've noticed is exactly what you said, Patrick. She loves this town, and this town loves her. She belongs here and has a home and a family. Something I've never had."

I gestured toward the kitchen. "That loser in there's my father, and if you didn't notice, I call him by his first name. He's never been a father to me or my siblings. The only family I've ever had are now living their lives far away, and I'm glad." I stood and grabbed my wallet to pay my bill. I needed to go somewhere, but not here. "I guess what I'm saying is Kora needs better than me. She can have anyone, and . . ."

"And you are being stupid." Bryson placed his arm over my shoulders.

"Where did you come from?" I asked. I didn't hear anyone walk in the pub.

"From the front door. You were wallowing in self-pity too much to hear me enter. Are the wings and jalapeño poppers ready?" Bryson asked Patrick.

"I told Nico two o'clock. It's about two, so it should be any time." Patrick popped open a beer and pushed it across the bar to Bryson.

"That's fine. I'm not in a rush. I'm glad I had somewhere to go. Charles and Jamison are manning the grill, and between the kids running wild and the women all over Kora, I had to get out of there. Trevor, are you stopping by when you close?"

"Yep. We close at five, and since Nico has a new dish washer, I think I'll be able to get out of here on time, unless we're empty before then."

The bell by the window to the kitchen rang.

"Orders up," Trevor said as he went to grab the bags.

Patrick grabbed them from Trevor and held them high. "Let's go. Kai, that includes you. If you're the one Kora has her heart set on, then you better be willing to fill her heart with happiness, because you're one lucky bastard."

"I agree. And the more guys I have there, the happier I'll be." Bryson downed his beer and waved to Trevor. "Trev, see you soon. Kai, will we see you there?"

I rubbed my hand over my forehead. Maybe what they said was right. Kora was an adult. She could figure out who she wanted. If she wanted me, why would I fight it? I sure as hell wanted her. I shrugged. "Maybe. I want to make sure everything here is settled."

As soon as they were gone, I leaned on the bar and gestured toward the kitchen. "I can stay and keep my eye on him."

Trevor chuckled and filled a pitcher of beer for a couple of men, gave it to them, held up a finger, and walked to the kitchen.

My mind wandered as I sat there. Patrick seemed to be a great guy. He was focused and a good friend. Why did he and Kora not work out?

Trevor came back. "Your dad and Nico are having a great discussion in there. Seems as if they were both in Desert Storm and have some things in common. Nico said he had no issue with taking Terry back to your place after they close."

The thought of Terry alone in my RV did not sit well with me, and I guess my face showed my concern.

"I promise, Nico's a great guy, and like I said, he's been a member of AA for some time. I'm sure he'll be going to his meeting later. You never know. Maybe your dad will go also."

Hearing Terry being referred to as my dad churned my stomach, but like so much where Terry was concerned, I chose to ignore it. "So, Patrick works for the police department, and weren't you part of the fire department?"

"I still am but work only on an on-call basis. I run this bar mostly. Patrick's only been in Orlinda Valley about six years. Honestly, I think that's what interested Kora in him the most. He was new, and she didn't grow up with him. She always had issues with knowing everyone."

My stomach fell and a lump grew. "So, you're saying that she's probably only interested in me because I'm new. That's it."

Trevor stood tall as a laugh escaped him. "God no. I've known Kora my entire life. Hell, we dated for two years. We were even prom king and queen, so the only other people who know her better than I do would be Summer and Darlene. And I promise you." He took a long sip of beer. "She's never looked at anyone the way she looks at you."

The lump shrunk a little, and my shoulders relaxed. Trevor was telling the truth. I could do this. I had to go to Kora and apologize for being a major asshole.

"She has a big heart and knows everyone is not a product of their family," Trevor said. "Don't think that because Terry is one way, you're destined to turn out the same. She'll understand if you tell her that your past bothers you, and anyway—she's worth fighting for."

Everything Trevor said was right. I knew that. I stood and placed money on the counter for my and Terry's lunch. "Thanks, man. Call me if he gets on your nerves." I wrote my number on a napkin. I needed to get to Kaye's and talk to Kora. *Hopefully, what Trevor said was true, and Kora's heart is as big as it seems.*

"You got it, but I'm sure things will be fine."

I walked quickly to the door and jumped into the truck. *You can't go there and ask her to forgive you. You need to come clean first and tell her everything before Terry does.* "Shit." I laid my face in my hand and gripped handfuls of hair. "What are you doing?" I came here to live quietly by myself and learn to deal with my past. I never thought I'd have feelings for someone, especially this quickly.

I've got to figure out my shit. What do I truly want? How am I going to come clean about my past? I can't go to her. Not yet. I've got to figure my shit out first.

Chapter 25

KORA

The great thing about summer break was I had all day to do whatever I wanted. The bad thing about summer break was I had all summer to do whatever I wanted, and I was already bored. I had hoped Kai would show up at Kaye's. Bryson told me he talked to him, and he thought he was going to be there, but as the night went on and he never showed his face, I got quieter and quieter.

I couldn't lie, I was disappointed, and I guessed it showed. Darlene got on to me and told me to stop moping around and insisted I needed to give Kai space, and no matter how hard it was, that's what I was going to do. If things didn't start looking up, though, I might need to go visit my dad in Florida earlier than I planned and maybe stay there as long as possible.

But that was this past weekend, and today, Darlene and I had a girls' day planned. She insisted I needed it to get my mind off Kai, and with James in Mother's Day Out, she had the free time she usually lacked.

She pulled up my driveway at eleven o'clock sharp just as I walked out my back door.

"You've looked better," she acknowledged as she pulled me in for a hug.

"Gee, thanks." I pushed away and climbed in her car.

"I guess you haven't talked to Kai?"

"Or seen him," I added and bit on the inside of my cheek to hold my feelings in check.

Darlene sat behind the wheel, and I could feel her gaze on me.

"We can talk as you drive." I gestured for her to start the car, then I shut down any other questions by turning away, snapping on my seatbelt, and staring out the window. God, I was frustrated with myself and how much I wanted to see him, and it wasn't hard to tell my frustration level had ticked up to that of being plain old pissed. I didn't think he'd go all weekend and not talk to me. That's why I shouldn't have been thinking. It was summer after all.

He said he needed space. Fine. He'll get his space. "It's in his court now. I'm giving him what he asked for."

I didn't look at Darlene but heard her frustration. "I'm sorry." She sighed and put the car in drive. "Hopefully everything works out."

"I don't know. He's having issues with his father, and I know things weren't easy when he was growing up. I can't act like I understand because I don't." I waved my hand in the air like I was erasing the discussion. "It doesn't matter. Where are we going to eat?"

Darlene pulled out of my driveway and onto the road. "Don't get mad, but I promised Bryson I'd meet him at the pub. I have to drop his wallet off. He left it at home when he left this morning."

"What? It's girls' day." What was Darlene thinking? "We can't hang with guys on girls' day."

"I know. He's helping with something at the pub. I'm not really sure what, but I have to give it to him. Then we can leave. Promise."

I shook my head and sighed heavily. "Whatever." We sat in silence for the rest of the drive. I kept my thoughts busy by counting the cows we passed. Busywork to keep from thinking about someone I was over thinking about.

"There were fifty-two cows between my house and here," I announced to Darlene when we got out of her car and walked into the pub.

She scrunched her face at me. "What?"

"Don't worry about it. It's not important." I followed behind her as she walked toward Bryson. He and Trevor were behind the bar in deep conversation about something by the beer taps.

"Hey, handsome. I got something you need." Darlene slapped Bryson's wallet on the bar.

He leaned across it toward her. "You ain't kidding, baby. You got a lot that I need." He smiled wickedly and kissed her.

"It's too early in the day to watch you two go at each other," Trevor said.

"No kidding. And we have places to go. We can't have a girls' day here," I added.

Darlene sat on a bar stool.

Great. Looks like we're staying a while. I plopped heavily on the stool next to her and listened as Trevor and Bryson told us about how they were planning on adding more taps so they could include some local craft beers.

I was only half listening, as I didn't drink beer and didn't really care, when a man exited the kitchen. He looked vaguely familiar, though I couldn't place him and scrunched my brow in thought. He had gray hair and deep wrinkles under his eyes like someone did when they had a hard life. "Trevor, who's that?" I tipped my head in the man's direction.

"That's Terry. He's working off some time with Nico."

"Kai's father, Terry?" I asked. I watched him hard as he wiped down tables. The first time I saw him was brief and it was dark. Now that I had a clear view of him, the only possible resemblance I could make out between him and Kai could be their height. Nothing else was remotely the same.

"Yeah. He's been working here to pay back the damage he caused during his drunken rage. Honestly, he and Nico get along great, and he's been working hard."

I pursed my lips and watched Terry as Trevor tapped in a table's order. Trevor said something to him, and Terry glanced up.

Our gazes locked. Recognition flashed in his eyes before he tore his gaze from mine and said something to Trevor. "Darlene, I'll be right back." I didn't know what I was going to do, but I felt compelled to acknowledge him and see what he was like.

"Terry?" I caught him right before he entered the kitchen.

He stopped and turned. "Yes? What can I do for you?" His eyes raked up and down my body quickly and then the same recognition I noticed earlier dawned in his eyes. "Aren't you Kora?"

I nodded.

"I'm Kai's father. We sort of met once." He wiped his hands with the rag he was holding repeatedly like he was nervous.

I nodded. "I remember." As I looked at the man in front of me, heat grew in my gut. I don't know why. Maybe it was because he was the reason Kai walked away from me. I didn't know if I could say anything without being rude.

Luckily, I didn't have to say a word. "Look. I surprised Kai by showing up here, and I sure haven't made it easy on him. Getting arrested, buying beer and getting drunk at his property. I'm sure he told you all about me and nothing was good."

I wasn't going to lie or make things easy for him, so I just shrugged.

"I want you to know that Nico took me to an AA meeting with him. I know I have a drinking problem. I've always had a drinking problem, and I'm going to try harder than ever to fix it and get sober for good. I've told Kai, but he doesn't believe me. I didn't expect him to. But he's being Kai, as always—nice to a fault—and is willing to let me stay with him as long as I stay sober."

Terry chuckled and relaxed a little. "He's always been a caring person. Sometimes a little too caring. When he was young, I teased him relentlessly and called him a wuss. He has so much of his mother in him. That was her downside. She cared too much. I'd tell him that heart of his would get him in trouble one day, and eventually it did. His need to care for his siblings at all costs got him three years behind bars. I laughed at the time. I was glad that my goody-goody of a son was more like his old man than he wanted to admit. I can see him now, though, for what he really was. A strong man who cared so much about others he was willing to do whatever was necessary to take care of the ones he loved."

Hold on. I reeled back a bit and cocked my head to the side. I was trying to register what Terry just said, but it was hard because he didn't stop talking.

"The truth is, what I thought made him like me really made him so much better than me. I spent my time in jail when I was young but didn't care at all, and it made me harsher. It didn't do that to Kai."

"Stop. Just stop." I held my palm up and shook my head. I had to have time to register what I'd just heard.

I turned and took a few steps away. *Kai spent time in jail? Why? What did he do? Why did he not say anything to me?* My head was spinning. I rubbed my temples to relax the pressure that was building.

"I guess he never mentioned anything about that." Terry's voice was kind.

I turned toward him, my emotions everywhere. "No. He didn't. He told me he left Georgia as soon as his sister graduated, and his brother got stationed in Alaska."

Terry's shoulders lifted. "Technically not wrong."

My mouth dropped. "Technically not *wrong*?" My voice went up a bit.

Terry shook his head. "Look, I shouldn't have said anything. I just thought he had." He hesitated. "No, that's wrong. I didn't think he did, and if I really thought about it, I should have known he hadn't mentioned a thing. He . . ." Again, he stopped and put his hands out. "Look, this isn't my story to tell. But it's true. He did what he did for his brother and sister, and he didn't leave until they were both gone and settled."

I was speechless. "I don't know how to react to this. The Kai I know is an amazing person. He wants everyone to be happy. It's too bad he's not willing to see that he deserves to be happy also." Terry pissed me off, and anger churned deep in my gut. What if what he said was true? Had Terry treated Kai and his brother and sister so badly that Kai had to break the law to keep food on the table? It was possible, and I totally believed Kai would put himself in harm's way for those he loved. That, I knew.

"Look, I don't know what happened between you two. He doesn't talk to me," Terry said.

I raised my brow and stood straighter.

"I know. Surprising, isn't it?" Terry laughed again, but it was uneasy. "But he hasn't been happy lately, not that I've seen him happy much in his life, but he's been doing work like crazy around the property. It's like when he was a teenager, and he would get lost in deep cleaning when I was drunk." He leaned on the counter.

My gaze met his, and I hoped he could feel how irritated I was. "Do you realize how you affect him?" I asked. "He was different before you arrived. You being here throws the weight of the world back on his shoulders. He's stressed and irritated." I gazed at the ceiling and took a deep breath. "Now you tell me all this."

"I know. You're right. That's why I'm going to try hard this time. I'm going to AA and will see the program through. I've already stopped drinking." A smile filled his face, but when I didn't give a congratulatory smile in return, it melted. "I'm going to my court date tomorrow and will do whatever I'm told. I hope to be able to stay here and continue working. It's not a great job, but Nico's a good man to work for, and I'm busy and being busy is good."

Nico called for him.

"Right there." Terry looked back at me. "Look. I'm sorry I spilled Kai's secret. I'm sure he was going to tell you, then with me showing up... just try and give him some time. I know he cares for you. He's worth the trouble. Not that I'm one to listen to. He's my son, and I barely know anything about him. That's no one's fault but my own. But what I know about him, I can tell you, it's worth knowing." Terry nodded and went back to the kitchen.

I plopped onto a stool. That was unexpected. Shocking. I rubbed my forehead and sighed. "Trev, send a couple margaritas to Darlene, please."

"Thought you weren't staying."

I shot him a hard death glare.

He gave me a thumbs-up, and I walked back to the bar and fell heavily onto the stool by Darlene.

"That looked like an intense conversation," Darlene said. She was eating chips and queso.

"Yeah, you could say that."

Trevor set the margaritas down. "Here ya go. Is everything okay, Kora?"

I nodded. "Yeah, I was ready to give him a piece of my mind for how rude he's been to Kai since he showed up, but I couldn't." I sipped the margarita in a daze over the news I was trying to digest.

"Yeah. One AA meeting with Nico, and he's been a different person. Quieter and more focused. His attitude and the chip that he had superglued on his shoulder are both gone."

I nodded. That wasn't what I meant, but I wasn't going to let them in on the news I just received.

"Maybe things will work out. They say that sometimes age changes a person," Trevor said.

"Really?" I already had half my margarita drank and was feeling it. "Who is this all- knowing *they*? *They* always have all the perfect answers." I sloshed the ice around in my glass.

"Right!" Darlene agreed. "Too bad it wasn't me. I'd be mom of the year."

"I thought you already were." Trevor chuckled as he walked away.

We sat quietly for a bit. I sipped my margarita, and Darlene nibbled at the chips.

"You know, you could go see Kai. Give him the benefit of the doubt."

I glanced at Darlene and held her gaze. I could. But what would I say to him? Should I let him know I knew his secret or wait to see if he ever got around to telling me? Was I mad that he hadn't told me, or did I feel like he lied about it? Should I give him the *benefit of the doubt* as Darlene just suggested? "Benefit of the doubt is yet another overused saying, which makes no sense."

Darlene glanced up at the ceiling; her lips pursed in thought. "True. It really doesn't."

"He knows where I am. I'm sure he has a lot going on. I don't want to get in his way. Once he decides what he wants to do about us, what he wants to let me know, he can find me."

"What do you mean?"

I shrugged off that comment. "Nothing."

Darlene watched me as she took a long sip of her drink.

I tried hard to ignore her. She could always tell when something bothered me, and if she questioned me too much, she knew I'd break. But I didn't want to say anything until I heard it from Kai.

"What are you going to do all week then to pass your time?" Darlene asked as she relaxed her gaze.

"Well, right now, we need to go shop, and in the next couple days I have plenty of work to do around the farm to keep me occupied. Friday night is a barbecue at my wonderful aunt's house."

"Friday night barbecues are back." Darlene lifted her margarita glass.

"To summertime," I said as I clinked my glass to hers.

I could act happy. All I had to do was keep busy and keep Kai far from my mind. The ball was in his court—yet another stupid cliché.

Chapter 26

KAI

"What am I doing here?" I wondered aloud as I pulled into Tonya's driveway Friday night.

I had stopped by the salon Thursday after work to make sure everything was still in working order, possibly hoping to see Kora or at least have someone tell her I had been there, but instead was invited to Tonya's weekly barbecue. I hadn't planned on going, as I was avoiding Kora and trying to get things going at the property, but after I left, I received a message from Bryson telling me I better show up. He needed a partner for cornhole. I decided why not.

As I drove up Tonya's driveway, my eyes wandered along the tree line. On the other side was Kora's place, and my pulse picked up. It had been a long week. Between work and dealing with Terry's court case, I stayed busy. It was a lot to deal with, and I never contacted her, and as with most things in life, the more time that passed, the harder things became.

During the court case, Trevor spoke up for Terry. He decided not to press charges, and with Terry's sudden focus on AA and getting sober, the judge gave him a fine which he was going to work off with community service for the town. As long as he kept his job as kitchen help at the pub and stayed focused on his community service and sobriety, after six months he would be off probation and his debt to Orlinda Valley would be paid.

He was here to stay for six months. I don't know what got into me, but I insisted that he stay with me. After much arguing, he thanked me profusely and promised to help me around the property and stay sober.

So, the septic and water lines were being put in this weekend, then I would be able to start on the foundation and framing. It wasn't the life I thought it would be when I pulled out of Georgia and first moved to Orlinda Valley. I'd hoped to get away from the past and my father, but it was possible for people to change. Maybe it would finally happen for Terry.

I heard the music and laughter coming from the backyard as soon as I climbed out of the truck. I smoothed my shirt and checked my hair in the side mirror.

This was crazy. I felt like a high school kid on the way to pick up a date instead of a grown man going to a barbecue at a friend's house. Yes, Kora would be there, and God, I wanted to see her, but it had been a long week and I'd never reached out. What if I messed things up?

I lost count of the number of times this past week I texted her just to delete the message. I knew I needed to tell her everything about me. The good, the bad, and the really ugly.

Terry told me he accidentally let it slip about me being in prison. At least that skeleton was out of the closet. It was totally possible she wouldn't want a relationship with me after she found out the details of why I spent three years behind bars. If she decided she couldn't be with me because of that, I'd accept it and move on. But no matter what, I was making Orlinda Valley my home with Kora or without her.

My feelings thudded around in my body, and my pulse raced. I took a deep breath, threw my shoulders back, and headed for the house. "You got this." I walked around the back and was wrapped in Tonya's hug just as I stepped into the yard. "I'm so glad you're here," she cooed.

I laughed. How could I not? "Lord, Tonya. Were you watching for me?" I pulled away, and she draped her arm over my shoulder. "Honestly, I wasn't going to come, but Bryson talked me into it."

"Well, I'm glad he did. Come on and say hi to everyone." She led me to the crowd. Her yard was large and bordered with trees and rose bushes. There were children running everywhere. I recognized James, Darlene and Bryson's son, but there were a couple of little girls he was running with whom I didn't know.

I glanced around the yard, and my heart thumped hard the second I saw Kora off in the back corner with Darlene and Summer. There was something different about her. Something in her expression.

"She's confused."

I turned away and gave Tonya my full attention. "Excuse me?"

"Kora. She's confused. She doesn't understand why you shut her out. And there's something else bothering her, but she didn't tell me what that was."

Just then, Kaye and Charles joined us. We said hello, and I got a hug from Kaye and shook Charles's hand. Diane joined us and introduced me to her husband, Tom. There were so many people and so many names, I doubted I'd be able to remember everyone. Just when I thought I would explode from information overload, Bryson and Jamison saved me.

"Glad you made it." Bryson offered me a beer, but I opted for a Coke instead.

"Thanks. Trevor and Nico have Terry occupied for the night at the pub, and I figured, why should I deny myself a free meal?" I joked. Maybe if I tried to forget that Kora was there, I'd have more fun, but the fact that we weren't together made a crater form inside my gut.

Lance joined us, and we moved away from the book club and took up residence at the back corner of the yard.

"So, all of you grew up together?" I asked. I wanted to understand what it was like with an extended family. Friends who were so close, like brothers.

"Yep," Jamison answered. "Bryson, Rowan, Kora and I are actual cousins, but Lance, Lilly—Lance's sister who lives with her husband in New York— and Rose, Ruth's daughter, were all brought up like cousins. One big happy, unrelated family."

I nodded and lifted my brow.

"With our moms being best friends, we've been together since birth," Lance added. "We have great stories about Kora if you ever want some dirt on her."

"Seriously, Lance. You'd throw me under the bus?"

My breath stuck in my chest. When the breeze blew, I could smell her strawberry and vanilla lotion. Our eyes met and my heart thudded harder. "Hey."

"Hey." Her voice was short, and her eyes were shrouded. The side of her cheek sucked in like she was chewing on it.

I struggled to contain the rush of emotions flooding my body—relief, longing, attraction, and a deep ache for reconciliation. I reached out, unable to suppress the overwhelming desire to pull her into my arms, then pulled back. "Can we talk?"

Kora held my gaze yet said nothing. Darlene elbowed her, and the look she shot at Darlene was all attitude—there's the Kora I missed.

"Yeah, go," Summer said. "You've been annoying the hell out of us. Go talk to him."

"Summer," Kora whispered, her eyes wide.

Summer shrugged and pulled Darlene away.

A smile ticked up the corners of my mouth. My dimple must have popped because Kora's gaze fell to my cheek and became softer. "Please?" I asked again, and this time I held my hand out.

Kora shrugged and placed her hand in mine. A shock of electricity traveled from her touch, making my pulse race. That was all the proof I needed that there was something between us, and I needed to make things right. I could try to ignore my feelings and think she deserved better, but it wouldn't work. I had to be honest with her and face whatever happened head-on.

I led her under a tree in the opposite corner of the yard, as far from listening ears as we could get. The sun reflected in her hair, and I didn't know how it was possible, but she was even more beautiful than I remembered. "Kora. I'm sorry for how I've acted. I know I was rude, and you deserved more explanation than I gave." I could feel eyes watching us. I turned my head and Tonya, Kaye, Ruth, and Diane were there, whispering and watching. "Is there somewhere more private we could go?"

Kora followed my gaze and rolled her eyes. "Seriously. They all need a life." She shook her head and pulled me by the hand out of the yard to the front of the house.

This was better. It was quieter here, perfect, and for now, we were alone.

"Kora..." I started, but she put up her hand. I closed my mouth.

"Look, I know things in your past were hard. That scar under your eye holds a story I could never understand. I'm sure all of this"—she gestured toward all the cars and the subdivision— "is something new to you. You mentioned never having a family. I can't picture that. Here in Orlinda Valley, family is more than just blood. Everyone stands up for each other. I don't know what it's like to not have all this. To not be accepted, to not be around people who love me, and I'm not going to pretend I do. But I can't make you believe you're good enough for me. If you don't believe it yourself, that's something you're going to have to figure out."

"Kora." I took her hands. I needed to tell her now. Just do it. Get my baggage out in the open. "Everything you just said is spot on. My life sucked, and I never imagined anyone actually had all this." I gestured around me. "This was a dream I thought only existed in movies. But there's more I need to tell you." I stared off in the distance and took in some breaths. "I was running from more than just Terry when I left Georgia, and I thought if I left my past, I wouldn't have to face everything. I should have realized that was a mistake. Unfortunately, it's a part of who I am, and I can't hide from the truth any longer."

I moved my gaze back to her brown eyes, and for the first time in my life, I saw concern, and someone who truly cared—about me.

I licked my lips and puffed out a breath. *Just do it.* "I didn't tell you the whole truth about me. I know Terry told you some, but it's my story to tell." I grasped her hands tighter, needing—no, hoping—her strength and courage would seep into my skin. "As I was growing up, I needed to make sure Sebastian and Susie had everything they needed. Clothes for school, pencils and paper, food. The basics. At first, Terry had enough money stashed away and I would take it and buy things, but by my junior year, things became worse. His drinking took a new turn and he never had money. We became desperate. I needed to do anything I could to get money so we could survive." I could hear my heart beating in my ears. I looked down at the grass and closed my eyes. *Relax. Once she knows, it's in her court. She'll get to decide. You owe it to her.*

"Kai?" Kora's voice was soft and concerned.

I glanced up into those beautiful orbs and felt my world start turning. Giving me the nerve to continue.

It will all be good. I took a deep breath. "I started dealing drugs. Pot at first. It was easy to get into and easy to be profitable. I made money and was able to put food back on the table and give the twins what they needed. It didn't take long before I was offered pills to sell. Those were even easier to get rid of than the pot. I dropped out of high school the moment I turned eighteen and pushed pills instead. My thought process was—more time making money, and it seemed to work for a while. I made enough money to keep us fed and fulfill the twins' basic needs. Unfortunately, one night I sold to an undercover cop and was arrested. Sebastian and Susie were in college, so the money I'd made helped them a lot. But then I found myself behind bars."

My pulse was racing, and I had been rambling. I took another deep breath. "Three years later, I got out. Sebastian was in basic training, and Susie had just graduated. I made it to Sebastian's basic training graduation, saw him off to Alaska, and helped Susie get set for South Dakota, then I hightailed it out of there myself. I needed to start over. I found a construction job where my record didn't matter, and I've been working there ever since."

There. I said it. All of it. Now she knew. I waited for a response. Yelling. Anything.

Finally, after what felt like eons but was probably just a couple minutes, Kora squeezed my hands.

"Wow," she said, her eyes on mine. "I'm sorry that happened, but I'm more sorry you had to do that for you and your siblings."

I needed to add more and make her understand why I acted like I did. "I've worked hard to not be stuck in my past. When Terry showed up and had already caused issues, it took me back. He made several comments that reminded me why I didn't want him to be a part of my life, and I allowed him to get under my skin. Again."

I glanced around at the trees and the pastures. People cared for each other in Orlinda Valley. This is the type of place I wished I would have grown up in. That's why I was here. I wanted this for my future.

I looked down at Kora and my heart did a somersault. I brushed my hand through her hair, which caught the light, causing the red to shine bright. "All this threw me. It's what I've always wanted. A family. A place to belong, but I never believed it really existed, and when I witnessed how people can love each other unconditionally,

I was overwhelmed. Everything about you and about this scares me. What I feel for you scares me. Ever since I saw you on the side of the road, I've been attracted to you, unlike anything I've ever experienced."

I cupped her face and lifted her eyes to mine. "I should never have walked away from you without telling you everything. My true past, my feelings, and why I felt that way, and I can't promise I won't screw up again, but I want to try to make this work. Make us work. If you want me."

I couldn't read Kora's expression, but she sucked her bottom lip in and bit on it. God, how I wanted to be the one biting on that lip. My pulse raced. There was a chance she wouldn't want me. That she didn't want to deal with my baggage and my skeletons. If that's what she decided, I'd understand, and I'd let her go. Somehow.

"Kai, when I met Terry at the bar, we had a talk about you." She reached out and traced my scar. "Tell me about this." She removed my hands from her face and held them tight.

Her hands were soft, and my pulse seemed to calm at her touch. She wanted to know about the scar. I'd already told her so much. What's one more thing?

I took a deep breath and blew it out. "I was a teenager. Maybe thirteen or fourteen. Our mother had been gone for a good while, and Terry's alcoholism was out of control. If the twins were going to be taken care of, I was going to be the one doing it. They were about seven. I was cleaning the kitchen after dinner, and the twins were at the table working on their homework. Sebastian had his backpack on the floor, and I didn't notice. I was in my own world. I had a big test in Algebra the next day and needed to get the chores done so I could get to studying. At some point, Terry walked in and fell over Sebastian's backpack."

I shook my head. I could still see the fear in Sebastian's eyes like it was yesterday. "Terry jumped at him and pulled him up out of his chair and pushed him . . . well, almost threw him against the wall. I grabbed the first thing I got my hand on, and it was Terry's beer bottle. He must have just put it on the counter. I screamed at him to get his hands off Sebastian. I called him all types of names. He turned toward me and laughed. He grabbed the bottle from my hand, and I punched him. The bottle fell to the floor and smashed to pieces. He punched me, and when I fell, he held a piece of the jagged glass to my face and cut me."

Kora's eyes were wide, and a tear fell silently. I wiped the tear from her cheek. "I told him to do it. I told him to cut me and leave the twins alone. He did, and as I screamed, it was like he was slapped. He just froze. I don't know what happened, but I pushed him off me, and he never hit or attacked any of us again. He just sort of existed in the house." I shrugged. "It was after that when things started getting worse, and the food disappeared from the cupboards. Not long after, I was selling pot." I touched my scar. "This scar is a reminder of my past, but also it reminds me that because I stood up to him and pushed him to cut me, I saved Sebastian and Susie from further abuse. I swore then I'd never let anyone hurt any of us again, and I'd never be like him. I worked hard to follow through, and I made some bad decisions along the way, and in the end, things became worse for the twins after I was locked up, but it all ended up okay. Sometimes when things are at their worst and we can't see a way out, we are proven wrong."

Kora traced her finger along my scar. "I'm sorry." Her voice was soft.

"I don't want you to be sorry. I've worked my entire life to not be anything like Terry. That's one reason I don't drink much. The other reason is when I used to drink, I made bad choices. I went from buzzed to belligerent pretty damn quickly, and I didn't like myself the next morning."

I placed my hands on Kora's waist. "I've kept myself shrouded in mystery and away from people, but I was attracted to you that very first moment I saw you. And it scared me. That's why I tried to push you away, but your stubbornness had already gotten under my skin, and I couldn't forget you."

"That's because there's something here. And I don't want to be without you." She closed the small gap between us and wrapped her arms around my neck.

I closed my eyes and breathed her in.

"Kai, thank you for sharing with me and being honest. I know it was hard. But understand something. I don't feel sorry for you. I don't judge you. You did what you had to do to survive. I can't say I understand because I don't. I just want you to know I care, and everyone here cares."

Her deep brown eyes held me tight, and I got lost in them.

"Kiss me, Kai," she whispered.

I didn't wait for her to ask again. I closed my lips desperately over hers and kissed her long and deep. God, I'd missed this all week. Her soft lips, her taste. My fingers tangled in her hair, and I held her tighter. I needed her closer, and soon, my tongue found hers.

I broke the kiss and held her steamy gaze. "Kora, I've never been good at expressing my feelings, and I have no idea how to be in a healthy relationship. What if I mess up? What if I fail you and fall back to what I know? What if I turn out like Terry?"

"Kai, if you mess up and if you fall, I'll be here to catch you. Every time." Her eyes shone bright and made my heart skip a beat.

"Thank you," I said.

"And don't worry. You're nothing like Terry. You're kind, loving, and so much more." She pushed up on her toes and kissed me softly.

It was a perfect kiss. A kiss that told me things would be okay. We were okay. My shoulders became lighter as the tension I stored in them evaporated.

"Let's go," she said when our lips parted. "I'm sure Aunt Tonya and the book club gossips will want to know what's going on."

I laughed and wrapped my arm around her waist, and we walked back to the yard. As soon as we turned the corner, we ran right into the book club.

"Wow. What a surprise. We never would have guessed you four would be eavesdropping on our conversation," Kora said with a laugh.

Kaye and Ruth glanced down at the ground while Diane and Tonya faced us head on.

"We weren't eavesdropping," Diane said, her head high.

"Yeah, Kaye was showing us a bird's nest, and we were wondering what kind of bird made it," Tonya said.

Kora looked at Kaye, then the bush. "Kaye, why don't I believe her? You and Ruth both look guilty."

"Don't know what you're talking about." Kaye entwined her arm through Ruth's.

"Yeah, don't give us that teacher voice." Ruth pulled Kaye's arm, and they walked away. Ruth never could hold strong under pressure.

I laughed. Couldn't help it. These book club ladies were too much. "Y'all are awesome."

Diane walked away. "Yeah, we are, and it looks like all things worked out."

Tonya nodded at them, winked, and followed her friends.

Chapter 27

KORA

I tried to wipe away the goofy smile I knew was plastered on my face but couldn't. After our talk, my muscles relaxed again. My heart was bursting, and I was on cloud nine. It might sound corny, but there was no other way to describe it. I felt like I could accomplish anything right now. I was invincible. It was funny how a talk and a kiss from an outrageously handsome man could do that.

I watched Kai play cornhole with the guys. His face was lit up with laughter as he and Bryson high-fived their perfect throws. He was cutting up with them like he had grown up here. Like they were family. He was in his element. He and Bryson were again dominating, this time though in the backyard.

He looked more relaxed than I had seen before. Maybe it was because his past was out in the open. He wasn't hiding anything from me, could be himself, and I was still interested. Damn was I ever.

"Someone's happy." Darlene said as she sat on the chaise lounge and joined me and Summer.

My eyes didn't leave Kai, and I took a sip of wine. "Yeah. I guess you could say that." I gave her a crooked smile.

"Well, I'm glad you worked things out with him," Summer added. "I know I give you a lot of shit, but you really are good together."

I exchanged a wide-eyed glance with Darlene, and we busted out laughing. It wasn't often Summer said something sweet.

Summer stood. "Whatever. See if I'm nice anymore. I gotta go."

I wrapped Summer in a large hug. "Oh, Summer." I squeezed her extra hard, mainly because I knew it would aggravate her. "Thank you. That means a lot."

She smiled as she pulled away. "You deserve to be happy Kora."

"You do too, Summer," Darlene said as she wrapped her arms around both of us.

"Yeah, well I don't think there's any man who can handle me, so I'll just need to keep you two close."

We watched her walk toward Tonya and Kaye and give them hugs, and Darlene and I settled back into our chairs.

"I wish she'd find someone who could get underneath that harsh exterior of hers, and get to know the Summer we know and love," Darlene said.

"One day it'll happen. I have no doubt," I said as I sipped my wine.

We sat enjoying the afternoon for a while and laughed at the kids playing in the sand box and watched the men across the yard.

"Maybe we finally got our wish," Darlene said in a quiet voice.

I scrunched my brow. "About?"

"We always wanted guys who were friends and got along so we could grow old together and our kids would be like family."

I nodded. We always did say that. "Let's not jump to any conclusions."

"You're right, and with how you're going, James will be in high school before you have any kids."

"Okay, let's slow your roll. I'm not going to argue. Right now, I'm just happy Kai and I are good."

Darlene's face lit up. "And I'm happy for you."

The guys finished their game and joined us. Bryson had his arms full with James. "I think someone's getting tired."

James leaned toward Darlene, who took him and flattened out his hair with her hand. "Yeah, it looks like he's beat."

Bryson helped her up, and they walked together to say goodnight.

"It is getting late," I said as I cuddled into Kai. "Do you want to come to my house? Maybe spend the night?" After watching him across the yard, and not being with him over a week, I really missed him and wanted to show him how much.

He rubbed my back, sparking goosebumps across my skin and a tingling in my groin. Just a simple touch and a look from those crystal eyes was all it took. I was putty in his hands and wanted him to mold me into anything he desired. But the look on his face stopped me in my tracks. "What's wrong?"

He wrapped his arms around me and pulled me close. "Even though I'd love nothing more than to be with you all night, I need to go home and check on Terry. I left him washing dishes at the pub with Nico, and I want to make sure he didn't heist any of Trevor's liquor."

My smile reached my eyes. "I thought things were going better?"

"They are, but I'm still concerned when he's alone. I feel like the tables have turned and I'm the father and he's my responsibility."

"And that's why Trevor brought me by."

I turned quickly, and there was Terry. He looked good. He had shaved and cleaned up a little since the last time I saw him.

Tonya, Kaye, and Charles came over. Charles held out his hand. "I'm Charles. You must be Terry."

"I am. Nice to meet you," Terry replied as he returned the handshake.

"Well, Terry, come on and grab a burger and a Coke. We're getting ready to play cards. I need a partner." Tonya wrapped her hand around his arm and pulled him off to the patio table where the cards were set up.

It didn't take long for laughter and joking to fill the air as the book club and men played cards. "Things look good here. I've gotta go check on the animals. Want to go for a walk?" I asked Kai.

"Of course."

We walked down the path leading to my place in silence. I could hear Tonya's and Terry's voices above the others.

We fed the goats and got them settled for the night, then Kai grabbed my waist and turned me to him.

"Thank you for being so amazing."

My insides fluttered as his crystal eyes ate me up. "You're welcome," I replied in a wispy voice. I stood on my tiptoes and brushed my lips against his in a sweet, soft kiss.

Kai, though, had other ideas and took the kiss up a couple notches—okay, a bunch of notches. It was hot enough to cause my knees to become like jelly. I placed my hand on his chest, then behind his neck, and pulled us closer still.

Percy and Jackson made a noise and placed their front hooves on my back. I tried to ignore them, but eventually, goat hooves hurt. I smiled against Kai's lips. "I almost forgot we had an audience."

"Not me," replied Kai as he went in for a deeper kiss. "I was hoping for the exact response we got."

"Trying to start something?"

"Nope." Kai shook his head. "Just letting them know how we feel."

"Oh, I'm sure that's not too hard to guess." I pulled him out of the goat enclosure and latched the gate behind us. "But this would be so much nicer in my house. Maybe even in my bed."

"Sounds great to me."

Chapter 28

KAI

After a lot of prodding, Kora got me out of bed early the next morning. Waking up with her wrapped in my arms was something I could totally get used to. Getting out of the house with her and into the truck was even better. My smile seemed to be a permanent fixture, and I wasn't going to complain. Kora sat close to me. A major plus of an older truck. There was no console in the middle of the front seat.

Matilda roared to life, and we headed down the driveway and to the diner to meet Tonya for brunch. I had no clue there was going to be brunch. Hell, I didn't even know what brunch really was, but if it meant I got to spend more time with Kora, I was all for it.

"What the hell? I thought it would be just the three of us," I said as we walked to the back of the small restaurant which must have served an amazing weekend brunch if the number of people here was any indication. The table held the entire book club and their husbands, including Terry. Not that he was a husband, but I was surprised when I didn't get a stone lodged in my stomach at the sight of him.

"Good morning, you two. Looks like someone had a good night," Kaye greeted us.

"Shit. It looks like they both had a good night." Tonya wrapped Kora in a hug. "Orgasms do a woman wonders."

"Seriously?" Kora's face was hot, and a blush appeared on her cheeks. "In front of the book club at Shear Perfection is one thing. But in front of all the husbands, and Terry also? And in public?"

I chuckled. I couldn't help it. "It's all good." I squeezed her shoulder and pulled out her chair. "It's not like we're the only ones at this table who ever had amazing sex in our life."

Kora's eyes went wide as cheers and a toast with mimosas went around the table.

I chuckled. These women were great. I turned to my father. "Terry, I'm surprised to see you," I said. "I didn't think you had your car back yet. Isn't it still at the lot where it was towed after your arrest?"

"Well, after my court appearance, and with Trevor dropping all the charges, I paid the tow fee and got my car back yesterday. I need a way to get to work and AA meetings after all."

Charles stepped in. "And after our game last night, he fit in perfectly, so we invited him along this morning."

"Now I'm not the fifth wheel," Tonya added. "So I don't feel left out."

"Like we've ever left you out," Diane retorted.

"Seriously. What are you talking about?" Kaye replied.

The book club group bickered for a bit. "Okay, whatever. It doesn't matter." Tonya turned to us. "You two look happy, and that was our goal."

"Yes, it was," Kaye agreed.

"Looks like the book club does more than read books and drink wine," Diane said.

"Okay, now I'm confused," Kora said. "What are y'all talking about?"

"We planned for y'all to be at my house last night. If it wasn't for us, y'all two may never have talked again," Tonya said.

"So true, and y'all are the cutest couple," Diane agreed.

"We always had hope for you to find an amazing guy, Kora," Kaye said. "And it seems to have finally happened."

My arm went around Kora's chair. "Look, I have to say, I don't know if we fixed things because of y'all, but thanks for whatever you did." I kissed Kora's cheek. "My life wasn't the best, and I made some really stupid decisions in my past, but driving into Orlinda Valley seems to be the best thing I've ever done."

Kora's face became one big smile that caused her to look more beautiful, and I didn't even know that was possible.

"I agree. Driving into Orlinda Valley was the best thing you've ever done. And me getting a flat tire wasn't that bad a day after all. It was the day I met you. Sometimes what feels like a negative can turn out to be a positive," Kora said.

"Kai, we're going to tell you what we told Terry last night. We are so glad you're a part of our little town, and Kora has never seemed happier than when you're together," Tonya said.

Kaye jumped right in. "I absolutely agree with T. Welcome to our little family, Kai."

"We're glad to have you," Diane agreed.

I looked around the table at the men and women who, along with their grown kids, were an extended family of Kora's. My gaze went to Terry. I might not have had any of this when I grew up, but I couldn't live in the past.

I had no clue what would come of my relationship with Terry, but he already looked cleaner and better kept than I ever remember him looking, and now he seemed to have friends. One day at a time was all I could give him.

Kora's hand squeezed my leg, and I turned to her. Her big brown eyes grabbed a hold of mine and held on. "I'm really glad to have you," she said in her soft voice that always raised my pulse a notch.

A smile filled my face and my gaze took in this beautiful woman next to me. "I'm glad I have you, and am so glad to be here. To be a part of this. I feel like I finally found a home." I placed my hand on her cheek. "You are the best thing that has ever happened to me." I held her gaze until the pull between us became too much and our lips met.

Our kiss was warm and sweet, and I knew without a doubt that these were the last lips I would ever kiss.

The day I met Kora changed my life for the better. I was a part of an extended family now. Yes, they were a bit crazy, yet were a lot of fun, and filled with love for each other. And that's all that mattered.

Epilogue

6 Months Later—Kora

"What the hell was I thinking?" I felt like a frazzled mess, and driving Matilda didn't make me feel much better. I had to use Matilda for an emergency trip to the vet for Percy. He ate something and hadn't been his usual pain in the ass self. But of course, as soon as I made the appointment and got him all the way there, he was fine. So fine, he chewed on everything he could get his mouth on in the vet's office and caused all kinds of chaos. I called Tonya on my drive home. I had to vent to someone. She said that was just like a baby. Not that I would know anything about that. But maybe one day.

I stopped at home and dropped off Percy and had to pick up Kai.

I finally turned into his driveway, and the gravel bounced me around. I hated driving his truck, but he had to talk with his crew about the construction and couldn't take time away.

The house came into view and so did Kai's sexy body. He stood with his hands in his back pockets as he talked with a few of the men. My lips curled up and butterflies fluttered in my stomach. I hoped he would always have this effect on me.

I looked in awe at the structure going up across the field. The walls were complete, and it finally started to look like a house.

I pulled to a stop and was wrapped in Kai's arms as soon as I climbed out of his truck.

"Was Matilda good to you?" he asked when we stopped our kiss.

"Matilda was fine. Percy on the other hand." I laid my head on his chest and felt it vibrate as he laughed.

"He's a goat. How bad could it have been?"

I lifted my head, and my eyebrows shot up. "Do you really want to know?"

"Nope. Not now." He shook his head. "I want to give you a tour." His eyes gleamed like a child's on Christmas morning, and he pulled me through the front door.

"Okay, now use your imagination." He gestured around.

Though the walls were up on the outside, the inside was still a skeleton.

"This is the living room, of course. There will be a fireplace here." He pointed to the corner. "The kitchen will overlook the living room with a bar counter here so we can watch the kids play as we make dinner."

I laughed out loud. "I think you're jumping the gun a little." He was so wrapped up in the house and my tour, he didn't hear me, and I followed him up steps, down what was going to be a hall, and passed two future spare bedrooms.

We entered the back bedroom. It was huge, and three windows took up the back wall.

I walked up next to him, and my jaw dropped. "Kai, this view is beautiful." I stared in wonder at the view out those windows. I could see the river meandering slowly through the trees. The opposite bank was met with fields, and now they were filled with the yellow flowers of soybeans. As far as the eye could see. Just beyond the field were hills green and lush with trees. In the fall, the colors would be magical. "This is everything I love about Orlinda Valley. The hills and fields, the river." I turned toward Kai. "It's perfect."

I froze. Kai's eyes were down, and his chest was moving fast like he was having difficulty breathing. "Kai, what's wrong?" I hadn't seen him look this pained and confused in a long time.

He shook his head and his eyes met mine. "Nothing's wrong." He rubbed his hand across his face. "Tonya and Kaye are going to kill me."

"What?" He muttered the words so low I almost didn't hear them. "Why would Tonya and Kaye kill you?"

My question was cut off when his lips crushed against mine. My breath caught but quickly caught up and my nerves stood at attention as I met his kiss. Those amazing lips drew me in. The kiss softened as quickly as it started. Our lips lingered on each other before Kai broke away and I was left breathless.

He hovered close and brushed his knuckles against my jaw.

"I love you, Kora." His voice was deep and raspy and caused my pulse to kick up a notch.

"I know—" My words were interrupted before I could finish my sentence. He placed his fingers over my mouth.

"I never knew this type of love was possible until you. You are my everything. You're the reason I breathe. You've given me a reason to live."

My heart thumped hard against my chest. "Kai," I whispered. His behavior made me nervous.

"You say this view is perfect. I say it could be. It could be if I wake up and get to look at you every day for the rest of my life."

My breath caught as Kai put his hand in his pocket and—*oh shit!* "Kai." His name was just a whisper as he got down on one knee.

"Everything would be perfect if you said yes. Kora, I didn't know real family, or real love, until I changed your tire. I want to change your tires forever. I want to be with you forever. Will you marry me?"

It was difficult to see him behind the wall of tears that blurred my vision, but that was the easiest question I'd ever had to answer. "Of course. There's no one else I want to change my tires or see the river with."

Kai jumped up from the ground and wrapped me in a hug. He spun us around and kissed me surprisingly softly for the joy that raged like an uncontrolled wildfire throughout my body.

Then he slipped the ring on my finger and my breath caught. It was beautiful. It was an oval diamond that glittered brilliantly when it caught the sunlight. It was perfect. "I love it."

Words he said earlier came back to me and I pulled slightly away from him. "Why would Tonya and Kaye kill you?"

"Shit. We gotta go." He pulled me to the truck.

Kai opened my door, and I hopped in. He drove like a bat out of hell, and I braced myself against Matilda's dash. I tried to make eye contact with him, but he was focused on the road.

"What the hell?" I asked as we pulled up my driveway and it was filled.

"Yeah. So, I invited everyone over earlier than usual. Don't worry. They're doing everything," Kai said as he turned the truck off and turned toward me. "They're expecting me to propose in front of them, but I couldn't wait."

I brushed my finger against his scar and gazed deep into his eyes. "They'll get over it. They just want us both happy." A smile spread across my face as I absently played with the ring on my finger. It already seemed like it was always there.

My heart was filled to overflowing. Everything was perfect. "I love you." I said as I stared into Kai's crystal eyes. He was proof that you aren't always the product of your environment. He was the sweetest and most loving man I knew, and he was going to be mine forever.

His smile met his eyes, and he cupped my face in his hands. "Nothing could make me happier than having you as my wife forever. You and these crazy people are my family."

His lips touched mine in the softest, sweetest kiss.

"I love you too, Kora," he whispered. Then his dimple popped. "Let's go tell the family our news."

Notes to the Reader

Thank you for taking your time and reading *No One But You*. I hope you enjoyed reading it as much as I enjoyed writing it. If you loved the story and characters, I would be so grateful to you if you would take the time and leave a review wherever you purchased the book. Reviews help authors and are so appreciated.

Orlinda Valley is a fictional town, yet a culmination of many of the small towns around my home. I hope you come back to Orlinda Valley again. The second book *No Love Like Yours* will be out later in 2024 and is now on pre-order.

I'd also love it if you would join my mailing list to find out about new releases in the Orlinda Valley series, and other happenings in my writing career. Visit my website https://donnarmadden.com/ to join my newsletter and see all my books.

I would love to hear from my readers, so please connect with me, on Instagram and Facebook—Donna R. Madden Writer, or email me at drmaddenauthor@outlook.com

Scan the QR code to find links to everything Donna R. Madden

About the Author

Donna R. Madden has been married to her husband for over 30 years.

They have raised 3 amazing boys in a small town north of Nashville. They share their house with chickens, their dog Lilly, and cat King Marcus Henry XXII, who they all affectionately call "Kitty Kitty."

Outside of reading, she enjoys hanging out with her family and friends, relaxing by the pool or on the beach, and of course reading–mostly romance.

Made in the USA
Monee, IL
16 October 2024